Teacher Is Kept After School

"Oh dear, oh dear," whispered Hildegarde Withers. She stood there by the door of the Teachers' Cloakroom while the old-fashioned gold watch on her old-fashioned bosom ticked away the best part of a minute.

She blinked, rapidly, but the dreadful vision still remained. Then at last the icy chill which had been travelling up her spine reached her brain. She shook her head, and assured herself that twelve times fourteen was still one hundred and sixty-eight.

It has been somewhere well written that amazement and terror are the most transient of emotions, and that within the space of a few seconds one must come to terms even with a gibbering ghost.

Miss Withers brought her teeth together with a slight click. Then her fingers felt again for the wall switch, and the room plunged into darkness.

This darkness was thick, black, and sticky. It blotted, mercifully, the picture of Anise Halloran in her last dreamless sleep, hiding the crimson gash that marred her white forehead and the rivulets that had barely ceased to flow across her cheek.

Bantam Books offers the finest in classic and modern American murder mysteries. Ask your bookseller for the books you have missed.

Stuart Palmer

The Penguin Pool Murder
The Puzzle of the Happy Hooligan
The Puzzle of the Red Stallion
The Puzzle of the Silver Persian
Murder on the Blackboard

Craig Rice

The Lucky Stiff

Rex Stout

Broken Vase
Death of a Dude
Death Times Three
Fer-de-Lance
The Final Deduction
Gambit
The Rubber Band

Max Allan Collins

The Dark City

William Kienzle

The Rosary Murders

Joseph Louis

Madelaine
The Trouble With Stephanie

M.J. Adamson

Not til a Hot January
A February Face
Remember March

Conrad Haynes

Bishop's Gambit, Declined
Perpetual Check

Barbara Paul

First Gravedigger
The Fourth Wall
Kill Fee
The Renewable Virgin
But He Was Already Dead When I Got There

P.M. Carlson

Murder Unrenovated
Rehearsal For Murder

Ross Macdonald

The Goodbye Look
Sleeping Beauty
The Name is Archer
The Drowning Pool
The Underground Man

Margaret Maron

The Right Jack

William Murray

When the Fat Man Sings

Robert Goldsborough

Murder in E Minor
Death on Deadline

Sue Grafton

"A" Is for Alibi
"B" Is for Burglar
"C" Is for Corpse

R. D. Brown

Hazzard
Villa Head

A. E. Maxwell

Just Another Day in Paradise
The Frog and the Scorpion

Rob Kantner

Back-Door Man
The Harder They Hit

Joseph Telushkin

The Unorthodox Murder of Rabbi Wahl

Richard Hilary

Snake in the Grasses
Pieces of Cream

Carolyn G. Hart

Design for Murder
Death on Demand

Lia Matera

Where Lawyers Fear to Tread
A Radical Departure

Robert Crais

The Monkey's Raincoat

Keith Peterson

The Trapdoor

Jim Stinson

Double Exposure

Murder on the Blackboard

Stuart Palmer

BANTAM BOOKS

TORONTO · NEW YORK · LONDON · SYDNEY · AUCKLAND

MURDER ON THE BLACKBOARD

A Bantam Book / published by arrangement with
the author's estate
Bantam edition / April 1988

ISBN 0-553-26796-5

Published simultaneously in the United States and Canada

Bantam Books are published by Bantam Books, a division of
Bantam Doubleday Dell Publishing Group, Inc. Its trademark,
consisting of the words "Bantam Books" and the portrayal of a
rooster, is Registered in U.S. Patent and Trademark Office and in
other countries. Marca Registrada. Bantam Books, 666 Fifth
Avenue, New York, New York 10103.

PRINTED IN THE UNITED STATES OF AMERICA

KR   0 9 8 7 6 5 4 3 2 1

Murder on the Blackboard

I

Teacher Is Kept After School

(11/15/32—3:55 P.M.)

The solitary prisoner sat quietly, his hands clasped in front of him. One shoe moved up and down against its mate, but there was no quivering of his lips. He'd show Them if he could take it or not! Only They weren't here to see.

His name was Leland Stanford Jones, but he preferred to be called "Buster"—a preference which cut no ice with the lady who looked down on him from the desk on the platform. The room was bleak and bare, and it smelled faintly of humanity and strongly of chalk-dust.

The solitary prisoner gave tongue. "Miss Withers. . . ."

"Why, Leland, you know better than to speak without raising your hand. That will do."

A small red palm, innocent of soap and water since seven-thirty that morning, waved uncertainly in the air. "Miss Withers. . . ."

Miss Hildegarde Withers raised her eyebrows, and looked as stern as it was possible for her to look. She seemed very formidable indeed to the nine year old who crouched there in his seat.

For those of my readers who are meeting Hildegarde Withers for the first time, let me inform them that she is in the neighborhood of forty—the close neighborhood—and that her face has something of the contour, and most of the characteristics, of a well-bred horse. Her nose, even without the pince-nez, would be a trifle thinnish, but the mouth is wise and friendly, and only a certain amount of effort keeps it from breaking into a smile at times like this.

The palm waved in the air for all of a minute, while Miss Withers listened to the bustle and the slamming of doors which marked the ending of the school day. She realized that

1

her fellow teachers at Jefferson School had most of them long since given up this old-fashioned method of discipline. All the same, it had worked well for twenty years, and Hildegarde Withers still kept little boys and girls, and incidentally herself, in after school, books on modern pedagogy to the contrary.

She heard a tremendous sneeze in the corridor outside. That would be Mr. Macfarland, the Principal. He had worn rubbers all his life, but coryza had him in its grip from September till May. She heard him pass down the first floor hall outside the door of 1B, and then for a moment there was silence.

Miss Withers pretended not to see the palm which Leland Stanford Jones still waved determinedly.

Someone else was passing along the hall. Light, quick heel-taps. That would be Anise Halloran, the music teacher, on her way to the Teachers' Cloakroom. Hildegarde Withers was thus reminded of something.

"What is it, Leland?"

"Miss Withers, can't I..."

"*Mayn't* I!"

"Miss Withers," he gulped a little, desperately. "Mayn't I go now? I didn't mean to say nothing—I mean anything. The fellows are waiting for me. They can't play without me, 'cause I'm the quarterback. I ap-pologize...."

"It is not my pardon you should beg, but Miss Halloran's," said Miss Withers sharply. "I don't like lies, and I don't like little boys who tell them."

"But it wasn't a lie, not exactly. All the kids say that Miss Halloran is sweet on Mister Macfarland!"

Miss Hildegarde Withers pushed back her chair sharply, and leaned across the desk. "Leland!"

She pointed a stern finger at the long blackboard which extended along two sides of the room.

"I told you that you had to stay after school, and after school you'll stay," she told him. "But I don't want to be unjust. Perhaps the other boys won't have to wait for you as long as you fear, if you are a good boy. Go to that blackboard and write the word 'discipline' one hundred times...then you may be excused."

"A *hundred* times?" Leland Stanford Jones intimated by

the tone of his voice that he considered the assigned number far beyond the scope of mortal imagination. "A whole hundred times?"

Miss Withers was implacable.

"There's plenty of chalk there," she told him, as he hesitated before the blackboard. "Take an eraser, and clear the board. Then write 'discipline' a hundred times. The sooner you finish, the sooner you may go."

With furrowed brow and protruding lip, Leland began to wipe away the accumulation of the day's scribblings. His languid eraser swept slowly through heiroglyphs, sums, spelling lists, and crudely drawn maps, in a swath that crept along the board. Being nine, his swath took in only the lower half of the expanse of polished slate.

Miss Withers spelled out the word for him. "Now don't dawdle so, Leland."

"Yes'm."

Miss Withers went back to her copy of the *Atlantic*, which she had camouflaged beneath a sheaf of uncorrected arithmetic papers.

Leland, casting a weather eye over his shoulder, decided that the coast was clear. Deftly he inserted three bits of chalk within the folds of his padded eraser, gripping them firmly with a grubby thumb and fingers. It was a discovery of his own—and of practically every boy who ever got in a similar jam—particularly suited to the conservation of energy. He did not know that a similar device is used in the White House when the First Citizen is called upon to sign several hundred state papers at the same time.

The eraser moved across the board waveringly, and three simultaneous "disciplines" appeared, in column form. Three more—

Miss Withers watched him over her glasses, and then hid a smile behind the article she was reading.

Discipline was discipline, and yet she wanted to get away tonight even worse than did the youngster. Only she couldn't have her children making such remarks in her classroom. The idea of little Leland's chattering nonsense about the principal and Miss Halloran! Well, this afternoon would be a lesson to him. It was, only not as Miss Withers had planned, exactly.

Hildegarde Withers liked the young music teacher. Her first name, Anise, was a little affected, perhaps. But the day was past when you could blame a young teacher for being beautiful and attractive. What if she did rouge her lips a little and wear French heels?

Three-inch heels weren't a sign of moral degradation any more, as Miss Withers was wont to remark when some of the older teachers got to talking. They talked too much. The children were bound to pick it up, just as Leland had done.

Miss Withers began to tap her front teeth with a pencil. Something vaguely troubled her, something that had to do with high heels. A little hammer pounded insistently at the back of her mind.

Oh yes, now she remembered. It had been a long time since Anise Halloran's heels had tapped down the hall toward the Teachers' Cloakroom. Unconsciously, Miss Withers had been waiting to hear them go back again up the hall toward the front door.

It wasn't like Anise Halloran to linger. Maybe she wasn't feeling well. She had been looking poorly, Miss Withers decided, during the last week. Suppose the girl had fainted. . . .

Miss Withers looked over her shoulder at the moonfaced clock on the wall. It was three fifty-five. Anise had passed down the hall as soon as the children burst out of the classrooms at three-thirty.

"Perhaps she went home without my hearing," Miss Withers told herself. "And yet—I wonder. I suppose I ought to look in there and see."

She listened. The deserted schoolhouse was less silent than the proverbial tomb, but in comparison with the noise of the day it was very quiet. Down in the dark reaches of the cellar she could hear the janitor, "Mister" Anderson, rattling a pail. Outside on the playground some girls were screaming delightedly, and farther on there was the thump of a stubby shoe against inflated pigskin. They hadn't waited for Leland.

The absence of the tapping heels of Anise Halloran seemed a minute discord in the quiet harmony of the building.

Leland had stopped to count his wordage. Miss Withers

stood up, flashed him a warning glance, and then sat down again in her chair.

The tapping heels were passing down the hall, past the door of 1B, and on toward the front door. Anise must be tired, for the steps were slower than usual . . . almost stumbling.

Miss Withers was glad she hadn't acted on her impulse. She wouldn't have liked Anise Halloran to think that she was another of the spying busybodies, like Miss Rennel upstairs, or Miss Hopkins on the third floor.

They talked about everybody. About Miss Halloran, about Mr. Macfarland, about Mr. Macfarland's pleasant young assistant who taught Manual Training . . . about everybody.

Miss Withers wasn't a chronic worrier about other people's business, but there had been a white, drawn look about Anise Halloran's face for the past week. "Maybe the girl is sick," she told herself. "She was in the Cloakroom a long time, and I distinctly heard her stumble. . . ." Miss Withers rose to her feet.

"Hurry up and finish, Leland," she said, and rose to her feet. It was only a step down the hall to the Cloakroom, which had a window on the street. If she hurried she could catch a glimpse of Anise Halloran outside. Maybe the child was ill and needed a taxi home or something.

Miss Withers had little use for the Cloakroom, since she kept her own neat sailor in a drawer on her desk in 1B, and since her nose had not been powdered since the Taft administration.

She opened the door quickly, but did not switch on the light, as she did not want everybody in the street to see her running to the window to look after another teacher. She was familiar enough with the room, though it was in half-darkness.

On one side were the chairs and the lounge, and on the other the coat lockers and the door of the lavatory. The frosted window was a dull blur of light across the room . . . with eight inches of daylight at the bottom where it was open for the sake of air.

Then her foot struck something soft on the floor. She stooped, and picked up a woman's shoe.

It was a gay, ridiculous bit of footwear, truly a sandal instead of a shoe. It consisted only of a tapering heel, a thin sole, and four or five straps. Only Anise Halloran wore shoes like that. And Anise Halloran had gone home five minutes ago—had she left her shoes here?

Miss Withers stood up, went back to the door, and turned on the light. On the floor lay the mate to the shoe she held in her hand, and on the couch was what was left of Anise Halloran.

II

Chalk and Eraser

(11/15/32—4:05 P.M.)

"Oh dear, oh dear," whispered Hildegarde Withers. She stood there by the door of the Teachers' Cloakroom while the old-fashioned gold watch on her old-fashioned bosom ticked away the best part of a minute.

She blinked, rapidly, but the dreadful vision still remained. Then at last the icy chill which had been travelling up her spine reached her brain. She shook her head, and assured herself that twelve times fourteen was still one hundred and sixty-eight.

It has been somewhere well written that amazement and terror are the most transient of emotions, and that within the space of a few seconds one must come to terms even with a gibbering ghost.

Miss Withers brought her teeth together with a slight click. Then her fingers felt again for the wall switch, and the room plunged into darkness.

This darkness was thick, black, and sticky. It blotted, mercifully, the picture of Anise Halloran in her last dreamless sleep, hiding the crimson gash that marred her white forehead and the rivulets that had barely ceased to flow across her cheek.

Instantly the darkness itself was peopled with a thousand vague and terrible shapes—shapes far more fearful than the quiet body of the young singing teacher, stretched out face upward on the couch.

Miss Withers nodded slowly to herself, and then stepped out into the hall and closed the door. She looked around her with something of a shiver, but whatever she had feared to see was not lying there in wait.

She came in safety to the door of her own classroom,

7

paused for a moment to compose herself, and then stepped inside.

This was the first, and quite probably the last moment in the life of Leland Stanford Jones that anyone but his mother had looked on his freckled face and found it beautiful. As Miss Withers stood there, her mind already wrestling with the one incongruous detail of that nearby room of death, Leland turned toward her, pleadingly.

"Teàcher, I wrote it seventy-one times already!"

Miss Withers nodded. "Seventy-one will be sufficient, Leland," she conceded.

Daylight dawned in his face. "An' I can go?"

She nodded again. "But first I want you to run an errand."

His face fell. "But the kids are waiting for me . . ."

"It's too dark to see a football anyway," she reminded him. "I want you to run across the street to Tobey's store. Here's a dime for the telephone. Call Inspector Piper at Headquarters . . ."

Leland snapped out of it like a rubber band.

"Yes, teacher!" It was a legend among pupils of Jefferson School that twice in the past their own Miss Withers had played a part in the activities of the New York Homicide Squad.

"Tell him where I am, and tell him to come quickly and quietly," added Miss Withers. "Hurry now—and don't stop for—for anything or high water."

Leland did not know that the watchful eye of his teacher followed him down the hall, across the windswept street, and through the yellow oblong that was the door of Tobey's Candy and Notions Store.

Back in 1B again, Miss Withers took a deep breath, and then consulted the moon-faced clock. It was, in spite of the early twilight of November in Manhattan, only ten minutes after four. Forty minutes had passed since the heels of Anise Halloran had tapped their way down the hall to the Cloak-room, and only a little more than ten since they had scuffled their way back.

With her eyes on the clock, Miss Withers waited there for five of the longest minutes in her life. There was not a sound from the vast emptiness of the school building around her, but she waited all the same.

Then she reached toward the drawer of her desk which held her sailor—gasping a little to discover that in her excitement she still held in her hand the blue sandal that was Anise Halloran's.

Swiftly she acted. The blue sandal was enclosed in examination papers, and tucked under her arm. On her head she planted the neat sailor, at a rakish angle, and in her right hand she clutched with a grip of steel the handle of her cotton umbrella.

For a moment she paused outside the door of 1B. She looked a little longingly back down toward the door of the Cloakroom, and then shook her head. It was too late for that. The best thing was for her to act naturally now.

She strode serenely down the hall and out through the front door into the street. It is an evidence of a certain latent histrionic ability in the lady that on this memorable night she left Jefferson School in identically the same manner that had been hers some two hundred-odd times every year for the past decade.

Nor did she hesitate on the steps of the building, but turned to the left and walked briskly along Avenue A. She did not appear to be counting windows—but at the sixth from the main door she paused. There was an eight-inch space at the top of that window—eight inches of jetty darkness.

Miss Withers swung her arm, and that darkness swallowed up a girl's blue sandal. The school teacher made an abrupt about-face. Calmly she marched back and across the street to Tobey's, the little notion store opposite the main entrance of Jefferson School.

The freckled face of Leland Stanford Jones appeared above the glass of the phone booth. He stood on his tiptoes to hang up the receiver and then came out.

"I called him, teacher!"

"Leland! Did it take all this time . . . ?"

"Mister Tobey wasn't in," Leland interrupted defensively. "The door was open, but he wasn't in. I couldn't get change out of your dime for the phone till he got back."

"But he's here now?"

"Oh, yes'm. In the back room. Mister Tobey!"

A short, bald toad of a man appeared in the curtained entrance of the rear room. The nails of one fat hand continually scratched his bald pate, and with the other he tapped suggestively upon the glass counter.

"Someding?"

Miss Withers joined Leland at the counter, above the assortment of brownish licorice, octogenarian peppermints, and furry horehound.

There was something very wary and defensive in Tobey's attitude toward this new customer. It didn't stand to reason that this angular lady had come to buy candy. More likely she was going to squawk about the quality of his product, like the young teacher across the street who had complained to the Board of Health about him when one of her pupils took a cramp in singing class. Just because of the bright colors in his hard candies! Aniline dyes, his eye! As if kids got any sicker from one kind of candy than another! Besides, the brighter it was the better they like it. Tobey knew.

He fidgeted, mumbled, and rubbed his hands raspingly together, but still this tall lady with the umbrella waited there, seemingly intent upon a choice between lemon drops and chocolate-covered peanuts.

He did not know that the curved, cloudy glass of the show counter reflected the dimly-lit doorway across the street. Whatever it may have been that Miss Withers had hoped to see, her vision was suddenly blotted out by a looming gray figure.

She whirled around, with her finger on her lips. "Oscar!"

Let me explain to those of my readers who are having their first introduction to Oscar Piper, Inspector of Detectives, that he is a leanish, grayish man of somewhat indeterminate age, with a pugnacious lower lip and a pair of very chilly blue-gray eyes. A badly-lighted cigar usually hangs from one corner of his mouth, and his speech, perhaps because he has risen from the ranks and is proud of it, smacks a little of Broadway, West Broadway.

There was a cigar in his mouth as he entered Tobey's store on this memorable evening, and he neglected to remove it before addressing Miss Withers. He was pleasantly surprised to have that lady grasp his hands in hers, with a warning look toward the candy proprietor and the waiting urchin.

She placed a quarter on the counter. "Anything you like, Leland," she said. Then she led the Inspector into the street.

He followed, docile enough. These two had once become engaged to be married—in the flush of excitement after the successful termination of a gruelling murder case—for the space of half an hour. Their friendship had ripened in spite of, or perhaps because of, the fact that the Inspector's zeal for the enforcement of the more intelligible of the state's laws had led him on a sudden chase that gave Miss Withers the opportunity to change her mind.

"Sorry to break up your whole afternoon," Miss Withers told him. "But now and then a dead body is apt to interfere with the daily pinochle game."

The Inspector took the cigar out of his mouth, but he was not given a chance to speak.

"I'm serious," she went on. She told him what she had seen in the Teachers' Cloakroom.

The Inspector teetered quietly on his toes. "Murder, eh? When did it happen?"

"You don't understand," Miss Withers exploded. "It's still happening! That's why I sent word to you to come quietly. This is no time for a squad car to scream bloody murder through the streets. Somebody smashed Anise Halloran's skull in that schoolhouse a little while ago—and that somebody is still in there!"

She tugged at his arm. "Come on!"

The Inspector held back. "This is irregular as—well, it's irregular," he told her. "I have to notify the local precinct station of the murder, and have two plainclothes men sent out here, and the Medical Examiner . . ."

"Botheration!" Miss Withers still pulled at his arm. "While you're doing all that, the murderer will wash up all traces and disappear. This is no ordinary crime, Oscar Piper. The murderer knew what he was doing, and he waited for me to go home!"

The Inspector threw his cigar away. "Where's the body?"

She pointed. "Got a gun, Oscar?"

He shook his head. "You know I haven't carried a gat since I took off my uniform."

"Well, then you can take my umbrella," she offered. Stealthily, they approached the schoolhouse.

One dim bulb was burning, as usual, above the entrance to the main hall. They came into the building, with its musty smells of chalk dust and humanity. Quickly Miss Withers led the way down the long hall toward the rear—past the door of 1B and down to the Teachers' Cloakroom.

The door was still closed. Inspector Piper listened outside it for a moment, and then thrust it open. He stepped back quickly out of range, but nothing happened.

A second later he found the light switch. There was a long, silent pause, and then he whirled on Miss Withers.

"Hildegarde! Is this your idea of humor?"

The room, Miss Withers saw to her amazement, was empty—as calm and quiet as it had ever been.

There was only the flapping curtain, blown by the breeze which came in through an eight-inch opening at the top of the window. The couch, on which Anise Halloran's body had lain, was not only empty, but its cotton print covering was orderly and neat.

Miss Withers pointed toward it. "There! There's where it was!"

Piper came closer. He took the couch cover in his fingers and inspected it closely. "Nonsense! You say that she had been bleeding? Well, there hasn't been time for anybody to wash stains out of this cover and get it dry. There's not a sign of blood."

Miss Withers shook her head doggedly. "I don't care. I saw what I saw. I'm not given to hallucinations. Nor do I indulge in the flowing bowl. You know that, Oscar. And I say that there was a dead body here less than ten minutes ago."

"Where could it go?" The Inspector drew a thin dark cigar from his pocket. "A corpse doesn't get up and wander about, as a rule. Unless this girl was only wounded, and managed to come to herself and get out of here . . ."

Miss Withers shook her head. "She was dead, sure enough. Her face—yes, she was dead. I can see her yet—with her face so calm and peaceful under that gaping wound. She must have died without knowing what struck her, Oscar . . ."

"Not necessarily. Fiction to the contrary, there is complete relaxation of all muscles in the face—and body, too— immediately after death, and it lasts till rigor mortis sets in. All expression leaves the face of a corpse within a few minutes—seconds, even. But go on. Try to remember . . ."

"She lay there, with her head toward the window."

"How was she dressed? Coat on?"

"I—I don't remember. Yes, I guess so. She had on a hat, I know that. It was a dark helmet that fitted the head, and it was drawn a little back to show the forehead."

Piper nodded. "I see. They couldn't have got her out of that window . . . no, that's as far as it opens. Well, your dead body is still in this building somewhere, and so is the murderer unless he—or she—made a getaway damn recently."

"Nobody made a getaway. I watched the hall while I was here, and the main and only door wasn't out of my sight while I was across the street."

"Good." The Inspector rubbed his hands. "I'm beginning to think you're right. Maybe the body was parked here for awhile. But why, I don't see . . . nor how the murderer managed not to leave a blood stain on the couch . . ."

"Wait," interrupted Miss Withers. "I think I've got it! There was something white under the body—I thought it was a towel, and it puzzled me. Now I know. The murderer intended to take the body away and leave no trace. He had it pillowed on newspapers!"

"Insulated, huh?" The Inspector chewed his cigar. His voice was tense and eager, for all its being pitched hardly above a whisper.

"The murderer is probably trying to hide the body somewhere else in the building, or else get it out of a rear window onto the playground. Lord, I've got a chance to catch him in the act!"

"You mean *we* have," Miss Withers corrected. She took a firmer grip on her umbrella. "Come on!"

Piper shook his head. "Two of us moving around in the building are sure to make some noise, and probably startle him. Besides, you've got to turn in the alarm. We must have a thorough search of this building, and quickly. There is such a thing as routine, too, and the local precinct has a right to get in on this. You run to the phone across the street, and start the boys this way. I'll lie low here and see if I can get wise to anything. Vamoose!"

"But, Oscar . . ."

"Hurry, will you? This thing is likely to get too big for us to handle. Go on, Hildegarde!"

"Just my luck not to be in at the finish," whispered Miss Withers sadly. She departed, swiftly and silently.

Inspector Oscar Piper paused in the Cloakroom long enough to light his cigar. Its pungent smoke comforted him. It didn't seem as if he had company, living or dead. The schoolhouse was quiet as a tomb—indeed, it *was* a tomb if Miss Withers was correct. And she had a way of being correct.

He had about made up his mind to start a systematic search of the place when the faintest of sounds reached his ears. It was no more than the whisper of a sound—a far-away clink of metal against stone. He stiffened

"Probably rats," he told himself. "The cellar must be full of them."

There it came again . . . followed by a muffled thump.

"It's certainly rats," the Inspector decided. "But I wonder—"

Slowly he moved on tiptoe down the hall, away from the main door. A red light burned feebly above a swinging door at the end of the hall. He pushed the door aside . . . and the noise of the rats came more clearly.

He was standing on the top of the cellar stairs—looking down a flight of concrete steps into the realm sacred to the janitor of Jefferson School and his battery of furnace and coal bins and storage rooms and all the rest of it. There were dank and unpleasant odors in the air that welled up from the abyss, and the Inspector began to pick his way down without any particular eagerness.

Finally at the the bottom, he put away his flashlight. He'd not need it after all, as the place was hung ahead of him with low-power incandescent bulbs, which gave more glow than real light. He could see, on either side of him and straight ahead, long lanes of roughly boarded flooring between thick arched pillars of concrete that supported the upper floors.

Slowly the Inspector made his way along the flooring, trying to avoid creaking boards, and keeping his ears wide open. The noise of the rats had stopped—evidently his coming had frightened them away.

His ears were also attuned to the first sound of the police sirens that within the space of a few minutes should be shattering the stillness of his lonely section. But he was not to hear it.

There came the faintest of movements behind him, a mere

rustling of cloth or the drawing of a breath. It was not rats—the Inspector knew that much. Tense as a steel spring, he swung to one side and whirled about, but it was too late.

A thousand bolts of lightning struck him on the back of the had, with reverberating echoes of thunder that mercifully died away . . . away . . . .

Outside in the street two squad cars were already blaring their sirens as they roared up to the door of Jefferson School. But Oscar Piper did not hear them. He lay on his face in a gathering pool of blood. His crumpled cigar, still firmly grasped in his mouth, hissed and went out.

III

Ink and Inklings

(11/15/32—4:45 P.M.)

"Don't stand there like stone statues!" Miss Withers was saying. "Do something!"

There wasn't much to do, not yet at any rate. The ambulance was on its way—Miss Withers dabbed futilely at the Inspector's gory head with her handkerchief—and officers swarmed through the cellar of Jefferson School.

"Let me get my two hands around the neck of the sonovitch . . ." prayed McTeague earnestly. His watery blue eyes were narrow and unhappy, like those of a caged animal. "Just my two hands . . ."

Sergeant Taylor, of the Inspector's office, shook his head. He shivered a little, stared distastefully around at the dank and ill-smelling place, and for the dozenth time he loosened the big six-shooter that he wore in a shoulder holster.

"Wait till we get the Inspector out of here," he promised her, "and then we'll start doing something. We'll tear this building down to the ground until we find whoever was fool enough to try this. And when we get him we'll give him a lesson in what not to try on cops. There hasn't a cop killer got away in this town in twenty years . . ."

He stopped short at the look on Miss Withers' face. "Of course, I don't mean that they can't pull the Inspector through, y'understand. He's a tough bird, and I've seen men live with bigger holes than that in their skull. Hey—you ain't going to faint, are you?"

"I am not," said Hildegarde Withers. "But to come back and find him like this! I didn't want him to stay here alone, but he insisted. And I tried to make him take my umbrella . . ."

"Never mind that now," said the Sergeant. "As soon as

16

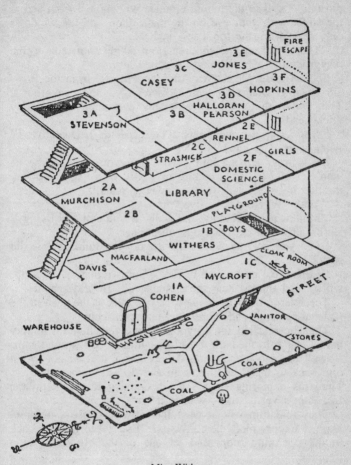

Miss Withers
Draws a Plan
of
JEFFERSON
SCHOOL

the ambulance comes we'll start work in earnest. Whoever did this is still in the building, since you phoned from across the street with your eye on the main door, and the windows only open from the top a few inches. . . .''

"That's to keep the children from taking short cuts to the playground," Miss Withers informed him.

Second-grade Detectives Allen and Burns, from the Bowery Precinct Station, hovered discreetly in the background. This whole thing was considerably over their respectively thick heads.

"If Piper croaks, who gets to be Inspector of Detectives?" Allen wanted to know.

His partner hushed him. "Not you, you sap. Maybe he won't croak. I seen a picture of a guy who had a crowbar through his skull and lived for twenty years.'

"Yeah? Where did he live?''

"Mattewan—chained to the wall—if you call that living," Burns informed the persistent questioner.

"Did you see the wound? What do you think it was did with?''

"Looks like an axe job to me," Burns replied. "Shut up, will you? I think I hear the ambulance." He did hear it.

The interne from Bellevue took one look at the gash in the Inspector's skull and rubbed his unshaven chin.

Then he reached for a hypo. "Something hit him mighty hard," he informed the breathless little group around him. "Swell piece of concussion if I ever saw it. I've got to get him back to the operating room and do a trephine job. . . ." Then his exploring fingers touched the gold badge on the Inspector's vest. "Say—who is it?'

They told him who it was. Instantly he chose a different hypo. "Excuse me," he corrected. "I've got to get him back to the operating room and let one of the big shots do a trephine.''

Miss Withers was close beside him. "Doctor, what chance does he have?''

The interne shrugged. "A swell chance—if we can keep him breathing for a while. They forget to breathe sometimes under a whack like that. Anyway, he won't need any ether for the operation—he'll be out stone cold for hours. All right, boys, lift him easy.''

Miss Withers leaned over the limp figure for a moment, then she stood erect. "You want to ride along with him?" asked the interne.

She shook her head. Sergeant Taylor stood beside her as they carried Oscar Piper away.

"I'm glad you stayed," said the Sergeant. "You can show us through this place. I know how you feel."

"Do you?" asked Miss Withers woodenly.

"From now on I'm playing understudy," she announced. "We're working together?"

"A hundred per cent," said Taylor, but his voice lacked enthusiasm.

"If I could only get me two hands around the neck . . ." McTeague intoned, hopefully.

And the chase went on.

Sergeant Taylor dispatched Allen and Burns, together with several husky uniformed men, to go through the cellar with a fine-tooth comb. "Though there's not much chance that the murdering blackguard stayed down here," he added, "we'll take McTeague and go through the building from the roof down."

"We won't get far at that," Miss Withers told him. "Most, if not all, of the teachers here lock their classrooms at the end of the day." She was thoughtful. "The janitor has a master-key . . . ."

"Janitor, hey? Well, where is this janitor?"

"Anderson may have gone home—no, because the lights were on down here and the main door was open. He wouldn't go home and leave them that way—but he doesn't seem to be around anywhere. Never mind him for now—I know where the duplicate master-key is kept."

Swiftly Miss Withers led the way up the stairs, down the hall past the door of the Teachers' Cloakroom, past the door of her own schoolroom, to a large office on the first floor, nearest the main entrance. The door bore a legend "Principal" and it was locked.

McTeague swung his massive brogan, and the door swung inward. They came into a small reception room, with a typewriter desk in one corner where, Miss Withers explained, the Principal's secretary, one Janey Davis, presided. Everything here was strictly in order—Miss Withers led the way into the main office and designated the middle drawer of the big oak desk.

Out they went into the hall again, and up the stairs at the right. The second-floor hall was pitch dark, and McTeague's flash cast ghostly shadows. It lighted for a moment on a tall glass-fronted show case built into one wall.

"What's that?" the Sergeant wanted to know. He was staring through the glass upon an assortment of seemingly unrelated objects.

Miss Withers pointed out a small label atop the case. "Lives of the Presidents" was the legend.

"An idea of Mr. Ballantyne, who taught shop work here last year, before Mr. Stevenson came," she explained. "He had the upper-class boys whittle out models of objects closely related to the presidents of the United States. They made everything of pine and then painted them."

The Sergeant rubbed his chin. "Not bad, eh?" Inside the case he could make out a rude log cabin and a life-size shovel, its blade marked with sums in chalk. Miss Withers did not need to tell him that these represented the early life of Abraham Lincoln.

George Washington, too, was represented by the hacked-off stump of a little tree, and a bright-handled hatchet beside it. Farther on stood a model of Mount Vernon, slightly askew as to pillars, a pair of duelling pistols labelled "Hamilton and Burr," and a silk-hat marked "Woodrow Wilson."

"Kids have more fun nowadays than we did when I went to school," the Sergeant informed Miss Withers. "Whittling out toy models, huh? They should have made an empty dinner pail in memory of Herb Hoover, and completed the list."

"Hoover's been blamed for everything else," Miss Withers remarked acidly. "I suppose this murder is his fault, too? Come on, we're wasting time." They climbed another flight of stairs.

"This is the top, huh? No way to the roof?"

Miss Withers nodded, then shook her head. "No way at all. And if anybody did get up there, he couldn't get down. there's a fenced-in playground on two sides of the school, the street out in front, and a twenty-story warehouse on the other side."

"We'll start at the end of the hall and work back," Taylor

decided. "You keep out of this, Miss Withers. This is one bad hombre, and if we flush him he's likely to swing at you."

"No more me than you," she pointed out. But the Sergeant was studying a peculiar door at the end of the hall.

"Thought you said there was only a playground here on this side of the building?" Taylor queried. "Then where's this funny little door go?"

Rudely he pushed on the swinging door, but it held fast. He looked at Miss Withers.

"That? Oh, I forgot to tell you. It's a fire escape. A little old-fashioned, perhaps, but it was the latest thing when Jefferson School was built, back in the time of Boss Tweed. We have fire drill every week, and the children file into this doorway, one by one, and slide down and out onto the playground. They love the excitement of roller-coasting down, chute-the-chute fashion, and the building can be emptied in five minutes."

McTeague thrust his bulk forward. "Say—if the kids can get out that way, why couldn't the murderer? If I could only get me hands on him. . . ."

"I don't think he got out that way—" began Miss Withers. She was interrupted by the sound of running feet on the stair.

Taylor jerked at his gun, but replaced it when he saw the perspiring face of Allen, the precinct plainclothes man. His mouth was working.

"Hey, what do you think we found down in the cellar?"

Miss Withers' eyes narrowed. "The body of Anise Halloran!"

He shook his head. "No, no body. There ain't no body in the cellar at all. But somebody's been digging a good-sized grave down there, in the soft dirt under the arches. We found the shovel and everything!"

"Well, I'll be everlastingly—" Sergeant Taylor set out, on the run, with Allen at his heels. McTeague followed, with a reluctant look at the door of the fire escape, which had slammed shut.

But Miss Withers let them go. She wasn't interested in open graves. This was her chance to do a little quiet sleuthing on the side, and she leaped at it. Oddly enough, she forgot for the moment that a bloodthirsty murderer was supposed to be hiding somewhere in the shadows of the deserted school-house. The lure of the chase was upon her.

Using the master-key which she still held in her hand, she proceeded to unlock each of the third floor rooms in turn, beginning with 3F, which was sacred to Miss Hopkins and her sixth grade.

There was little here which seemed of interest. The well-worn chair behind the desk on the platform wore a gay cushion of chintz. That was typical of Mattie Hopkins, who weighed two hundred pounds and preferred comfort to every-thing else. There was a pair of carpet slippers beneath the desk, and several hundred spit balls had dried upon the long blackboards. Miss Withers shook her head. Mattie Hopkins was getting slack with her pupils.

Miss Withers passed on to 3E, across the hall. Here the saturnine Agatha Jones dispensed English and allied subjects to the seventh and eighth graders. The room was neat as a pin, except for the blackboards, which still bore scrawlings of the day's work in sentence structure. Idly Miss Withers went through the drawers of the desks, unearthing a sling shot, three packages of chewing gum, and other booty no doubt gathered by Miss Jones during the day and unreturned to its juvenile owners. None of this seemed to have any bearing on the situation.

Miss Casey's room, 3C, was hardly more productive. Here the seventh and eighth graders were exposed to arithmetic, history, and civics. No murderer lurked within its common-place walls, and the face of one George Washington looked down benignly from above the window.

Miss Withers came to 3D—a double room shared by Miss Pearson, the young drawing teacher, and she who had taught music until today in Jefferson School—beautiful Anise Halloran herself.

This was not primarily a schoolroom but in reality only a joint office, as both the young teachers had gone into other classrooms as a rule to give their work. It contained a piano and some wooden benches for the Glee Club, a portable Victrola and cabinet of classical records and march music, which was moved throughout the building as needed, and a blackboard upon which Miss Petarson had evidently been engaged in drawing a fearful and wonderful Thanksgiving turkey, in colored chalk.

Natalie Pearson's desk was nearest the door. Miss Withers hesitated at prying into its contents, for she liked the boyish young drawing teacher. But this was no time for a consideration of ethics. Within a few moments Sergeant Taylor was bound to rejoin her, and Miss Withers had a secret desire to do her sleuthing alone.

She found two vanity cases—both in disrepair—several boxes of pastels and colored chalk, a large box of water colors, its cakes badly mixed and muddied, and a theater program, undated, for a revival of Florenz Ziegfeld's *Show Boat,* still running at the Casino Theater. Within the pages of the program was pressed a limp greenish-white cattelya orchid. Miss Withers sniffed, and then smiled and raised it to her nose. Then she made a grimace, for a faint odor of putridity clung to it.

Carefully she replaced the token, leaving everything as she had found them. Then she passed on to the desk that had been Anise Halloran's.

Much to her surprise, Miss Withers found it locked. For a moment she debated with herself, and then went into action with a hairpin. She had met locks like this one before, and it was only a few seconds until the main drawer slid out, releasing the others.

Sheet music, mostly folk songs and marches, covered a well-thumbed copy of the French classic *Mon Homme,* sung so successfully in this country some years ago by Fannie Brice . . . that was all she found in the top drawer.

The top sides disclosed a box of Kleenex, a gold and enamel vanity with a cracked mirror, two packs of Life Savers, a large bottle labelled "Aspirin" which was nearly empty, a bottle labelled "Bromo Seltzer" which was quite empty, and an envelope containing two season tickets to the Lewisohn Stadium concerts of the past summer, both well-used.

Miss Withers puzzled a moment over the aspirin and bromo. What was a young and beautiful girl like Anise Halloran doing with headache remedies? She hadn't looked as if she ever had a headache in the world until the last few weeks. Well, her headache would trouble her no more. Miss

Withers shivered as she thought of that broken body she had seen in the Cloakroom, two floors below. Where was it now? Into what dark recess had the murderer carried it, and when would the shadows give up their secret?

The bottom drawer on the right brought the first real surprise of Miss Withers' search. There she came upon a fat bottle labelled "Dewar's Dew of Kirkintilloch." The label was discolored, as if it had lain in salt water, and the contents of the bottle, to Miss Withers' somewhat amateurish nose, seemed to be a reasonably close approximation of Scotch whiskey.

She sniffed, and replaced the bottle, carefully covering it with the newspapers in which it had been wrapped. There was also a box of paper cups, of the type furnished in metal cases above the water containers of the school.

Miss Withers frowned. That didn't seem like Anise Halloran, somehow. She would as soon have believed that liquor was the secret vice of Mr. Macfarland himself.

The desk yielded nothing more of interest, and Miss Withers slammed the drawers shut.

It was at that moment that stealthy footsteps outside reminded her that a murderer was quite possibly stalking her through these deserted halls. Miss Withers reached the light switch in one second, flat, and cast the room into darkness. Then, with her umbrella poised for action, she waited.

Slowly the door opened, and a man's dark figure showed itself. Steadily she poked forward the umbrella, until its bone handled pressed sharply against the back of the figure which was moving past her into the room.

"One move out of you and I'll shoot," she promised. Then she switched on the light. Sergeant Taylor, his hands high above his head, turned to face her.

"Oh," she remarked, in a disappointed tone. "It's only you."

He wore a heartfelt look of relief. "Thank God it's you," he told her fervently. "Say, what have you been doing up here alone? I thought you were coming with us . . ."

"Never mind that," Miss Withers interrupted. "Did you find anything in that grave?"

Sergeant Taylor shook his head. "It wasn't very deep," he admitted. "But it was a good beginning. Six feet long, two feet wide, and about two or three feet deep, cut down into the soft dirt under the pillars in the unfinished part of the cellar. There's no flooring there, you know."

Miss Withers nodded, thoughtfully. "Anything else?"

"Nothing to speak of. No sign of that janitor fellow. They did come on a box half filled with women's wornout shoes, hidden in the clothes closet of the janitor's room under the stairs. And that's a funny thing for a man to collect."

Miss Withers moved back and forth, restlessly. "It doesn't make sense!" she protested. "Oh, I wish Oscar Piper were here. He was almost always wrong, but he was so positive about everything that it was almost as good as being right. He'd have some explanation for this. An hour ago I saw a body here—now there's a grave and the body is gone."

"Come on down and have a look at the grave," invited Taylor. "I'd feel better about this if you stuck with us until we find the guy we're looking for."

"Then you'll stick with me," Hildegarde Withers told him. "Because I'm going to go through the one remaining room on this floor if it kills me." She led the way to the door nearest the staircase, which bore the joint labels 3A and 3B. They came into a long, bare room partially filled with benches and littered with tools. "Mr. Stevenson, the assistant principal, teaches shopwork and science to the older boys in this room," she explained. "That door farther on is his private office."

Taylor nodded. He crossed over to a a a bench and picked up a shining chisel. "Now do you suppose the Inspector was beaned with one of these?"

Miss Withers hesitated. "Maybe. You'd better have McTeague check over these tools and see if anything is missing."

Taylor nodded. "Yes, ma'am. Shall I have him do it now? I ordered him to patrol the stairs and the upper hall here until we got through. . . ."

"Later will do," Miss Withers decided. "I don't want him poking around here until we see all there is to be seen."

The end of the room used for the science classes boasted only of a double row of chairs facing a long table against the windows, which was littered with aquaria, plant specimens, cases containing frogs and turtles, and a hutch containing nothing but sodden straw.

"You are standing on the scene of a recent tragedy," Miss Withers remarked as she paused before the hutch. "Amos and Andy, two guinea pigs, used to live here, the pets of the school. They were purchased for dissection purposes, I suppose, but the children got to love them so much that Mr. Stevenson didn't have the heart to use them in his demonstrations. For some reason or other, they up and died a few days ago. That is, Amos died. Andy was sick, but he lingered on and had to be put out of his misery."

Taylor scented a mystery. "Say! Do you think they could have been poisoned?"

Miss Withers was dubious. "I'm afraid it's nothing exciting like that, Sergeant. They were fine and fat and healthy looking, but they gradually grew too weak to stand up. Something deficient in their diet, I suppose, or else lack of sunlight. Mr. Stevenson explained it to the children, but I don't remember. It doesn't matter. Shall we go on into his office?"

Sergeant Taylor followed her, but he was puzzled. "See here," he said, "I don't get this straight. Are we hunting for clues in desk drawers, or for a murderer that's supposed to be hiding somewhere in this schoolhouse?"

"We're just hunting," Miss Withers told him. Swiftly she went through the big oaken desk in the middle of the room. There were only the usual papers, pamphlets, and teaching paraphernalia. Everything was unusually neat and tidy.

"Good for Stevenson," she observed. "I didn't think he was the sort who'd keep everything so shipshape."

The desk top bore only a large green blotter, a fountain pen set in malachite, and, standing beside a heavy glass inkwell, a small nickel-plated cigarette lighter.

"I don't know what he had that for," Miss Withers told the Sergeant. "Smoking is never permitted inside the schoolhouse during school hours, because it's a bad example for the older boys."

Taylor shrugged his shoulders. "Maybe the assistant principal used to work nights a lot." He drew a cigarette from a tattered pack in the breast pocket of his coat, and offered another to Miss Withers. "I need one of these, how about you?"

"Me? Mercy sakes, no. The idea of me smoking one of those nasty things!"

Taylor grinned, and quoted a current advertisement. "It happens that I don't smoke, but some of my debutante friends who do tell me that Luckies are parched, not toasted. . . ."

Idly he picked up the lighter from the desk and snapped it, with no appreciable result. Again, and again. . . .

"These things never work," he informed Miss Withers. He replaced it on the desk, and lit his cigarette with a match from his capacious coat pocket.

Miss Withers was surveying a shelf between the windows, on which stood an assortment of various and sundry bottles. "These look harmless enough," she observed. "Here's a can of the lighter fluid that they put in those little jiggers, and it's nearly empty. I suppose that's why the lighter won't work, he's forgotten to fill it . . ."

She stopped short, as a distant metallic booming broke the stillness. "What's that?"

The Sergeant relaxed again, with a chuckle. "I'm getting as nervous as you. That's only a radiator banging."

"Oh!" Miss Withers was thoughtful. "A radiator? But . . ."

She moved toward the radiator across the room, but stopped short in front of a little wash stand which stood in the corner, behind a screen. It was quite evidently used for the cleaning of scientific apparatus, as the sink was littered with retorts, glasses, and cups.

Here her sharp eyes caught sight of something. She raised one of the glasses.

It was of the type sold in ten-cent stores everywhere, and sometimes used by otherwise law-abiding citizens of this great nation in the imbibing of highballs.

This glass differed from its fellows in one particular. It was inhabited.

Much to Miss Withers' surprise, a solitary red ant lay in the bottom of the glass.

Further examination disclosed the fact that this red ant was a dead red ant. Had he climbed to this dizzy height from the playground outside, Miss Withers wondered, in search of water, only to die of exhaustion on the slippery inside of the glass with a single drop almost within his reach?

She raised the glass to her nose, but dropped it to shatter

on the floor as the silence of the evening was violated by a hideous crescendo of sound.

Outside in the hall, in every hall of the building, a powerful gong was ringing.

"Hey," burst forth the Sergeant. "They've found the murderer—or the body!"

IV

Hide and Go Seek

(11/15/32—6:15 P.M.)

Miss Withers put out a restraining hand and caught the Sergeant as he was in the doorway.

"Wait," she told him. "That's the school fire alarm."

"What? You mean, to top everything else, that the place is burning down?" Sergeant Taylor had to raise his voice to make himself heard above the din.

Miss Withers shook her head. "I doubt if the building is afire. But I know what's happened. Come on."

She led the way swiftly down the hall, with her palms pressed firmly over her ears.

"I don't get you," the Sergeant complained.

"I'll show you," she said. They had come at last to the end of the hall, where the solitary window opened out beside the narrow door that led to the old-fashioned fire escape.

Miss Withers tugged at the sash. "Remember my saying that I doubted very much if the murderer got away via this fire escape? You were skeptical."

"I wasn't exactly skeptical, but I had a hunch you were screwy," Taylor admitted.

"Well," went on Miss Withers, as she finally raised the sash, "McTeague didn't take my word for it, either. He's tried it for himself, and therefore the ungodly din. Because whenever the fire alarm is rung in this building, it automatically opens this door. Vice versa, when the door is forced, the alarm goes off."

Sergeant Taylor heaved a sigh of relief. 'You had me scared for a minute, ma'am. So it's only good old McTeague, huh? He's always letting his bump of curiosity lead him astray."

Miss Withers peered out into the darkness of the playground. There was only a faint glow from a distant street light, and for a moment she could see nothing.

"Call to him and tell him how to get back here," she advised. "There's no connection between the playground and the building—he'll have to go north around the teeter-totters and through the gate to the street, and then come back through the main entrance. The playground has a fifteen-foot wire fence around it to keep the children from getting out into the street and being run over."

The siren was dying down. Sergeant Taylor put his head out of the window.

"McTeague! Hey, McTeague!" There was no answer.

The Sergeant turned to Miss Withers. "Say, he couldn't be hurt, could he? Strike his thick head against a rock or something like that as he slid out of the chute?"

"I don't see how," Miss Withers retorted. "The children slide down it every week and I've never had a casualty yet. Wait—isn't that he there?"

She pointed into the darkness. A blurred figure was disappearing toward the gate, around the teeter-totter.

"McTeague!" shouted the Sergeant again. Then, to Miss Withers—"I guess he's wise to the way out. Hey, McTeague!"

There was the shuffle of footsteps behind them, and Miss Withers whirled around to stare into the placid countenance of—McTeague!

"Here I am," said the big Irish copper. "Who wants me?"

Miss Withers and the Sergeant both turned to the window again, but the blurred figure was gone. They looked at each other in silence.

Then Miss Withers whirled on the hapless McTeague. "Say, didn't the Sergeant tell you to patrol the stairway and this upper hall? Where were you? You went off duty and let somebody sneak through here. . . ."

McTeague blinked. "But I heard a suspicious noise, ma'am. A sort of knocking. . . ."

"Yes? Where was it?"

"Well . . ." McTeague removed his uniform cap and scratched his head. "It wasn't no place. I mean it was every place. It was in the radiators, ma'am. Just steam."

"Just steam, eh? Well, we heard that, too, Taylor. Steam rattling in the radiators."

Miss Withers looked around, quickly. There was a large radiator of the flat type hung on the ceiling over their heads, well out of the way.

"Will one of you jump up and touch that?"

McTeague willingly boosted himself up the wall and brought a large red palm in contact with the metal, He withdrew it, redder than it was before, and used a word not common in polite society.

"I beg your pardon, ma'am," he added. "But that's hotter than hell."

Miss Withers nodded slowly and wearily. Her face was drawn, and the excitement of the chase was gone.

"None of us thought it was unusual for a schoolhouse to have steam coming on at this hour of the day," she said slowly. "The weather has been so warm that there's only been a small fire in the morning, to take the chill off the place. I suppose you and those stupid men of yours who are down in the basement thought that somehow the janitor had come in and built up a fire for your comfort this evening?"

Sergeant Taylor was puzzled. "Huh?" He frowned. "Say, I'd like to find that janitor fellow. Allen and Burns don't seem to be getting anywhere with their search downstairs—they haven't got either the janitor or the body."

"You'd better go on down to the basement," Miss Withers told him, "and tip them off that they need only search for the janitor now. I know where the body is."

The Sergeant's mouth dropped open in unison with McTeague's. "You know *what . . . where?*"

Miss Withers told him.

"Good God! Come on, McTeague! You coming, Miss Withers?"

She shook her head. "Not for anything in the world."

"But, ma'am, with all this going on I'd feel safer about you if you'd stick with us. . . ."

"There's nothing to worry about now," Hildegarde Withers told him calmly. "We know where the body is—and the murderer is safely out of here and far away. He—or she, for that matter—happened to know his way out of the building. And out of the playground, even if it was dark."

Sergeant Taylor's face brightened. "Then all we got to do

is to find out the people who know their way around this place, and the murder is solved!''

"Simple, isn't it?" Miss Withers agreed as they walked down the hall. ''You've narrowed the suspects down to thirty or forty thousand. Don't you realize that New York is full of men and women who spent the best part of eight years of their childhood in Jefferson School?''

They came down the stair, and Miss Withers paused outside the door of the Principal's office. ''I'll be here,'' she informed the Sergeant. ''I want to make a phone call.''

Downstairs Taylor came upon the two detectives, Allen and Burns, in a hot argument.

They were standing beside a rude grave in the far corner of the long basement. It was a dark corner, between heavy stone arches that supported the floors above, and had never been completed or floored. There was hardly room for the Sergeant to stand erect, and McTeague was bent almost double.

"I tell you, this hole was dug this afternoon at the latest," Burns was insisting. "Look at the shovel marks. Look at the dirt. It's not dried, is it? Say, you can't fool me about dirt. I used to be on a farm when I was a kid. I've walked plenty of miles behind a plow, and I tell you that dirt is black when it's just dug, and then it dries out and gets grayish-like.''

"Never mind that, boys," Taylor told them. "We got to get busy. Quick, where's the furnace down here?''

Allen pointed with his thumb. "Over there in the corner. Why? Looking for a hot scent?''

"You don't know how hot," the Sergeant told him. "Come on.''

Back under the arches they went, past three gaping coal bins, and along a board walk to where a squat black furnace stood.

"I don't see why we're monkeying around here," Allen complained. "We got to get busy and find whatever there is to be found in this place. Doc Levin is outside, and he says he's going home. He figures the whole thing is a false alarm, and he isn't going to set around and wait . . .''

Allen suddenly paused, as he saw the expression on Sergeant Taylor's face.

"Wha-what's up?''

"Plenty. You searched this basement, didn't you? Well,

you'd be a good one to send after trouble. Because you couldn't find anything. You couldn't find Times Square if you came out of the Paramount.''

Gingerly, the Sergeant caught the handle of the furnace door and threw it open.

A horrible, sickening odor burst out in their faces, and they drew back. McTeague crossed himself, and his lips moved wordlessly.

They were a hardened little group, those four policemen, who stood there aghast at the contents of that flaming bubble of iron. The life of a metropolitan policeman is not such as to make for squeamishness, and those four had looked on death, sudden death, in most of its more horrible forms.

But never in all their lives had they seen a sight like this one. Within the furnace a blackened, fleshless horror grinned out at them, through billows of murky yellow smoke and flame.

They had found the body of Anise Halloran.

V

Do-re-mi

(11/15/32—6:30 P.M.)

"Inspector Piper?" said the voice at the other end of the line, very sweetly. "Oh, yes, Inspector Piper. He's resting quietly, madam."

"Oh, he is, is he? Well, you listen to me, young woman. That resting quietly stuff may go well with most of your telephone enquiries, but it won't do for me. I want you to put down your magazine and take that gum out of your mouth and go to the floor nurse and find out how the Inspector is, do you hear me?" Miss Withers was rapidly losing her temper.

"But, madam . . ."

"Don't you 'but' me! Or I'll come over there to Bellevue Hospital and put you over my knee and spank you."

There was a gasp, and then a long silence. Then the voice came again, still sweet.

"Inspector Piper is in the operating room now, madam. They say he has a comminuted fracture of the skull, and severe concussion, but that he is doing as well as can be expected. His heart is stronger. But of course he isn't conscious yet. He may not be conscious for a day or more, the doctors say. Is there anything else?"

The harshness went out of Miss Withers' voice. "No, thank you, child. Good night." It took her three trials to get the telephone back on its hook, and her face was drawn with weariness as she slowly rose to her feet.

Outside in the hall she could hear Detective Allen's voice, hysterical and high. He was evidently talking to the police photographer. ". . . and believe it or not, we used three fire extinguishers before we could draw it out of the furnace. There won't be much for you to take pictures of. . . ."

They passed onward, toward the cellar stair, and Miss

34

Withers pulled her sailor down over her ears. It was a traditional gesture of defiance with her, a sort of nailing her colors to the mast-head.

She was resolved not to go near the cellar as long—as long as the body was down there. Miss Withers had seen enough of violence and sudden death for one evening. There remained the classrooms of the second floor to search. The police would do it eventually, but Miss Withers was a firm believer in the idea of striking while the iron is hot. The Inspector had always said that more sleuthing could be done in the first twenty-four hours after a murder than in all the time following. Here she was, given the opportunity of being almost an eye-witness to the murder—and as yet not one ray of light penetrated the mystery.

She started for the stairs again, and then thought better of it. She had little respect for the intelligence of the police when Oscar Piper was in charge of a case, and none at all now that he lay on the operating table in the emergency ward at Bellevue.

"I've got to make hay while the sun shines," she resolved. Acting on impulse, she went back into the Principal's office. Somewhere there ought to be a record of the home addresses and telephone numbers of the faculty of Jefferson School. It might be in Mr. Macfarland's desk—no, there was no sign of it. She came back into the outer office and leaned over Janey Davis' typewriter desk.

She tried the upper right-hand drawer...to find only stationery, stamps, an old letter or two, and a package of lemon mints. The second disclosed a small red pasteboard file box, the object of her search.

But Hildegarde Withers had no eyes for the address file now—for just behind it, wrapped in a gold and blue scarf, was a businesslike little automatic pistol.

She picked it up gingerly. The Inspector had once showed her the workings of an automatic, if she could only remember. She adjusted her pince-nez carefully, and then scrutinized the weapon. "This—and that—and then this...."

With a click the magazine slid out of the gun. It was fully loaded—but Miss Withers frowned in perplexity. The shell in the chamber, and all but one in the magazine, were blanks!

One solitary cartridge was complete, with a wicked looking copper sheath over its leaden slug.

It was the third in succession, allowing for the shell already in the chamber. In other words, this little gun would have to be fired twice before it would do anything but make noise.

Miss Withers squinted down the barrel. The gun looked as bright and clean as a new penny. There was no soot in the barrel, and no odor of powder.

"Never been fired, I'll be bound," Miss Withers decided. All the same, it might play some part in this mystery of mysteries.

"If I leave it here, it will only get Janey Davis into trouble," she decided. "Besides, I may need it myself before this night is over." Acting on the thought, she replaced the magazine, and tucked it away in her dress.

Then she picked up the address file, skimming rapidly through the colored cards it contained.

There was supposed to be, Miss Withers realized, a card here bearing the home address and telephone number of every teacher and every employee of Jefferson School. Anderson, the janitor, led off the list with an address far down on East Fourteenth Street. Natalie Pearson was listed as a resident of the Martha Washington. Mr. Macfarland himself was here, with a number on Central Park West, and the assistant principal, Mr. A. Robert Stevenson, gave an address which Miss Withers recognized as one of the quieter sections of the Village, and Betty Curran, the half-time domestic science teacher, was listed as residing at a well-known Brooklyn boarding house.

Then she came at last to the card for which she had been searching. "Anise Halloran, phone Morningside 2-2333, apartment 3C, 441 West 74th St."

Miss Withers added this to her notes, and then skimmed on rapidly through the list until she reached her own name, the end. Then she frowned.

Janey Davis' own address was not listed here. She went back to make sure.

That was strange. There must be a record somewhere . . . suddenly Miss Withers thought of the letter that she had seen in the top drawer. That might have it. It did.

The envelope was of the glassine window type, and she drew forth its contents.

The letter was the usual formal greeting from the Metropolitan Gas and Coke Company, congratulating Miss Davis on becoming a new customer of the company and assuring her that the Metropolitan Gas and Coke Company wished to be known, not as a business institution, but as a personal friend of hers—"please ask our meter readers to show their credentials, thank you. . . ."

It was addressed to Miss Jane Davis, apartment 3C, 441 West 74th Street, and dated two weeks before. Miss Withers had it copied on her list before she realized that the address and apartment number were identical with what she had written just above!

Then Janey Davis and Anise Halloran were roommates—or had been, until today! Not that there was anything so strange about it. Most of the teachers at Jefferson School shared apartments with someone.

Miss Withers carefully put the address file where she had found it, and straightened the desk. Then she bustled out into the hall, confidently hoping that the bulky gun next her body was not too evident.

She drew back into the office doorway again to let pass a canvas-covered stretcher, with two burly morgue attendants grasping the poles. Sergeant Taylor was close behind, in the company of a thin, yellow-faced little man in a blue serge suit.

"Hello, there," greeted the Sergeant. "You know Dr. Levin, don't you?"

Miss Withers admitted that she had had the pleasure. "And what do you find, Doctor?"

The Assistant Medical Examiner shrugged his narrow shoulders. "So what should I find? How can I tell? Even a full autopsy can't give us much information when the body has been burning merrily for half an hour or so. Death appears to be caused by a blow on the forehead with a sharp instrument. But that's not official. See you tomorrow."

His little black case swinging on his arm, Dr. Levin bowed his way out past the bluecoat at the main door. Miss Withers did not envy him the night's work which lay ahead.

"The body was there where you said it would be," the

Sergeant admitted to Miss Withers. "I don't know why the boys didn't find it before then, though. I guess they never thought of looking for it in the furnace."

"They couldn't find anything unless it had a thirty-foot neon sign over it," Miss Withers told him sharply. "It's a wonder those nitwits even found the furnace. Where are they now?"

"We're about through for tonight," the Sergeant confessed. "Allen and Burns searched the second floor classrooms, and now they're going through these on the ground floor."

"I hope they managed to find the second floor without difficulty," Miss Withers remarked. "Did they find anything else of moment?"

The Sergeant drew himself up to his full five foot six. "They certainly did find something," he retorted. "And it may have a deep bearing on this case. There was a full bottle of veronal in the desk of 2E!"

"Well, what of it? Why shouldn't Alice Rennel quiet her nerves with veronal if she wants to? I'm sure if I had her fifth graders day in and day out, I'd need it, too."

"Yeah," said the Sergeant. "But veronal is a pretty strong sleeping powder. Why, you can't even buy it in this state without a prescription from a doctor, and they give 'em out damn seldom." He took a large round bottle from his pocket. "This was bought over in Jersey, according to the label."

Miss Withers studied it. "What is more to the point, it's still a full bottle. As far as I can see, you couldn't cram another tablet in here with a crowbar. Besides, you don't think that Anise Halloran was killed with poison, do you?"

"I'm not thinking, yet," the Sergeant announced.

"Let me know when you start," Miss Withers said softly. "Any time you're ready, this case could use it." Suddenly she changed her tone. "Any sign of the weapon?"

He shook his head. "Not unless the murderer used that shovel for hitting his victims and digging the grave, both. We're having the thing taken to the analyst for bloodstains. No fingerprints on it, worse luck. Hey, Mulholland!" He turned and shouted down the hall.

"Bring that shovel here a minute!"

A sandy-haired man in a new and well-filled blue uniform

marched down the hall from the rear. Over one wide shoulder, military fashion, was the tool in question.

"That's a gardener's spade, not a shovel," Miss Withers informed the Sergeant. She looked at it, gingerly. There were no obvious signs of blood on its rusty blade. But all the same she drew away.

"Take it along," she said. "There's something worse about it than there would be about a bloody knife or a smoking pistol. A nice peaceful garden tool put to such a purpose . . ."

"I know what you mean, ma'am," put in Mulholland. "My sisters's cousin tamed wild horses on a ranch out west for years. Then he came back east and got run over by a brewery team on the street. He wasn't bad hurt, but faith, it like to broke his heart . . ."

"That'll do, Mulholland," said the Sergeant.

Miss Withers tidied her back hair. "I think I'm going home," she announced.

"I wish I was," the Sergeant told her. "I don't know whether I'm officially in charge of this case or not, but I'm going right ahead as if I was, in the place of the Inspector. We're all through here for tonight. I'll station a man in the hall outside the Cloakroom where the murder took place, and another at the main door. As soon as Allen and Burns get through with combing the ground floor I'll take 'em with me and we'll start the third degree."

"Oh, yes? You're going to question somebody?" Miss Withers stopped dead.

"We sure are. I'll find out where this wren lived, and who her boy friends were, and we'll soon be on the trail. Maybe she'll have a roommate, and a good sock in the nose or two ought to make anybody talk."

The Sergeant was strictly of the old school of detective investigation. Miss Withers was suddenly very thoughtful.

Her thoughts were interrupted by the raucous voices of the two precinct detectives, who burst out of the door of room 1A, across the hall, and approached excitedly.

"What d'you think, Sergeant, we found the dead dame's office! This is it, right here."

Miss Withers raised her eyebrows. "What makes you think

that this was Miss Halloran's room? I tell you, you're mistaken.''

"Mistaken my eye," said Burns doggedly. "She was the music teacher here, wasn't she? Well, right in this room there's a lot of music written on the blackboard. You can't kid me—I used to be a choir boy.''

"The classroom you have just left belongs to Miss Vera Cohen, of the second grade,'' Miss Withers told him.

"Well, what's the notes doing there then?''

"Listen to me a moment, and I'll enlighten you,'' Miss Withers began. "Miss Halloran had a little office on the third floor, but most of her music work was given in the respective classrooms. Let me see—yes, tomorrow morning would be her morning with the second graders. She was just being beforehand tonight, and putting her scales and charts and things on the board so as to have everything in readiness for the morrow.''

"Let's have a look at that room,'' Sergeant Taylor decided. Miss Withers was already ahead of him.

Everything seemed to be strictly in order within the domain of Miss Vera Cohen. Miss Withers' keen eyes fell at once upon the marking which graced the blackboard in the front of the room.

It was here, then, that poor Anise Halloran had remained, after most of the other teachers had gone for the day, to prepare her work for tomorrow. It was here that she had drawn her last breaths of the murky, chalk-filled air of Jefferson School—and it was from this barren room that she had gone out into the hall to click on her high heels past Miss Withers' door and down to the Teachers' Cloakroom—with the shadow already upon her face, and the beating of vast invisible wings in her ears.

Had the girl a premonition of what awaited her there when she made these notations on the blackboard? Miss Withers wondered, for there was something wavery and irregular about the spacing of the lines, and something erratic about the notes, which was not like the neat work of Anise Halloran in the past.

Particularly was this true of the last line of music on the board, beneath the scales and the rendition of the hackneyed rondel, "Are you sleeping—are you sleeping, brother John?''

The phases in question seemed to have been added in a hurry, as if Anise Halloran had been in haste to keep her appointment with Death.

This little tune, which ran off unfinished at the end, looked simple enough even for Miss Cohen's second graders. But all the same, Miss Withers copied it into her notebook.

"Why are you bothering with that?" the Sergeant wanted to know. "I suppose you're going to whistle up the murderer, the way sailors are supposed to whistle up a wind when they want one?"

"Maybe I am," Miss Withers said. She was beginning to have her doubts about the Sergeant. This was his first taste of authority, and it was going to his head.

Well, it would do no harm to tell him this. "You want to know the reason I copied down this last bit of music? I'll tell you, though you won't take it seriously. It was the last thing Anise Halloran wrote. I like the feeling of something she used, something she touched, something that occupied her mind near the end. Not that I believe in second sight or anything like that—but you never can tell. There are fakirs in India, and even in this country, who can look at a ring, and tell you the personality of the person who wore it last."

"It's over my head," Sergeant Taylor insisted. "I'm a practical man, I am. Well, we've done everything here that can be done. Just a minute while I make sure my men are stationed for the night, and we'll clear out of here." He went out into the hall.

"Mulholland!" A man stepped clear of the far doorway.

"Yes, sir?"

"Okay. Just wanted to make sure you were there. Where's Tolliver?"

"Here, sir."

Another bluecoat put in an appearance, a brawny bulk of beef with feet like scows.

"Mulholland, you're stationed in the hall here, outside the

Cloakroom. You and Tolliver will do guard duty tonight. Nobody goes in or out, you know enough to know that. You'll be relieved in the morning some time. That is all.''

He swung on Miss Withers, authority resting upon his shoulders like a mantle. This was the Sergeant's big hour.

"Say," he queried, "do you happen to know where I can dig up the address of this girl who was bumped off? Have they got a record or something around the place?"

Miss Withers assured him that they had. "Wait here a moment," she said, authoritatively.

Quickly she disappeared into the Principal's office. Before the Sergeant could make up his mind to follow her, she had drawn out the file box from Janey Davis' desk again.

Snatching a pen and dipping it in a nearby inkwell, she drew a tiny streamer at the top of the figure "1" in Anise Halloran's street number. Now the card read "apartment 3C, 447 West 74th Street."

"That ought to give me half an hour's head start," she figured rapidly. She came out into the hall and handed the card to the Sergeant.

Her mind was busy in an effort to discover some means of keeping this little Hawkshaw from tagging along. "By the way, Sergeant," she suggested, "are you sure that you've found all there is to be found in the basement? I have a very strong hunch that the murder weapon is still down there—and that your shovel doesn't mean a thing. Hadn't you better look again?"

Sergeant Taylor drew himself up to his full height. "Say, listen," he told the school-mistress. "Maybe we did slip up at first on the body and a few things like that. But don't kid yourself. One thing my boys know how to do, and that's to search a place. They've been over every inch of the floor downstairs with a filter and a fine-tooth comb, and unless the murder weapon was small enough for one of your red ants to carry down his ant-hole, I'll stake my life on it that it ain't there. No, ma'am, there ain't nothing nor nobody down in that basement now. Unless"—he ventured a heavy jest,—"unless the ghost of the dead little dame is wailing around the furnace!" He laughed, heartily.

It was a laugh in which Miss Withers did not join. Neither

did the joke seem to amuse Mulholland, he whose job tonight was to keep him on a lonely vigil here.

"Say, you don't believe—" he started to say.

But his question, and the Sergeant's hearty chuckles, were both clipped off as with a pair of shears.

From somewhere, out of the darkness and the loneliness of that ancient building, there came the sound of a human voice, raised in song. It was far away, and muffled, and there was a throaty, eerie note in it.

"There's somebody upstairs!" shouted Detective Allen.

"No, it's out on the playground . . ." Mulholland pointed wildly.

"You're both wrong," Miss Withers cut in. "Listen a moment."

The voice came louder. It was no ghost, that was certain. It was the voice of a man, a gay man, a man who had nothing heavier than a feather upon his conscience or his mind.

The song was of the simplest. "Oh, I know an old soldier an' he got a wooden leg, an' he hadn't no tobaccy and none could he beg. . . ." These were the words, or at least as many of the words as the singer wished to sing. Slowly he came closer.

"I'll get him," the Sergeant promised.

"Wait," Miss Withers put in. "He's coming this way." She looked at the Sergeant. "Are you sure that was a *fine-tooth* comb you combed the cellar with?"

The voice was very near now, rough and bawdy and boisterous. It was, of a certainty, coming up the basement stair . . . up from the basement that had been fine-combed so thoroughly and so often by the Sergeant and his men!

"Oh, there was an old soldier . . ."

The voice stopped, and an apparition in gray stared at the little group from the doorway at the end of the hall.

He was a man of medium size, with a thick head of colorless hair and a face that was seamed and wrinkled as a potato left too long in a damp, dark place. He wore a decent blue serge coat above denim overalls, and there was straw in his eyebrows and blood in his eye.

He swayed gently back and forth, like a wheat field in the breeze.

"Anderson!" gasped Hildegarde Withers breathlessly. "Anderson the janitor!"

Slowly Anderson came forward, putting each foot down carefully in front of the other, with his body as intense and rigid as if he were walking a tightrope.

He made a valiant and not too successful effort to stare them all in the face as he came to an abrupt halt against the wall.

"Whass comin' off here?" he questioned. "Mgoing close upaplace."

The Sergeant's mouth widened a little. He looked toward Mulholland. "Take him."

The big cop seized Anderson's arm, and the janitor immediately slumped, head down. "Gong home," he muttered. "Gong turnou' lights. . . ."

With a smile of satisfaction, the Sergeant pressed forward. He shook the man roughly by the shoulder. "Say, what do you know about this killing, huh? Come clean!"

Anderson blinked. "Abou' wha'?"

"Answer me, or I'll break your back! Where you been hiding out? Come on, or we'll help your memory with a night-stick."

"You can't do thiss to me," Anderson retorted, brightening a little. "'M a rich man. 'M a millionaire, if had m'rights." Tears suddenly burst from his bleary eyes. "I been cheated, I tell you. Cheated! Thirteen's m'lucky number. I tol' her so. I tol' her. . . ."

Slowly his body collapsed, like a deflated balloon. Mulholland lifted his grip and grunted with the weight.

The Sergeant looked at Miss Withers, but he got no help from her. "Frisk him and take him away," he ordered the precinct detectives, who stood ready. "Take him over to the station and give him the water-cure. He won't talk now."

"How we going to book him, Sergeant?"

"Book him?" The Sergeant was more than a little excited. "Book him for the murder of Anise Halloran . . . no, play safe. Book him for disorderly conduct, resisting an officer, parking in front of a fire hydrant. What do I care how you book him as long as he's safe behind the bars?"

"He appeared out of nowhere in the cellar," Miss Withers

suggested wickedly. "Maybe he'll disappear in the cell the same way."

"Oh, yeah? Well, put the cuffs on him, Allen. Now let's see you vanish, Mister Janitor."

Anderson gave no evidence of vanishing. He dangled in Mulholland's grasp like a limp rag.

The precinct detectives patted his pockets professionally. Suddenly Burns cried out.

"What you got?" The Sergeant was all ears. "Find the murder weapon, or a gun?"

"Naw." The detective extracted something from his prisoner's hip pocket. "But it bulged like a gun."

He tossed over to his superior a pair of white cotton gloves with blue wrists. The Sergeant surveyed them eagerly. Then he looked at Miss Withers.

When the wagon arrived, Anderson was still in what appeared to be an utter state of alcoholism. He was carried out, his face wreathed in a sodden smile. The Sergeant approached Miss Withers.

"You won't be needed after all," he told her. "I guess I've washed up this case, and in double-quick time, too. What a sap he was to walk right in on us! I suppose the dope thought I'd be fooled with his play-acting about being drunk. He's not as drunk as he looks."

"And how do you know that?"

"I'll tell you how I know that," Taylor confided. "There wasn't a single empty bottle, or a full one either, in the cellar. And he had nothing in his pockets to drink. A guy can't stay drunk without a source of supply, and he's been hiding out down there for some hours."

"How about the furnace? Glass melts, and fuses to a rough lump in intense heat."

Taylor shook his head. "Not a sign of it. We sifted the ashes, looking for anything that might have to do with the corpse. All we found was this."

He took a tiny blackened doughnut from his pocket and showed it to the schoolteacher. "Probably a ring from the girl's finger, before it got partly melted. Analysis will show what it is. Though there's no need of fussing much with that. This case is open and shut."

"Open and shut," Miss Withers repeated absently.

"Sure it is. The janitor's a moron. He got full of liquor—yes, he had a good load, though he wasn't as drunk as he pretended. Then he hit the girl over the head with a shovel, dragged her down cellar—and then burned the body. He was going to bury it, but the Inspector prevented that, by walking in too soon. Say, we've had dozens of these sex crimes lately. The papers are full of 'em."

The Sergeant wrapped up the gloves carefully, and put them in his inside pocket. "These're important," he announced.

Miss Withers wanted to know why.

"The murderer wore gloves so as not to leave his fingerprints on the shovel handle," Taylor announced triumphantly. "But microscopic analysis will show traces of this same cotton on the shovel, I'll bet anything."

"That'll prove a whole lot, seeing that the janitor naturally used that shovel every day of his life," Miss Withers pointed out. "Sergeant, you're making a mistake."

"I'm making a what?" The Sergeant was blank. "Oh, you mean we're not sure that the shovel was the weapon the janitor used to kill the girl and bean the Inspector?"

"I mean you're making a mistake in giving the janitor the third degree. I warn you, if any harm comes to Anderson while you have him in the station house, I'll see that a whole basketful of trouble unloads on you. Guilty or not guilty, you have no right to beat up a man to get a confession, and I'm opposed to it. Besides . . ."

"Besides what?" The Sergeant looked around him for support, and found it in the persons of his uniformed men, who were looking at Miss Withers with ill-concealed contempt.

"Besides, you didn't look at his eyebrows," she finished, and took her departure.

VI

Miss Withers Springs a Quiz

(11/15/32—7:30 P.M.)

The assuredly demented aide-de-camp of the Weather Man whose especial duty it is to send Manhattan's weather, had evidently been unable to decide between rain and snow, and had sent both that night for good measure. Miss Hildegarde Withers heaved a heartfelt sigh of relief as her taxi finally skidded to a stop before a sombre brownstone on West Seventy-fourth Street. Shielding her sailor from the drifting wet by means of a half-folded evening paper, she ran across the sidewalk and up a short flight of steps.

There was a line of bell-pushes beneath the row of mailboxes. Apartment 3C was at the end, evidently the top floor rear. There was a card, whose comparative whiteness signified that Halloran and Davis had not lived here for long.

Miss Withers leaned heavily on the buzzer. Her hand reached for the knob of the inner door, but no click came from upstairs to release the lock. She tried again, pressing the button until her thumb ached, but still she drew no reply.

"Botheration," snapped Miss Withers. She hadn't counted on this. She stood awhile, in thought. Her train of thought was rudely side-tracked by the noise of a taxi outside. She drew back against the inner door, and waited.

A girl and a man came up the steps, laughing at the gusty wind which drove rain into their fresh young faces.

The girl, her face an elfin white triangle above the turned-up collar of tweed sport coat, was Janey Davis. Her arm was crooked inside the elbow of a tall young man. For a moment Miss Withers did not see who he was, and then she raised her eyebrows. Young Bob Stevenson, shopwork and science instructor at Jefferson School, had better taste than she had credited him with.

47

The young couple paused outside and she could see Janey's lips forming a question. Would he come in? Evidently he would, for he followed Janey through the door. They looked up as one, to see Miss Withers facing them, her face white and drawn.

"Good evening," she opened, quaveringly.

"Good heavens!" said A. Robert Stevenson. "Miss Withers—what's wrong?"

"Plenty," said that lady, heavily. "Shall we go upstairs?"

They went upstairs, the trim little figure of Janey Davis leading the way, Miss Withers marching second, and Bob Stevenson bringing up the rear, his high white brow furrowed and his hair slightly askew. His topcoat was dripping, and his neat—almost dainty—oxfords were wet through. He shivered a little.

They came, through the door marked 3C, into a small squarish living room whose inner wall bore the tell-tale panelling of a folding bed. There were books and ashtrays scattered everywhere, and one comfortable chair into which Miss Withers lowered herself carefully.

"I came here to tell you that Anise Halloran has been murdered," she remarked in a strictly conversational tone. "We haven't much time before the police will come traipsing around asking questions. I though maybe you'd rather talk to me first—I have some connections at Headquarters, you know."

The two of them stared at her, blankly. Then Janey Davis grasped the back of a chair.

"Not Anise . . . murdered! No, no . . . that couldn't happen. Nobody would want to murder Anise. . . ."

"Then somebody did it unwillingly," Miss Withers told her, coldly.

Bob Stevenson lit a match, though he had no cigarette in his mouth. "Would you mind starting over from the beginning?" he asked quietly. "You're *sure* she's dead?" He hesitated a moment over the word as if he did not like the taste.

"She's dead all right," said Hildegarde Withers. "Dead and cremated." She told them the bare facts of what had happened.

Janey, half-hysterical, was mouthing sorrow and incredulity. But Bob Stevenson had more control.

"She was such a little thing," he said softly. "Why should anyone want to kill her? I don't understand it. It all seems so—so wrong. Why, we were expecting her to join us here tonight when we got back from dinner, and we were going to play three-handed bridge . . ."

"A beastly game," Miss Withers cut in. "Well, she won't be here. I can't waste words. You realize that everybody who knew her will be suspected until this thing is cleared up. I suppose the two of you have alibis?"

"Alibis?" Janey Davis's surprised eyes looked even more surprised than ever.

"You heard me," said Miss Withers. "You can prove where you were when the murder was committed?"

Janey looked blank. "Of course I can," said Bob Stevenson. "I went to the public library early this afternoon, and I stayed there in the Genealogy Room until I came here to take Janey out to supper. I do that often, it's a hobby of mine to trace back on my family tree. I'm preparing a paper on my mother's family. We put a lot of stock in those things down where I come from."

"And where's that?" Miss Withers wanted to know.

"Virginia," Stevenson told her. "I've got rid of the accent, being up north the way I have."

"We have been known to put a lot of stock in those things up where I come from, in Boston," Miss Withers reminded him. "Janey, what did you do this afternoon?"

The girl blinked. "Me? Why—just nothing. I sat around home, that's all. I was going to a gym class, but Anise promised she'd hurry home and go with me, and so I waited for her until it was too late. She hasn't been looking at all well lately, and I argued her into doing something about it. And now—"

"And now she's in the Morgue," Miss Withers observed. "It's too late to do anything about that—but we can find out who did it. Can either of you offer any suggestions?"

"I didn't know her so very well," Stevenson admitted. "This is her first year at Jefferson School, and mine, too. I've seen her around the building, and thought how nice looking she was—and then of course since I've been coming here to see Janey, we've got to be quite friends.''

Miss Withers looked at Janey Davis. "And you?"

"We've just roomed together this month," Janey admitted. "I had this place alone, and I thought it would be nice to cut the rent in two. Anise didn't like the place she was living in, because they frowned on boy friends, and so she moved in with me. I don't know much about her except that she came from somewhere in the middle west. Chicago, I think. She told me her parents were both dead."

Miss Withers was busy making shorthand notes. "And the 'boy friend,' as you call it—the one they objected to in Anise's last place. I suppose he's been here often?"

Janey hesitated. "Often? No, not at all—unless someone came when I was out. I never thought of it before, but maybe it is funny. Anise had lots of dates out, but I didn't know her well enough to ask her where she was going, and she never seemed to want to tell me. She's been strange lately . . . worried, and thin looking."

"Worried about what?"

"Her health, I guess. She complained that she wasn't ever hungry."

Miss Withers nodded. "I'd like to look through her room before the muddling detectives get here," she suggested. "Will you help me, Janey?"

"Of course!" Janey stood up. "But she didn't have any room. There's only this room, and the kitchen-dinette over there. That's her closet, and the little chest of drawers holds her things."

"I'd better be running along," said Bob Stevenson. "Unless there's something that I can do?"

Miss Withers appreciated his delicacy. There was something a little indecent and irreverent about unfolding the personal belongings of the dead girl in front of a man's alien eyes.

Stevenson paused at the door. "I wonder—you don't happen to know if school keeps tomorrow or not, do you?"

Miss Withers had her own ideas, but she did not expose them. "I'm going down there at the usual time in the morning," she said. "I think it would be best if we all did."

"Right!" He crossed the room and took Janey's hand. "This is tough for you," he said. "Good night."

Miss Withers watched Janey's blue eyes follow the young instructor as he went out. Unless she was very much mistaken, Janey Davis saw Sir Galahad, Rudolph Valentino, and H.R.H. Prince Charming incarnate in that well-muscled figure.

The two women stood for a moment facing each other, and then they set to work. A search of the closet and the chest of drawers brought nothing to light that should not have been there. Just a few clothes and dozens and dozens of shoes, the latter well-worn on the inside of the heel.

Strangely enough, there were no keepsakes, no letters, no personal photographs. "Anise told me she threw them all away when she moved," Janey confided. "She wanted to start over again, I guess."

Miss Withers nodded. With sure, deft fingers she refolded the silken garments that had covered and warmed Anise Halloran's round young body only a few hours before. She stood the pairs of high-heeled shoes back on their shelf. Then she rose to her feet.

Miss Withers moved across the room toward the kitchen. It was little more than a closet set in the wall, with one narrow window and an alcove with a built-in table and two benches.

"We didn't eat in much," Janey said. Miss Withers looked idly through the cupboard shelves. A tall dark bottle caught her eye. It bore no label, but it was half full of a pungent amber liquid. Miss Withers removed the cork, sniffed at it, and replaced it.

"That's Anise's medicine," Janey offered.

"Bad medicine," said Miss Withers. "Anise wasn't the type to have a taste for whiskey." Her eyes roamed the shelves, but there was no sign of cocktail shaker or even of mixing glasses. Just the tall brown bottle—

"She drank it straight, too," concluded the schoolteacher.

Janey Davis was defiant. "Well, what if she did? This isn't 1850, Miss Withers. What Anise did was her own business. Besides, she never drank at school, and it didn't affect her teaching."

Miss Withers, who knew differently, did not speak. She led the way back into the living room, glanced idly at the bath, and then came back to the easy chair.

"This is a nice apartment," she observed. "But didn't you find it a little lonely here for the two for you? Weren't you a little frightened sometimes?"

Janey Davis shook her head, innocently. "Frightened—of what?"

"Oh, burglars, prowlers, men—anybody. Weren't you?"

"Of course not!"

"Then why did you have this?" And from her breast Miss Withers drew out the little automatic that she had found in the drawer of Janey's desk at Jefferson School.

Janey's face showed that she was startled.

"That? Oh, yes, that. Why, I . . . I bought it for Anise. She didn't tell me why she wanted it, she just wanted it."

"She planned some target shooting, no doubt," Miss Withers suggested. "But why didn't she buy it herself?"

Janey almost smiled. "Only last week she came to me and asked me to get it for her. You see, my brother has a hardware and sporting-goods store over in Newark. And the laws are pretty strict about selling firearms in New York. So yesterday I had dinner with my brother and got the gun. But I forgot to bring it home."

Janey Davis stretched out her hand for the gun, but Miss Withers replaced it in its hidden resting place.

"Later, perhaps," she said. "Someone may want to look at it. This mystery isn't cleared up yet, you know."

Janey Davis, like everyone else at Jefferson School, knew of Miss Withers' occasional connection with the Police Department of New York, and so she submitted to the somewhat high-handed proceeding.

"It all seems so strange, so terrible," she said brokenly. "Why, Anise wasn't ready to die. I know she didn't want to die—she was afraid of dying. Who could have wanted to kill her? What motive could there be? Anise had nothing— nobody could have gained by her death!"

Miss Withers shook her head, slowly. In her hands she still held the newspaper which she had bought when she took the taxi, and which had served no purpose to this moment except to shield her hat.

Idly she began to refold it, and then her eagle eye caught, on the second page, a name that was all too deeply burned into her consciousness. She read the item in silence, and her face betrayed nothing. She fought for control, and then the room steadied again.

"Motive," she repeated calmly. "Motive—hm, let me see. Do you think this little news item could cast any light on the subject?"

She extended the folded paper to Janey Davis, with one long forefinger firmly pressed against the paragraph in question.

The girl read, and slowly the blood mounted to her neck and face. It was a very short item indeed. A headline announced "LUCKY NUMBER DRAWS FAVORITE IN IRISH SWEEPSTAKES."

Beneath the head were these words: "*Dublin, November tenth, AP* Lucky number 131313, according to an official announcement made by Mr. Shamus Donnell, president of the Irish Hospitals' Sweepstakes Commission at the conclusion of the drawing late today, won the name of Kangaroo Lad, favorite for the Midlands Derby. This last great race of the season will be run two weeks from today, and the holder of the lucky one-pound ticket, said to be one A. Halloran of New York City, is certain to receive a prize of from five hundred pounds if Kangaroo Lad merely enters the race, to a possible five thousand to ten thousand if he shows, places, or wins. Other tickets winning—"

Slowly Janey Davis put down the newspaper. Her red little mouth was open, and she expelled a deep breath.

Then she jumped to her feet and ran across the room to the mantel which hung above a fireplace boasting only a gas heater. She fumbled for a moment among a little pile of letters and papers there. Then she paused.

"Wait a minute," she said. "Wait—I remember." She ran to the bookcase, and searched busily through its shelves.

She found at last a little limp leather volume, with a gold cross on its cover. She brought it out to the table, and flipped through the leaves.

"Anise put it somewhere in her prayer book because she thought it would bring us good luck!" said Janey Davis. "Now if I can find it . . . I told her not to put it here. I said it was bad luck to use a prayer book for such a purpose, but I guess I was wrong. Here it is!"

She drew forth a large oblong stiff cardboard, bright cerise in color, with an emerald green border of tortuous engraving.

It bore the scrolled insignia of the Irish Hospitals' Sweep-stakes, and the number embossed across its face was 131313.

Janey Davis was breathless. "The prayer book brought her good luck after all!"

"Such good luck that tonight she lies, a blackened thing of horror, in the City Morgue," Miss Withers reminded her. "Such luck that her skull was broken in the darkness, and her face streaked with blood, and then cast into the fire. . . ."

"Stop! Stop, I tell you!" The girl drew back, her hands to her lips. The lottery ticket whirled to the floor like an autumn leaf. But Janey Davis stooped to snatch it.

"It's half mine," said the girl. "Why, I even loaned her the money for her half. She came home, all excited, saying that she had a chance to get a very lucky number, and would I go halves with her? The ticket was five dollars, and I paid it. They only allow space for one name, and she put hers down, but we were halves on it. Why—"

"You're going to have to prove that," Miss Withers told her. "Don't you see what a position this puts you in? Half of that ticket may be worth, let me see—even with taxes and things, it might mount up to twenty thousand dollars if that horse comes in ahead of the other horses."

Janey looked bewildered. "But—why should that have anything to do with me? My half is my half. We agreed on that. Bob Stevenson was here when we talked about it, he'll bear me witness. Why should her death have anything to do with this?"

"If she was dead—you had the ticket," Miss Withers pointed out. "The whole ticket is worth more than half, and I imagine one would have little difficulty in getting the name changed. Believe me, my dear, the police are going to make things very difficult for you, even if you can prove that you bought this ticket for Anise."

"I can! I can prove that. Look here!" Janey ran to the mantel, and took up a folded black leather oblong. "Here's my check book—the stub will show. See?"

She riffled the stubs, and then displayed one which gave evidence that on September sixth she had drawn a check for the amount of five dollars to Anise Halloran, lowering her account from eighty-seven dollars to eighty-two.

"And if the police won't believe that, they can look at the

cancelled check and see for themselves,'' Janey declared. She snatched up a long manila envelope, and dumped out its contents on the table. A moment later she presented a single bit of paper, riddled with bank perforations, to Miss Withers.

It was the check for five dollars, payable to Anise Halloran. Idly Miss Withers turned it over. There were three endorsements on the back of the check. The first was the thin, neat signature of Anise Halloran. The second was a heavy, almost illegible scrawl that Miss Withers made out to be "Olaf Anderson" and the last was "Palace Grocery, B. Cohen, cashier. . . ."

"Anderson?" Miss Withers frowned.

"Yes, the janitor at school. You know. He came through the building with these things, selling them."

"He didn't come to me," Miss Withers remarked. "But then, he wouldn't. I'm not the gambling type." She toyed with the check a moment.

"I guess that proves it," said Janey triumphantly.

"It proves something, anyway," Miss Withers agreed.

VII

In a Pig's Eye!

(11/15/32—10:00 P.M.)

It was late that evening when Hildegarde Withers finally inserted a key in her own door, and let herself into the little flat on Seventy-sixth Street which enclosed her Lares and Penates.

It was characteristic of the lady that she first methodically put away the damp copy of the *World-Telegram* which bore the news of the sweepstakes ticket. Then she cast a longing eye at the comfortable slippers which lay neatly beneath the head of the davenport that, when properly managed, became her bed.

But she crossed directly to the telephone. The girl at the hospital phone desk must have recognized her voice for she spoke quickly. "Oh, yes—Inspector Piper. He's resting quietly. I mean, he's really resting quietly. Yes, ma'am. Dr. Hampton operated at seven o'clock and it was a success. He's going to be all right in a little while . . ."

"Never mind that," cut in Miss Withers. "When will he be conscious?"

The nurse didn't know. "Perhaps tomorrow, perhaps it will be several days. Head injuries often are that way, you know. Perhaps if you'll phone tomorrow . . ."

"You can depend on it that I shall," Miss Withers promised. She hung up the receiver with a decided click,

She had her hat off, and her slippers and dressing gown on, when the telephone went off like an alarm clock across the room. She answered it wearily, and then suddenly the weariness went from her voice.

Her ears were filled with a tenor staccato which she recognized as belonging to Mr. Waldo Emerson Macfarland,

Principal of Jefferson School, and scholastically speaking, her superior officer.

Mr. Macfarland's meaning was not entirely clear, owing to the excitement under which he was laboring. But she gathered that he wished to inform her that there had been a regrettable accident at the School; that the police and the newspapers had been having him on the telephone; that it was of the utmost importance that within the next few minutes he have an interview with his third grade teacher.

"I'm coming over to see you at once," she was told. "Immediately. Without a moment's delay."

Miss Withers thought hastily. "Wait a minute!" She looked longingly at the comfortable davenport, and then at the door to the inner bedroom in which her two roommates were sleeping soundly after their day's labors over the river in Flatbush Junior High Number Two. This was not the time nor the place to receive Mr. Macfarland, or any other gentleman.

"I'll be over at your house in ten minutes," she promised. Off came the slippers, and back on went the serge suit and the sailor. Then she fared forth into the night again. It was lucky, she thought, that Mr. Macfarland's residence was only a matter of a few blocks north along the Park. It was less lucky, of course, that the rain and snow were still combining forces, and that as usual the myriad cruising taxicabs that always infest Manhattan in good weather had vanished at the first breath of bad.

Hildegarde Withers strode briskly north past the mammoth new apartment hotels, beneath sign after sign with their pitiful notices, "Vacancy—fourteen rooms, eight baths—at revised rates," until she came at last to the barren reaches above Eighty-first Street where some of the old brownstones still hold grimly on like a breakwater before the dark tide of Harlem to the north.

She climbed the steps of 444 and rang the bell, which jingled dismally somewhere in the dark interior. She had no long wait this time, in fact the door sprang away from her. There was Waldo Emerson Macfarland, in his shirt-sleeves. He spun his glasses wildly on their wide black cord, and his gray hair was a rumpled halo above his usually placid countenance.

"I answered the door myself, because I think Rosabelle is

asleep,'' he confided. This was a standing cliche in the Macfarland greeting. It was true enough, Miss Withers knew. The slatternly sepian lady who ''did for'' the Macfarlands was quite certainly sound asleep far away on Lenox Avenue, since it was a matter of years since the place had afforded a full-time servant.

She followed the Principal through a combination foyer-reception room, past the foot of the really magnificent staircase, and into a book-lined study in the rear. Macfarland dropped instantly into the leather chair behind the battered oak desk, and rapped busily on his fore-teeth with his fingernails. Miss Withers hesitated for a moment, and then sat down.

''I have received a telephone call from Sergeant Taylor of the Police,'' the Principal began. ''He wishes me to call at Headquarters first thing in the morning. I have also received telephone calls from several odd persons representing the newspapers. I am informed that a regrettable accident, a very regrettable accident, has befallen a young woman we both know. In short—''

''In short, Anise Halloran was killed this afternoon, and there was no accident about it,'' Miss Withers aided him. ''For heaven's sake, come to the point. You didn't bring me out into the rain to tell me what I knew hours ago.''

''Of course, of course.'' The man was swinging his eyeglasses so vigorously that Miss Withers feared he was about to let them go flying, discus fashion. ''Supposing for the sake of argument—supposing that this unfortunate happening does prove to be—to be murder''—he tasted the word carefully—''I was wondering if you would be willing, in the light of your previous experience in such matters . . .''

''Willing to what?'' Miss Withers' nerves had stood about all they intended to stand, for one day.

''I was wondering, as I was saying, if you, in the light of your previous experience in such matters, would be willing to act in my behalf and in the behalf of the Board of Trustees, who are very upset over the matter, as a sort of—as a sort of—''

''You mean, you want me to play detective?''

''Exactly!'' Mr. Macfarland was not a beaming person, but he was very close to beaming now. ''You would, of course, be relieved of your duties for the length of time necessary to clear up the unpleasantness. A substitute would be provided, and any expenses—any really necessary expenses . . ." He sneezed in his cupped hand.

Miss Withers was both pleased and puzzled. "I suppose this is an honor," she said. "But I'm not a detective. I was mixed up in one murder case because I happened to be at the Aquarium when a dead body appeared in the penguin tank upside down, and in another because I was having tea with the Inspector when he heard the alarm. But—"

"I should consider it the greatest of favors," said Waldo Emerson Macfarland. "In fact, if this matter could be settled expeditiously and quietly, I should be willing to consider making a change in the staff of the faculty at Jefferson School. It has always been the custom to have a man as Assistant Principal, but I am not sure that a woman might not serve the purpose most admirably. Mr Stevenson has not been everything that I could wish, I must admit. In fact, Mr. Champney and Mr. Velie, of the Board, have agreed to follow out any recommendations I might make for a change at the end of the semester."

"Mercy sakes," said Hildegarde Withers. Birnam Wood had come to Dunsinane with a vengeance.

"Then we'll consider it settled? Of course, you will keep me informed of all developments and so forth. It has always been my belief that the intellect can easily triumph over force, and perhaps I can aid and guide you."

Miss Withers said nothing to that.

"It is a deep mystery to me," went on Macfarland in his high, excited voice, "a very deep mystery why a crime was committed in Jefferson School when the murderer must have known, as everyone associated with the school from the janitor to myself knows, of your remarkable success in solving such cases in the past. It was a terrible mistake he made. . . ."

Miss Withers frowned. "I've just begun to wonder if it was a mistake," she said softly. But Macfarland did not hear her.

"We shall simply put it down as the intervention of Divine Providence," said the Principal. "He was ignorant, or else he forgot. In either case, you were on the spot when the deed was done, and you must have heard or seen things which will lead you quite easily to a solution of the crime. Eh?"

"I'm afraid not," Miss Withers admitted. "It looks as though I was deaf, dumb and blind this afternoon."

Mr. Macfarland was seemingly able to conceal his disappointment at this. "I shall always regret," he went on, "that I hurried away from the school at two o'clock this afternoon, cancelling my last class in eighth grade history, and came home to nurse my cold." He sniffed, and sought a handkerchief, while Miss Withers mumble polite wishes. "If I had only been there, as is my custom, until five o'clock or so, this unfortunate accident would never had occurred. To think that I sat calmly here writing at my daily essay while the quiet halls of learning entrusted to me were being violated. . . ."

He motioned toward the large ledger-like book which graced the exact center of his desk. Miss Withers knew that Macfarland prided himself upon having written, every day for the past dozen years or so, an essay upon any subject that struck his fancy. One whole shelf of his library was devoted to the ledgers, each page filled from margin to binding with microscopic script. Miss Withers had seen them, had even been permitted to read as many of them as she could manage. "Twilight," "My Garden," "Eternal Youth," "Children," "The Orient," "Friendship" . . . the range of Waldo Emerson Macfarland's subjects was as wide as his experience was limited.

"Anyway," ventured Miss Withers a little daringly, "you'll have a new subject for tomorrow's essay, won't you? *Murder as a Fine Art,* perhaps?"

Macfarland looked pained. "But my dear Miss Withers, that title was used by De Quincey some years ago."

She knew that. She also knew Danny Ahearn's recent classic "How to Commit a Murder" was much more interesting and to the point, but she did not mention the fact to the Principal.

Miss Withers rose to her feet. "I'll do what I can, of course," she agreed. "I'm not making any rash promises but I'll try, if I'm allowed a free hand. You'll excuse me now. I've had a very hard and exciting day."

Instantly Macfarland was bursting with sympathy. "Of course! Of course, my dear Miss Withers! And you came 'way up here in the midst of all this inclement weather. I shan't let you go until you have some refreshment. A cup of tea, of course." He raised his voice. "Chrystal!"

"Mrs. Macfarland will be most happy to join us," he confided. "Oh, Chrystal!" He began bustling about with a spirit lamp on the table behind his desk, and at that moment a heavy lacquer screen across the room swung aside and a tall and formidable person appeared. Miss Withers greeted the better half of Mr. Macfarland.

She wore a loose cotton coolie-coat ornamented with brilliant dragons biting their tails, and her hair was thin and curly. Her bare feet were displayed through woven sandals of some sort of yellow grass, and in one hand she carried a sickly peony.

"I'm so *very* happy!" said Mrs. Macfarland. Her voice was very throaty and full. She moved the peony to her left hand and offered her right to Miss Withers, who found it very like a dead fish in texture and temperature.

Chrystal Macfarland—she preferred to be known as "Madame Chrysanthemum" since a venture into Numerology— was the result of a lifetime spent in pursuing the bypaths, the isms and the ologies of this world. She had begun as a choir singer in a little Methodist church in Minnesota, had studied Brahmanism, become a convert to Sister Aimee, Prince Rhadipore, Margery the Medium, Mrs. Eddy, and Nicholas Roerich in the order named, and now was enjoying a peaceful existence halfway between hypochondria and New Thought, combining, Miss Withers thought, the worst features of both. She was also a determined Orientalist, and her fingers bore multitudinous rings of Nevada jade and Fourteenth Street scarabs.

She sank languorously upon a long couch which stood beside a teakwood coffee table. "There is something tremendous in the rite of pouring tea," she contributed to the conversation. "I vibrate strangely to tea."

Miss Withers thought to herself that no one should laugh at the Principal's interminable essays and the other queer quirks of his personality without at least imagining what his life with this dim-witted semi-invalid must have been.

With a can of Sterno blazing merrily beneath the copper pot, Macfarland looked up at the guest. He held a lemon in his hand.

"You like your tea Russian fashion, of course?"

She hesitated the fraction of a second. "If it isn't too much trouble, I'd like cream, please. . . ."

He put the lemon down. "It's in the ice-box downstairs. No trouble at all." He disappeared.

Madame Chrysanthemum dabbled at the air with the peony. "Ah, tea!" she murmured. "What should I do without its blessing? Waldo has always left me much alone, you see, but while I have flowers and tea . . ."

"Alone?" Miss Withers prompted.

"Ah, yes! In the summers, when he goes to our place in Connecticut. Do you know, all this afternoon, while my Waldo was out gathering atmosphere for his essay on 'Sidewalks,' I lay on my couch here absorbing the fragrance, even the very soul, of a bowl of peonies!"

"Um," said Hildegarde Withers. She rose from her chair and moved idly toward the desk. Madame Chrysanthemum, deep in the soul of her peony, was oblivious to everything else. Deftly the schoolteacher leaned against the oak desk and extended her hand toward the ledger, drawing it closer. She flipped it open . . . to today's date. "November fifteenth" was written in Macfarland's fine hand. Beneath it, scrolled and rescrolled, was the title "Sidewalks." The rest of the page was blank.

"Um," said Miss Withers again. She returned to her chair, and after a few moments of tea seasoned with Macfarland's long sentences and his wife's moonings, she took her departure.

The Principal walked with her to the door. "I am happy that you consent to serve Jefferson School and of course the cause of justice and right by taking this case upon your own shoulders," he concluded. "I shall arrange for a substitute to assume your third grade tomorrow.'

Miss Withers shook her head. "I don't think that will be necessary, Mr. Macfarland. I'll be able to learn more if I keep to the usual routine, and don't give the murderer any warning that I'm on his trail. Don't you think so?"

Mr. Macfarland hemmed and hawed a moment. "My thought was this," he finally told her. "In your investigation it will quite possibly be necessary for you to leave the city. In fact, I was going to advise that you start at once for Mr. Stevenson's home in the south, Virginia I think it was. I'm very much in doubt about that young man, and I think a few days spent investigating his past would throw much light on this case."

Miss Withers was thoughtful. "Perhaps you are right. I'll have to consider it. Of course, you promised me a free hand if I took the case . . ."

"Of course," Macfarland agreed. "Certainly, beyond a doubt. Just an idea."

She left him, and went out into the rain. At the next corner she stopped and looked back at the old brownstone house.

"Just an idea, indeed!" she said aloud. "I go to Virginia on a wild-goose chase, and when I get back the case is stale potatoes!" Turning her face southward again, Miss Withers used a phrase that would have brought instant reprimand upon young Leland Stanford Jones.

"In a pig's eye!" she announced to the night and the storm.

VIII

Recess

(11/16/32—7:00 A.M.)

All through the long hours of that night, Detectives Allen and Burns had leaned over the stolid figure of Olaf Anderson, sending wave after wave of questions over his head, and after each wave Olaf Anderson remained, eyes glazed, mouth open, as impregnable as Gibraltar.

Sweat poured down the red faces of the two inquisitors, wilting their collars. Slowly their voices grew hoarser, and their tempers more short. But Olaf Anderson's cropped, knobby head remained unbloody and unbowed.

They gave him, aided by recruits from the station reserves, what is known as "the works." A bright, unfrosted bulb beneath a glaring reflector cast a hundred watts into his faded blue eyes. He sat in a hard chair, denied even the grace of a table to lean his arms upon. Cigarettes lay just out of his reach, a water cooler stood across the room, denied to him until such time as he should decide to make a voluntary confession of his own free will.

Everything had been tried. Anderson had been locked in a cell with a detective masquerading as a fellow-felon. His thick lips had never opened. He had seen a supposed suspect—also a masquerading detective—dragged into an inner room, and howls and bellows of pain issuing therefrom. He had even been given fatherly, kindly advice by the venerable Desk Sergeant, but even then he had shown no interest in the idea of "coming clean and making things easy for yourself. . . ."

His eyes were glazed and bloodshot, but so were Allen's and Burns'. His lips were cracked and dry, but so were the two detectives'. Finally, as a last resort, a tall bottle of whiskey was brought before him, together with a pair of glasses. This bait held even less lure for the big Swede. He shut both his eyes very tightly and turned his head away.

Finally Burns reached in the pocket of his coat and removed two unusual looking bits of paraphernalia. One was a ten-inch length of garden hose, plugged at the ends. The other was a man's sock, the toe and part of the foot stuffed, Santa Claus fashion, with sand. The detective laid these objects on the table, in full view of Anderson.

"Go ahead, sock him," urged Allen. "The Captain says it's all right as long as we know he pulled the job. If that won't make him talk, I got other ideas that will."

Anderson the janitor, staring straight ahead of him, opened his mouth wide enough to say "I told you I kill nobody," and closed it again.

Burns leaned closer. "I'll give you one more chance," he offered. "You killed that Halloran kid, didn't you? And then stuffed her body in the furnace? And then you hit the Inspector over the bean with a shovel and hid out in the cellar? Come on, where did you hide out?"

"I kill nobody that I remember," Anderson insisted.

"All right, you asked for it," Allen told him. He caressed the stuffed sock lovingly, and then brought it down across the Swede's forehead.

The prisoner blinked and shook his head. The sock burst, and sand flowed down the front of the denim overalls.

"Will you talk now?"

Anderson seemed stirred out of his lethargy. "I tell you if I kill anybody I don't remember," he insisted. "I was drinking."

"Yeah? Well, we'll help your memory for you. How'd you like to be put on the floor and dangled up and down by the drawers, huh? We got another trick we call the rocking-chair. You'd go crazy over the rocking-chair. Want to know what it is?"

Anderson showed no enthusiasm.

"Well," explained Allen, "it's a great little stunt to bring back bad memories. We lay you on your back on the floor, and then I put my right foot on your Adam's apple and my left foot in your gut. Then I stand on the right foot and ask if you'll talk, and then I rock over on the other foot and give you a chance to talk. And if you don't, then I rock back and forth until you do. Wanta try that game for awhile?"

But the detectives' ideas of playfulness were rudely interrupted. The uniformed man whose broad back had blotted out the light behind the glass of the door now interposed his head.

"That school-marm is upstairs," he informed them. "I can hear her arguing with the Captain."

Detective Burns replaced the garden hose in his pocket, and his teammate identified Miss Withers profanely and colorfully. But all the same—

"She's like this with the Inspector," Allen reminded him. He held up two fingers. "And Oscar Piper hasn't kicked in yet." They came to attention.

The voice was coming closer. "They say it's down this way, Doctor. And of all the dark, damp, and gloomy holes I ever saw in all my born days—"

Hildegarde Withers was not in the best of tempers. She was not accustomed to rising with the sun, and its pale beams had only begun to tinge the street outside.

She entered the room like a squadron of cavalry with banners flying. "So here you are! Up to your old tricks, you two! I suppose you have a basket full of useless confessions?"

There was a man with her, a weary little man whom both the detectives knew. They saluted, awkwardly. A police-surgeon is far above the rank of Second-grade Detective.

"Dr. Farnsworth, I demand that you examine this man," she said, pointing to Olaf Anderson. "Thoroughly. . . ."

"Yes, yes," agreed the Doctor. "But I've been up all night at the hospital with Inspector Piper," he reminded her. "Any time today would have done as well for this."

"Say, there ain't a mark on him," Allen objected. "We only been talking to the guy. You don't need to—"

"I want him examined for drunkenness and alcoholism," snapped the schoolteacher. "Any time today would certainly not do as well. He's probably sobered up now, if he was drunk. But it ought to be established whether or not he was as drunk as he says he was."

Dr. Farnsworth rubbed his head. "As a rule, in cases of this kind we establish soberness or the contrary by making the examined person try to walk a chalk line twelve feet long. If he makes it without wobbling, he's sober. But—"

"But it won't work vice versa," Miss Withers completed

his sentence. "Because if this man is faking his drunkenness he could wobble, too. Aren't there other tests?"

The Doctor nodded. "The best of all is to analyze the brain for alcohol," he informed her. "It's a regular part of a thorough autopsy. Dr. Bloom or Dr. Levin over at the Medical Examiner's Office could tell you about that. But I can't analyze the brain of a living subject."

He reached for his little black case. For the first time during that long and gruelling ordeal, Janitor Anderson looked worried.

Then the Doctor shook his head. "I have a better idea than that," he offered. "I'll send for a stomach pump and analyze his digestive tract. The by-products of alcohol are easy to define. Want to stay and watch it?"

Miss Withers emphatically did not. "I've got to get down to my school," she informed him. "And I've got an errand or two to do first. Would you be kind enough to telephone me at the school when you make an official decision in this matter?"

The Doctor would.

As Miss Withers flounced out of the room, the lifeless bluish eyes of the janitor followed her. An expression filled them which might have been one of dumb animal gratitude, and which also might have been one of calm and calculated suspicion. But Miss Withers did not see, and Allen and Burns were not students of the subtle.

For all of thirty minutes Miss Hildegarde Withers stood on the steps of the New York Public Library, awaiting the august pleasure of its gray-clad minions in opening the doors for the day. Once inside, she crossed the wide marble rotunda, and stalked grimly up the stairs. On the third floor she turned west, through the almost-vacant catalogue room, and on toward the main reading rooms. Here she turned right, without a moment's hesitation. She marched on past the desks, with their uncomfortable chairs and their reading lamps undoubtedly designed to throw all the light off the book and in the eye for the benefit of the spectacle industry.

A narrow sign "Genealogy" graced the door. She came through into a smaller room, its walls filled with three tiers of ancient and musty books, mostly privately printed and bound in leather. Wrought iron stairs and scaffolds gave access to the upper levels, and already several old gentlemen, as ancient and musty as the books themselves, were roaming among the stacks or huddled in the little wall-recesses.

Miss Withers looked around, questioningly, and was signalled by the lady at the desk. "Sign the register, please. . . ."

"I'm not planning on taking out any books," Miss Withers admitted. But all the same, the gray-haired guardian of the books insisted.

"The volumes in this room are so valuable," she explained. "Most of them could never be replaced. We require everyone to sign."

Miss Withers signed. Then she looked up, an idea lighting her face. "Could you let me see yesterday afternoon's page, please? I want to check up on someone."

"Oh, now. The records of the library are confidential."

"Very well. I'll go and get an officer." Miss Withers spoke with the voice of authority.

The register was placed before her, with alacrity. Miss Withers took out her glasses, and went slowly down the page. Near the top of the list was the boyish scrawl—"A. R. Stevenson," followed by his address.

"Were you on duty here yesterday afternoon?" she asked the librarian.

"I was. I always am. I've been here, woman and girl, for thirty years come April. And if you ask me, I don't see . . ."

"I'm not asking you to see. I want you to remember." Miss Withers pointed out Stevenson's signature. "Do you know the man who wrote that?"

"Hm, let me see. Mr. Stevenson. Would that be a tall, elderly gentleman with a toupé?"

"It would not. It would be a youngish gentleman with glasses, and a pair of football shoulders, if you know what I mean. A sort of nice smile."

The librarian's face lit up. "Oh, yes! The young man with the smile. He comes here often, very often. I think he's doing some sort of special research. Perhaps he's writing a book. Everyone is, nowadays."

"Well, was he here yesterday afternoon?"

"Oh, yes." The lady consulted the register. "According to the records, he came in quite early, too. His name isn't far from the top of the list, and a new page is put out fresh at one o'clock. He must have arrived about two or three at the latest.''

"And what time did he leave?'' Miss Withers was eager.

The librarian frowned. ''I can't say, exactly. It seems to me that he was here until late, but of course I can't be sure. If I knew what books he was using, I could tell.''

"Doesn't the record show? I mean, don't people sign out, too?''

The librarian shook her head. ''Only *in*. But if I could remember what reference book he used, we could check it by that. We keep track of the time a book is in use, and after three hours, if another reader calls for it, the first person must give it up.''

"Hm, I see.'' Miss Withers toyed with a pencil. ''Well, can't you find out what book he was reading by means of the withdrawal slip? I see that every person has to sign one of those too, before he is allowed to take the book to a desk.''

The librarian looked blank. ''Yes, he must have signed a slip. But so did some thousand or so other readers yesterday. They keep the slips somewhere on file, but they are listed under the title of the book, and not under the name of the reader. It would be an impossible job to discover—''

"Impossible nothing,'' demanded Hildegarde Withers. ''A man's life may depend on this. Do I have to see the Head Librarian, or do I get the information I want?''

"Well,'' relented the white-haired lady, ''I suppose I can have one of the boys do it. But it may take hours.''

"I don't give a hoot if it takes days,'' said Miss Withers. ''I want it done. Find me the name of the book that Mr. Stevenson was reading yesterday, and the hour he took it out and brought it back. And as soon as you get it, phone me at either of these numbers.'' She scribbled on a piece of paper. ''Here—and, oh, yes. Do you happen to remember where Mr. Stevenson sat yesterday?''

"Where—oh, yes. Where he always sits, of course. Right over there.'' The librarian led the way across the room to a little recess between the cases. There was a bench-like chair, a narrow desk, and a dim reading light.

"He likes this because it is quiet and out of the way,'' the librarian explained. ''In the afternoon this place gets pretty

crowded, and most of the regular people leave the main tables
in the middle of the room and creep in one of these.''

''I see.'' Miss Withers poked at the light, rubbed her hand
over the back of the bench, and then pulled out the drawer of
the desk. It was narrow and shallow, and it bore only a
blotter—pristine and un-inked. Gently Miss Withers shoved it
shut, and bade her adieu to the white-haired librarian.

She came out of the library, descended to the Queens
subway for one stop as a substitute for the Crosstown, and
then took a Lexington local south. Five minutes later she was
ascending the steps of Jefferson School, surrounded by a
clamorous crowd of children.

''Miss Withers, don't we have any school today? The cop
says we can go home!''

''Miss Withers, did you see the murder? Was there lots of
blood, Miss Withers?''

Leland Stanford Jones was there, his face alight with
excitement. He clung to her hand as she came through the
mob of children at last. ''I guess you'll show 'em, Miss
Withers, won't you? I guess you'll find the criminal, won't
you? They can't get away from you!''

Miss Withers rapped him smartly on the top of the head
with her knuckles. ''Run home, you scamp,'' she ordered.
She approached the door, with its blue-clad guardian. ''They
can't get away from me,'' she repeated to herself. ''They
can't—I wish!''

She paused beside the man at the door. ''Good morning,
Tolliver. Did you and Mulholland have a pleasant vigil?''

''Not half so pleasant as if we'd been stationed next door,''
admitted the copper, with a wink and a twist of his thumb
toward the warehouse which loomed at the left of the doorway. Miss Withers looked at him blankly.

''You're to go in room 1A,'' Tolliver told her. ''I got
instructions to send all the teachers in there as they get here,
and to send the kids home. Only the kids say they want to
stay and see the fun.''

''I'll settle that quickly enough,'' Miss Withers promised.
She turned around and faced the swarm, clapping her hands
for silence.

''Children,'' she told them, ''if you all will wait quietly

here I am sure that we will be able to get back to our classes
and our work in an hour or two.''

Even as she spoke, the fringe of the crowd began to melt
away. Children scampered toward the playground, others
made a beeline for Tobey's candy store, and still others raced
down the street toward the distant elevated.

Miss Withers looked around again as she stood in the
doorway. Not an urchin remained in sight, with the single
exception of Leland Stanford Jones. ''Aw, I don't want to go
home and I don't want to go to classes,'' he announced.

''What in Heaven's name do you want to do?''

''I want to go with you,'' he announced bravely.

She took his hand and led him past the officer. ''That's just
where you're going,'' she promised him. ''I've got a job for
you.'' Tolliver looked surprised, but said nothing.

There were voices within Miss Cohen's room—1A—but
Miss Withers lingered a moment outside. Mulholland's bulky
figure graced the far end of the hall, but she had no thought
for him.

She searched in her handbag and extracted a key. She
pressed it into Leland's moist palm, with whispered instructions. He nodded, eagerly.

''Bring it, and the key, to me here,'' she told him.
''Scamper now, and let no one see you.''

She watched him race up the stairs toward the second floor,
and then drew a deep breath and plunged into the assembled
faculty meeting.

They were all there, every man jack of them. Miss Withers
felt vaguely disappointed at that fact. She had hoped that
some of them—the guilty one, of course—had made a bolt
for it, thereby proving the innocence of the others.

At that time, Hildegarde Withers put little or no faith in the
guilt of Anderson the janitor, in spite of the various unexplained
angles to the case. Later developments, as we shall see, bid
fair to change her mind.

As she took a seat toward the back of the room, she could
not help wondering if the murderer of Anise Halloran, and
the would-be murderer of her own friend the Inspector, was
perhaps sitting beside her, or across the aisle?

Could it be the young and handsome Bob Stevenson, who
was so busily engaged in separating the various thin leaves of

a built-up cardboard match from a paper before him? Could it be Alice Rennel, she of the sharp eyes and the sharper tongue, or Vera Cohen, so young and ambitious and buxom?

Miss Mycroft, motherly and placid, the guide and mentor of the first grade, looked upset and worried this morning. The cameo pin at her throat was pinned askew, and the beautiful gray hair was coming undone from its Greek knot at the back of her head. Miss Mycroft had taken a motherly interest, almost more than a motherly interest, in the young singing teacher.

They were none of them looking their best, Miss Withers decided. It must have been a problem in many an apartment that morning of what to wear under such tragic circumstances. Most of the "girls," as she called them, compromised on black or dark blue serge, unrelieved by the usual flounces and cuffs and collars of lace. Miss Hopkins, for some unknown reason, had blossomed out in bright peach. Miss Jones and Miss Casey, sitting together in one seat at the side, whispered incessantly, until Hildegarde Withers was almost moved to rap upon her desk with a ruler.

Natalie Pearson, she who had shared a top floor office with the dead girl, sat alone in a front seat, a tiny lace handkerchief to her mouth. Her eyes were red and swollen. Miss Withers found herself remembering, unreasonably, the pressed orchid in a theater program in Miss Pearson's desk. There must be a sentimental streak even in this stiff and starched young woman with her low-heeled oxfords and her tweed suits.

Across the aisle from Natalie Pearson sat Miss Murchison, whose duty it was to divide her time between the school library, in room 2D, and her own fourth graders in 2A and 2B combined. She was engaged at the moment in showing Miss Strasmick, she of the too-red hair and the too-pink dress, something written on the back of an envelope. Miss Withers would have given a good deal to have seen what it was—though she realized that she was getting to be nothing but an old snoop.

Waldo Emerson Macfarland sat on the platform, with Janey Davis at his side on a low chair. When he had waited long enough to make it very evident that Miss Withers was very, very tardy, he coughed, sneezed, and then tapped on the desk.

"Inspector Taylor has asked me . . ." he began.

"Sergeant," corrected Miss Withers, sotto voce.

"Sergeant Taylor has asked me to get you all together, in a body, in one place, as it were," he went on heavily. "Now that we are all together, of course with the exception of Miss Curran—"

Sergeant Taylor appeared in the doorway. "Say, who's this Curran dame who doesn't show up, huh?"

He was assured by the Principal that Miss Curran, who divided her time between this school and Washington Heights Number Two as an instructor in sewing and domestic science, was unavoidably absent due to an operation for appendicitis. "She has been at Brooklyn Hospital for more than ten days now," the Principal informed him, "so I think she can play no possible part in this investigation." Mr. Macfarland sniffled delicately. "We have not as yet got a substitute."

The Sergeant waved his hand, and Macfarland drew a deep breath and prepared to go on with his speech. The shrilling of the telephone across the hall interrupted the course of his thoughts.

Janey Davis took her eyes from Bob Stevenson's, and prepared to answer it, but the Sergeant waved her aside. "You go, Mulholland," he ordered.

A moment later the big copper was back at the door. "It's somebody for Miss Withers," he announced, and winked heavily.

With every eye focussed upon her, Hildegarde Withers rose from her seat and passed out of the room. She cast a look of gratitude toward Mulholland for not announcing before them all the name of her caller.

It was, strangely, the librarian of the genealogy room at the Library. "We found the information you wanted," she was told. "Luckily it was among the A's, so it only took a few minutes. According to the records, Mr. Stevenson took out volume one, a rare book titled 'The Addison Family Previous to 1812,' by Robert Addison. He signed for it yesterday afternoon at exactly three-thirty, and returned it to the desk at a quarter of six."

Miss Withers asked another question. "Oh, no. If Mr. Stevenson had left the library during the afternoon his book would have been collected by the pick-up boy and returned to the desk, since no books may be taken out. The boy makes his rounds every half hour. I'm sure you're very welcome. No, I won't speak of it to a soul."

Miss Withers hung up the receiver. There was a noise in the hall. She looked out and caught the eye of a fellow-conspirator. It was Leland Stanford Jones. He came at her whisper, and handed her a key. She looked at him questioningly. But he shook his head. "It's gone, teacher. I looked all through her desk!" Miss Withers patted his shoulder and motioned toward the door. Then she returned to the telephone, and made a call.

Surprised at the result, she made several more. Finally she put down the instrument and strode triumphantly back into the faculty meeting.

"I'd like to interrupt with one question," she said. Mr. Macfarland looked annoyed.

"Yes, Miss Withers?"

"I'd like to know where it was that you learned that Miss Betty Curran, our domestic science teacher, was convalescing from an appendicitis operation at Brooklyn Hospital."

Mr. Macfarland frowned. "She told me so, before she left. Why, we sent flowers—you remember that, Miss Withers! All the teachers contributed."

Miss Withers nodded. "But did anybody go to see her?"

There was a general shaking of heads. "Brooklyn is a long way by subway, and besides, she asked us not to. Said she'd rather be alone." Miss Strasmick looked at Hildegarde Withers. "Why?"

"Exactly. Well, perhaps Mr. Macfarland was wrong when he said that she could play no possible part in this investigation. Betty Curran was a good friend of Anise Halloran's, and Anise Halloran is dead. What's more, I just phoned Brooklyn Hospital, and four or five other big hospitals in that part of the city, and at none of them is there or was there a patient named Betty Curran!"

Mr. Macfarland gasped, audibly. "I never . . . heard of such a thing! Then where *is* Miss Curran? What's she been doing all this time?"

Miss Withers nodded. "I wonder!"

IX

That's What Little Girls Are Made Of

(11/16/32—10:00 A.M.)

Things were getting out of the Sergeant's depth. He looked at Miss Withers, but got no help from that lady. He looked at the Principal, who seemed in need of help himself.

Sergeant Taylor had gathered these teachers together in the hope of garnering from them information which would fasten the net tighter around Anderson the janitor. And now things seemed to be getting out of hand, what with the introduction of new names and new avenues of approach. Taylor liked his cases simple

"I don't see—" he began.

"Quite evidently," Miss Withers told him. "*Very* evidently you don't see."

There was a shuffling among the teachers, and an exchange of whispers.

The Sergeant pushed his hat up on his forehead. "I suppose you mean that this Curran dame is hiding out, and that she killed Anise Halloran? It don't make sense, to me. That sort of a killing ain't often done by a woman. Women kill each other with a gun or else with poison. Besides, where's a motive?"

"I mean nothing of the sort," said Hildegarde Withers. She surveyed the assemblage. "This is neither the time nor the place to tell you what I mean. But, Sergeant, I think you'd better stop this futile speech making and send out a broadcast to pick up Betty Curran. Check up on her boarding house or wherever she lived. Send out her description. That missing girl is important to this case, and don't forget that for a minute. The janitor is safe in a cell, and he'll keep. There'll be weeks to dig up evidence against him—but you may only have hours to find that girl." Miss Withers lowered her voice, so that only the Principal and the detective could hear. "You may be hours too late!"

The Sergeant's eyes narrowed. "You mean . . . say! A fiend, huh? Two victims instead of one! You don't think we'll find this Curran girl even if we do send out the alarm . . . not alive, anyway!" He turned to the gathering.

"Excuse me, folks. I've got to get to the telephone—you all wait right here."

The teachers settled back in their seats resignedly, all but Miss Strasmick, the wide-faced, red-lipped mistress of the fourth grade. She half rose in her seat.

"You can't do that!" she began. "Betty Curran is a friend of mine."

The Sergeant faced her. "I can't do what?"

"You can't sound the alarm as if she was a criminal or something. I—I'm sure she has nothing to do with this. It's cruel—it's . . ."

"Exactly," Bob Stevenson chimed in. "Suppose Miss Curran is simply in some other hospital? Isn't what she's doing her own business?"

"Well, for the—" But Miss Withers cut the Sergeant short.

"I'm afraid this is a murder inquiry, not a picnic," she suggested. The Sergeant was already at the door, bound for the office and the telephone. Miss Withers saw her chance.

"I'll have to be excused for a little while," she said to the Principal.

Macfarland was bending one of the wings of his stand-up collar back and forth.

"But Miss Withers . . . the Sergeant wants to question all of us. And I must speak with you privately."

She paused at the doorway. "Later, Mr. Macfarland."

"But I wanted to tell you . . . I thought, that in the light of the new developments in the case since I talked to you last night . . . it might not be necessary . . ."

"It is necessary," said Hildegarde Withers. She went out into the hall and down toward the main door.

Officer Mulholland interposed his bulk as she reached the doorway. "Sorry, ma'am. But the Sergeant says nobody was to leave this place till he gave the word."

"But for Heaven's sake, man, that doesn't apply to me."

Miss Withers smiled her prettiest smile, but Mulholland shook his head.

"It's as much as my job is worth, ma'am," he told her. "If the Sergeant says so. . . ."

Miss Withers could hear the Sergeant's voice booming out over the telephone. At the moment she wanted nothing less than an interview with that gentleman, unless it was an interview with Macfarland himself.

"All right, Mulholland," she said. "There are more ways to kill a cat than choking it to death with butter." And she turned on her heel.

As the officer went back to his post, Miss Withers paused outside the door marked "Principal."

She nodded, slowly. The Sergeant was giving the telephonic third degree to Betty Curran's landlady.

"You say she gave up her room with you at the beginning of last week? And she drew all her money out of the bank, huh? No forwarding address—what's that? Okay. Yeah. What color hair did she have?"

Miss Withers turned, and swiftly ran up the stairs to the third floor. She passed down the hall to the little square door at the end, took a deep breath, and forced it open.

Immediately the siren shattered the stillness of the big empty building, shrieking its alarm to high heaven.

But Hildegarde Withers was paying no attention to the disturbance she was creating. Swiftly and dizzily she was sliding down the old-fashioned spiral fire-escape, chute-the-chute fashion, her hat gripped in one hand and her bag in the other.

Round and round she went, until at last her brown oxfords struck the door at the bottom, and she slid out into the daylight.

She picked herself up, made a cursory examination of her skirt to make sure that there had not been an unfriendly nail or bit of jagged metal anywhere in the slide, and then strode swiftly across the playground, around the teeter-totters, and out into the street.

Five minutes later she was in a taxi-cab, bound across town.

Calling all cars . . . calling all cars . . . a missing girl . . . a missing girl . . . name Beth Curran . . . age twenty-three . . . blonde

*hair . . . height five feet two inches . . . weight a hundred and
fifteen pounds . . . last seen wearing a blue coat and blue
hat . . . mole on left cheek . . .*

Slowly, almost mournfully, the description droned itself out
through the invisible ether. Long black touring cars, two
hundred of them, pulled over to the curb while stubby pencils
took down the details.

Teletype mechanisms clicked furiously in every important
city of the nation, reproducing the words . . . *"Last seen
wearing a blue coat and hat. . . ."* Morgue attendants lifted
the white sheets from many a marble slab. Down at the
Bureau of Missing Persons an elderly gentleman in a Lieutenant's cap and shirt sleeves laboriously filled out a yellow
card. *". . . weight a hundred and fifteen pounds . . . last seen
wearing a blue coat and hat. . . ."*

Hildegarde Withers, all oblivious of the furore she had
created, was standing on the stoop of a remodelled tenement
on Barrow Street, in the heart of Greenwich Village.

Facing her, and resting comfortably on a fifty-pound
cake of ice, a swarthy person was fingering a fifty-cent
piece.

"Sure Mister Stevenson he is one of my customer, why
not? Two, three mont' I deliver his ice. He pay me every
week. Why he have anybody else when my place right down
here in his basement?"

Miss Withers nodded. "Did you deliver anything else to
him but ice?"

The swarthy man nodded. "Sometimes he phone me at
night when he want a fire. Hees fireplace, you know. I bring
a wood, cheap."

That wasn't what Miss Withers meant. "Oh, you mean da
gin?" Pietro shook his head vigorously "I have good gin,
cost dollar a fifth. Everybody else in these building, he's my
customer. But Mist' Stevenson, he's never order that. He
don't have wild parties, I 'guess. Just orders ice, and wood
when he have a lady guest and want it nice and cheerful and
warm."

"Aha!" Miss Withers herself was getting warmer. She
ventured a cautious question.

"No, signora. I never see Mister Stevenson with a little yellow-haired lady, no. He's not have any lady friend like you say, who wears a blue coat and hat. I know all about him. I live right here. I see everybody come in, everybody go out. Sometimes he have a tall, pretty lady, dark and thin, but no yellow-haired lady."

Well, that was that. There was nothing more she could do here, having already discovered Stevenson's apartment locked, and no evidence of a key under the mat or above the ledge of the door.

Miss Withers contributed another fifty-cent piece in consideration of the little Neapolitan's keeping quiet about her scouting foray, and then reentered her taxi.

She took stock for a moment, and then told the man to drive her down to Center Street. All her hunches in this case seemed to be leading her up blind alleys.

"I must be getting childish," she told herself, scoldingly. "In every case there's an essential clue, pointing straight to the murderer. But if there's one here, it's like the purloined letter in Poe's story—too obvious to be seen."

She climbed up the stone steps of the dreary building which is Police Headquarters, and went directly to the office which had been Inspector Oscar Piper's. The inner door was closed, but in the outer office Lieutenant Keller, her old acquaintance, was engaged with a container of brew and a sack of liverwurst sandwiches.

For a few moments they said the usual things about the Inspector. "I called the hospital this morning," Miss Withers confided, "and they said he was going out of it nicely. As soon as he's conscious I can see him for a minute, maybe tonight or tomorrow morning."

She accepted a sandwich. "Do you think there's any chance of his knowing what struck him?"

The Lieutenant shrugged his shoulders. "We know who struck him all right all right. That Swede janitor is going to get his. Only one thing I don't understand. The Inspector isn't as young as he used to be, but he's no weakling yet, and he knows how to take care of himself. I don't see how any drunken maniac could hit him over the head without the Inspector's doing anything about it."

Miss Withers nodded. "I agree with you. That's why I

talked the Police-Surgeon into going with me this morning to give Anderson a test, there in the precinct house. The Sergeant doesn't think Anderson was drunk.''

"Yeah, I know," Lieutenant Keller answered. "But he's wrong. I talked to Dr. Farnsworth on the phone a few minutes ago. He tried to call you, but you weren't at the number you gave him. He gave Anderson the works, and he says the ugly is still loaded up with alcohol. You could burn him for Sterno. The doc says that Anderson must have been crazy drunk last night. Of course, those big Swedes can hold twice as much liquor as anybody else. All the same . . . anyway, Allen and Burns are up a tree. If the guy was as drunk as the doc says he was, there's no use to third-degree him, because he won't remember what happened anyway.''

Miss Withers looked at the opposite wall and nodded. "I'd like to know how a man can get dead drunk in a cellar without letting the police see him when they search the place twice—and without even leaving one empty bottle around." She had another idea.

"Lieutenant, have you checked up on Tobey, the little man from across the street who sells candy and so forth? Not that he seems to be implicated, but I just wondered.''

"Sure we checked up on him," Keller answered. "There's no harm in little Tobey, ma'am. He's had that place for years. He sells cheap candy, and bootleg fireworks in the summer. Lately, according to what the boys dug up, he's been selling a little bootleg liquor, too. Though he doesn't seem to be hooked up with any gang. It's good stuff, not poison or anything like that. And as long as nobody dies from the stuff, we keep hands off. The Federal men can do their own snooping.''

"So his liquor is better than his candy, eh?" Miss Withers finished the last of her sandwich. "Well, I'd better be running along, Lieutenant.''

But she was to do no running along yet awhile. In the doorway she met a bustling young man.

It was Dr. Levin, Assistant Medical Examiner for the County of New York, and he was in a hurry.

"Hello, Miss Withers—how's the Inspector? Hello, Keller. Well, here's our report, such as it is. Want to look it over before it goes to the Commissioner?''

The Lieutenant wanted to look it over, and so did Miss Withers. "But where's the little package you were going to bring me?" asked the former.

"The package? Oh, you mean the teeth." Levin shook his head. "No use, Lieutenant. They wouldn't do you a bit of good in making an identification of the body."

"Why not? Say, I've got to have those teeth. We'll find out what dentist this Halloran dame went to, and let him identify them. It's a cinch . . . unless they were destroyed in the fire. . . ."

"It is not," Levin contradicted. "It is not a cinch at all. Because while the teeth of the body I just performed an autopsy on are uninjured by the fire, they're also uninjured by anything else, including dentists' drills. In other words, this girl never had a cavity in her life. So how are you going to prove anything with them?"

The Lieutenant was flabbergasted. "But how are we going to establish the identity of the corpse without them? Miss Withers here thinks she saw Anise Halloran dead in the Cloakroom, but how are we going to make a jury believe that the body in the furnace is the same girl? It stands to reason—but that isn't legal proof. We've got to show a corpus delicti . . . and when a body's been in the furnace for half an hour, blazing merrily, there isn't much corpus left."

Miss Withers picked up the report, on an official form of the Medical Examiner's Office. It stated, in medical terminology, that the cadaver examined was that of a young woman of the Caucasian race . . . that the cause of death was a fracture of the frontal bone of the skull by means of a heavy sharp instrument, probably an axe, and that death was instantaneous due to injury to the brain.

"It's not much of a report," Levin admitted. "There was less than ninety pounds weight in the cadaver. Everything burned off—hair, face, skin of the body—even both legs were consumed and one hand. Half an hour longer and there'd have been only the thorax, and not much of that."

"Whoever put that girl in the furnace knew how to work the drafts," Lieutenant Keller suggested. "If he gets out of the Chair, this janitor ought to get himself a job in a crematorium."

Miss Withers wrinkled her nose. "I'm beginning to be

convinced against my will, that this was the work of fiend, after all.''

Dr. Levin, lingering as if there was still something on his mind, nodded. "The funny part of it is that it was all so unnecessary," he said slowly.

"Unnecessary? But isn't murder usually unnecessary?"

"This one more than most. Because Anise Halloran—if this is the body of Anise Halloran—was in a pretty bad way before she was ever hit over the head.''

The young doctor leaned against the table. "It came up almost accidentally," he admitted. "I was making a little test of my own to determine how long the body had been exposed to extreme heat. There is a change in the structure of the bones after a certain length of time, and I was working with sulphuric acid on a specimen of the bone of the hand. I stumbled on an interesting little detail. The subject was pretty far gone with pernicious anaemia of the bones—one of the littlest known and most deadly forms of anaemia. She might have lived, but she would have been a hopeless invalid all her life. The animal structure of her bones was wasting away— and no amount of fire could cause that!''

He put on his hat. "So long, everybody. Give my regards to the Inspector when you see him. Good thing for the Department that he was hit with the flat side of the axe instead of the sharp. I suppose the boys will be chipping in one of these days to buy some flowers or something to send up to him. Don't forget, Lieutenant, I want a hand in it. . . .''

"Wait!" Miss Withers clutched his arm as he was making for the door. "Hand! That's it, *hand!* Didn't you say that the fire destroyed both legs and one hand of the body?''

Dr. Levin nodded. "What's that got to do with it?''

"Plenty!" Miss Hildegarde Withers drew herself up to her full height. "That leaves, if my count is right, one hand that wasn't burned?''

Levin nodded. "The left hand it was. According to the boys who dragged the body out of the furnace after using fire extinguishers on it, that hand escaped because it had fallen down, under the coal, so that it protruded into the ash-pit underneath. But what about it?''

"This about it," said Hildegarde Withers. "Anise Halloran was very dainty, very fussy about herself. The other teachers used to gossip about her because she always went to a beauty parlor over on Lexington Avenue for a manicure, instead of doing it for herself." Miss Withers pointed a long bony finger at the Lieutenant. "Get busy and find that manicurist, the one who was used to doing Anise Halloran's finger nails. Take her down and show her the unburned hand—she'll identify the body as well as any dentist could!"

The Lieutenant nodded, and then hitched up his belt. "Say! It might work at that. Where's this beauty parlor at? I'll put a man on it immediate."

"I suppose it's going to be just a little hard on the manicure girl," Miss Withers told Dr. Levin as the Lieutenant bent over the telephone across the room. "Identifying a partially cremated corpse!"

The young doctor grinned. "Say, dentists get calls to do it all the time. And I never saw a manicure girl yet who wasn't harder boiled than any dentist who ever breathed." He picked up his hat again. "This seems like a lot of red tape in order to prove that a body of a girl is really her own body, but that's the way these things have to be done."

Miss Withers nodded agreeably. "I don't suppose it has occurred to you that perhaps the body of this girl *isn't* really her own body? Another young teacher disappeared recently from Jefferson School. And before long I'm going to find out where and why!"

"You've got a nice day for it," said Dr. Levin as he went through the doorway.

X

Cinderella's Slippers

(11/16/32—12:30 P.M.)

"All right, all right." The Lieutenant moved wearily toward his telephone. "I didn't say I wouldn't have the shoes sent up here, did I? I just said you wouldn't get anywhere with them. Why that janitor fellow took it into his head to collect dames' shoes is more than I can figure out. But everybody to their own taste, as the old lady said when she kissed the cow."

"Maybe Anderson could furnish some explanation of the shoes," Miss Withers suggested.

But the Lieutenant shook his head. "He's foxy, that Swede. Just plays dumb and tells the boys he never heard of the shoes. Says somebody must have brought 'em in and hid 'em in his room, which is a fat chance." He bent closer to the inter-office phone.

"Hello, McTeague? Who's got the box of slippers the boys dug up in the janitor's room at Jefferson School the other night? Property clerk . . . oh, the D.A., huh? Well, leap over and get 'em, will you?"

A few minutes later Miss Withers bent above a small cardboard box, of the type used for packing groceries or druggists' notions. In it were five pairs of shoes. All were well-worn and of last year's mode, and all but one pair of oxfords were frivolous and light in weight. She took out an opera pump, surveyed its battered heel, and then placed it thoughtfully on her hand. She surveyed it from several angles, and then put it down and took up a strap of sandal. This also came in for close scrutiny.

The Lieutenant watched her. "I don't see what that'll get you, ma'am, I honestly don't. They're just old shoes that Anderson picked up in the garbage cans or somewhere. He's a queer duck—but the shoes haven't got anything to do with this case."

"No? That's what Sergeant Taylor thought, too." Miss Withers pushed the box toward the policeman. "Come, come, Lieutenant. See anything strange about these shoes that you think Anderson picked up from garbage pails or dump heaps?"

Keller shook his head. "Just shoes far as I'm concerned, ma'am. All dames' shoes look alike to me."

"That's just it! These shoes look too much alike. There's a reason—they've all been worn by the same feet. All five pairs are just the same size, and the heels are worn down the same peculiar way. What's more—" Miss Withers lowered her voice to a whisper—"what's more, I'll stake my life on it that the person was Anise Halloran!"

"But how . . . ?"

"I looked through Anise Halloran's closet last night," Miss Withers confessed. "I saw her shoes, and studied them closely. I always notice gloves and shoes. Well, these are not only of the same size and type, they're identical—even to the angle of the heel's wearing away!"

Miss Withers suddenly stood up. "Give me that telephone," she said abruptly. "This morning I objected to Allen and Burns giving the janitor a third-degree. That's why I brought the doctor up to examine him, for the most part. But now I'm going to call the precinct house and tell those two strong-arm detectives that they can go as far as they like with Anderson. They can knock the stuffing out of him, for all I care. Because there's no innocent reason why he could have started a collection of the dead girl's shoes. He's in this case up to his neck, Lieutenant."

But even as the Lieutenant was handing the phone across to her, it buzzed under his hand. "Hello? Oh, hello, Sergeant. No, no report on the Curran girl yet. Give the out of town boys more time. Who? Yeah, she's here. Oh, the Principal. Wait a minute." He looked up at Miss Withers.

"It's Sergeant Taylor, and he's hopping mad. Says you walked out on a quiz he was giving. And he says the Principal is there at the other end of the line and wants to talk to you."

"Well, I don't want to talk to him," Miss Withers decided.

"I can guess what he's got to say to me . . . no, I'll take it. I might as well get this over with." She picked up the receiver. "Hello, Mr. Macfarland?"

If that worthy gentleman was worried or irate he concealed it perfectly. "My dear Miss Withers," he began. "When I had our little interview last night, I did not know that the murderer of Anise Halloran had been apprehended. With the janitor safe in jail, there's hardly any need for you to undertake the case in our behalf. In fact, upon more mature consideration, I'm afraid that I shall have to ask you to disregard our little chat." He paused long enough to sneeze.

"Just supposing it wasn't the janitor?" Miss Withers suggested slyly. "You must have read enough mystery novels to know that the janitor and the butler never commit a murder. It's always the nice man who seemed so disinterested and helpful all through the progress of the story."

Macfarland hesitated a moment. "Yes, yes, of course. But after a chat with Mr. Champney and Mr. Velie, of the Board, I think best to ask you to drop the investigation you took up this morning at my request. The police assure us that the janitor is guilty and that there is an open and shut case against him."

"It's open, but it's not shut," Miss Withers said to herself. She murmured something over the wire, and then hung up.

"It isn't enough to know who did it," she said aloud. "We've got to know *how* and *why* and *when* and, in this case, even *where*."

She moved toward the door. "This office isn't the same without the Inspector sitting in there with his feet on the desk and a cigar clamped between his teeth," she said. "I think I'll go up to the hospital and find out if they'll let me see him yet. Oh—one more thing, Keller. What did the analyst decide about that little bit of melted metal found in the furnace with the body? You know, the little thing that looked like a lead doughnut?"

Lieutenant Keller shook his head. "Van Donnen isn't through with it yet, I suppose. Hasn't reported here, at any rate. I'll phone him, though, and ask him to come up."

Max Van Donnen was through with his analysis, after all. He brought back the bit of metal, together with two sheets of official pink paper.

"Simple," he announced. "Very simple. Now if this could haf been a bullet, ja, I could show you somedings. But this—it is merely a trinkety ring for the finger. White gold alloy, and the gold no more than five carat. Worth maybe five dollar, no more."

Miss Withers was hanging on his words. "No sign of a setting or a stone? Or would that have burned off? Diamonds burn, I've heard."

He shook his head. "The ring is intact, though the metal started to fuse," he told her. "It did not have a setting. It is a wedding ring, no doubt about it. The body was in the fire, ja? Well, the ring burn off the finger and finally fall through the coal and embers, which is why it was not completely burned. It iss all in my report."

Miss Withers was fingering the pink sheets. "Wait a minute . . . what's this?"

Dr. Van Donnen came back. "That? Oh, der second sheet? Sergeant Taylor brought me some liquor to analyze this morning. One bottle with a label, and one without."

Miss Withers knew without being told why Leland Stanford Jones had failed her. The Sergeant had happened upon the bottle in Anise Halloran's desk, and also on the brown bottle that she had left standing on a shelf in the kitchenette of the apartment uptown.

"Subject A," began the report. "One quart bottle labelled Dewar's Dew of Kirkintilloch. Contents ¾ quart. Label genuine, and at least yen years old. Fingerprints, none. Analysis of liquid contained in bottle shows pure aged Scotch Whiskey. Fusel oil, none. Alcoholic content, 60 per cent. Foreign substances, none."

Miss Withers passed on to the second paragraph. "Subject B . . . one brown glass bottle, originally used for bottled soft drinks, contents ⅕ of a gallon. No label, no prints. Half full, see above."

Miss Withers looked up in surprise. "What does that mean?"

"It means," explained the little old Doctor patiently, "that in so far as the laboratory can tell, the contents of both bottles are one and the same. Analysis shows the same percentage of alcohol and inert ingredients, and the same general texture, flavor—" the Doctor licked his lips—"and reaction to fluoroscope. It would be difficult to prove in a court of law, but I will stake my professional reputation that both bottles contained the same liquor. It is very seldom that such whiskey is discovered nowadays. It is far superior even to drugstore prescription liquor, ja. Goot-bye.''

Lieutenant Keller put the reports and the ring carefully away in a drawer of his desk. ''Private stock, eh? I wish I knew where that girl got her liquor.''

''I'm not worrying over that, yet,'' said Miss Withers. ''I'm interested in that wedding ring.''

''Oh, the wedding ring. Say—'' the Lieutenant had a bright idea. ''Did you ever see this Halloran dame wear a wedding ring?''

Miss Withers shook her head. ''I did not. But there's more to it than that.''

''Oh, you mean you don't think that the burned body was this Halloran dame's at all? You think somebody substituted the body of some other doll who happened to be married?''

And still Miss Withers was doubtful. ''I'm trying to figure out why the ring was half melted away when the left hand of the body in the furnace was almost uninjured. They wear wedding rings on the left hand, or so I've always understood.''

''Right you are.'' Lieutenant Keller sighed audibly. ''I ought to know, lady. I've bought three of 'em in my time. It would of been four, but my second died instead of leaving town like the others, so I got double mileage on that one.''

Miss Withers was deep in thought. ''If the ring was on her finger when she was thrown into the furnace, how did it get burned . . . and if it wasn't, how did it get in there? People don't go around tossing gold rings into furnaces.''

''At Reno when the dolls get their divorces they toss the wedding rings into the river somewhere outside of town,'' the Lieutenant offered. ''A cousin of mine who lived out there made a grappling iron out of fishhooks and did pretty good with it. He said—''

But Miss Withers was already in the hall, outward bound.

XI

Hildegarde Lifts the Lid

"Hello, Hildegarde," came weakly through the bandages.

Miss Withers surveyed her old friend from across the foot of the bed. "How do you feel, palsy-walsy?"

"Lousy," the Inspector muttered. "Got any idea who hit me?"

"The nurse says I'm not to talk to you about that," Miss Withers reminded him. "You haven't any ideas, yourself?"

The bandaged head shook. "Just a steam-roller as far as I was concerned. Whoever it was could move quicker than a cat, quicker than two cats."

Miss Withers' eyes narrowed. 'You were on your guard, then? It couldn't have been, let's say, a man who was drunk?"

"It could not! It tell you—"

"Never mind telling me. I'm doing my best to find out for myself. This is a personal matter with me, because it happened under my nose for one thing, and because you and I are friends for another. You lean back and relax."

"I will, but not for long." There was an impatient note in the Inspector's voice. "Say, the Commissioner is going to be sore at me for this."

"Why, because you're left out of the murder investigation?"

Piper shook his head. "Because I'm not going to be able to speak at the dinner he's going to give to welcome that big Viennese crime expert, Professor Pfoof or whatever his name is. It was scheduled for tonight, and the Commissioner was all steamed up. He won't mind Sergeant Taylor taking over the murder case, but can you see Taylor, or even good old Keller, doing my speech?"

"I can't see you doing it yourself, for that matter," said

Miss Withers. "But stop worrying about things. Professor Pfoof will have to be welcomed by somebody else. You just rest and get well. That must have been a terrible whack you got to make your thick head crack."

"It was." The Inspector lifted a weary hand. "Boy, what a headache I've got!"

"I'll be running along in a minute," she told him. "I just wanted to see for myself that you were still with us. I'll be back tomorrow. What do you want me to bring you, flowers or candy, or a radio or what?"

"Bring me the scalp of the gorilla who did this," Piper requested. "That dimwit of a Taylor will never get anywhere in a thousand years. I don't see why the Commissioner left him on the case."

"Nobody left *me* on it," said Hildegarde Withers. "But I'm there just the same. Maybe the janitor did it and maybe he didn't, but if he did it wasn't for the reasons they've dug up yet. I'm going to keep on snooping, whether the Sergeant likes it or not."

There was a rap at the door, and a white-capped nurse looked in. "You're time's up," she announced. Miss Withers rose obediently.

"Wait," said Piper. "Get me my clothes."

"I'll do nothing of the kind," said the nurse. "You're delirious. You won't put on your clothes for two weeks, anyway. Come, now."

"I don't want to put 'em on," Piper explained wearily. "I just want 'em." Something of the old command came back into his voice. "Hurry up!"

The nurse went across the room to a narrow closet, unlocked it with a key from her pocket, and brought out some well-worn gray tweeds.

"Just the vest," said Piper. She brought it to him. Waving away the proffered aid, he fumbled until he found what he was looking for. He unpinned it, polished it on his pillow, and then handed the golden shield to Miss Withers.

It was his badge of office, presented to him by subscription of the Force on the completion of his twentieth year as a police officer. "I want you to take it until I get on my feet," he told the surprised schoolteacher. "I'll send word to the

Commissioner that I want you sworn in as a special deputy or something."

Miss Withers took the badge, and pinned it beneath the lapel of her serge suit. "This is all I need," she informed him. "I'd rather I wasn't made a policewoman or anything like that. This way I'm responsible only to you. The more unofficial I am, the better I like it."

She caught his bloodless hand and pressed it. "I'm going now, because the young lady over there seems to think I've been here too long as it is. But I want to say just one thing, Oscar Piper. Maybe it sounds silly, coming from me. But I'm going straight home and thank God on my knees that you have such a thick skull. This would have been a lonely old town for me if you—if you—"

"Quit it," said the Inspector uncomfortably. "Go on, get out of here and see how that badge works for you. And if you don't come back tomorrow I'll send a squad car after you."

Miss Withers got out of there. As she came from the elevator on the first floor of the hospital she saw a familiar face.

Georgie Swarthout, the sole remainder of a squad of "college cops" taken on by the Commissioner in the previous year, was leaning against the desk in close conversation with the telephone girl.

Miss Withers paused. She knew that this boyish, ruddy-faced youth was intensely loyal to the Inspector, and that under his flippant exterior he had a good working knowledge of half a hundred trades and tricks.

He looked up and saw her. "Aha!" he said. "And they told me the Inspector couldn't be seen! Schoolteachers rush in where detectives fear to tread, or something. How's the boss?"

"He's doing all right, but he isn't to be seen," Miss Withers told him. "You'll have to cool your heels until tomorrow."

"Cooling my heels is what I do best," Swarthout admitted. "The worthy Sergeant doesn't seem to have much use for me on the Halloran case. Says it is all settled anyway, now that he's nabbed the janitor. I'm supposed to be looking for a missing girl named Curran, but that's not much of an assignment."

Miss Withers looked at him. "Maybe the case is all settled, as you say. And yet—"

"And yet you're going ahead on your own? I might have guessed that, after the way you mixed into the Stait murder last year and picked everything the Inspector and I did to little pieces." Georgie's face brightened.

Miss Withers showed him the gold badge. "I'm going ahead," she admitted. "But not entirely on my own. I don't happen to agree with the Sergeant, at least not with every point of his case. He hasn't scratched the surface of this business, young man. I'm starting in digging, this very day. Want to put a finger in the pie, and tag along?"

"Both hands," said Georgie Swarthout. "Head, neck, and heels. Let's go."

•   •   •   •   •   •   •

Another and even larger blue-coat stood in the doorway of Jefferson School, in Mulholland's place. But he stepped back smartly at the flash of the gold badge. "Hello, Sunshine," Swarthout greeted him, as they passed on. The sad-faced cop only grunted. Miss Withers calmly led the way back through the empty building to the cellar stair.

"Somewhere in this basement," she told Swarthout, "a man stepped out of nowhere, or maybe it was a woman for all we know, and struck the Inspector over the head with a blunt instrument. And somewhere in this basement Anderson the janitor managed to get himself very drunk, avoid two thorough police searches, and then walk calmly out into the midst of us upstairs."

The young detective nodded. "You don't think they were both the same person?"

"I do not. There's one thing Sergeant Taylor has forgotten. Somebody sneaked down the top-floor hall and slid out the fire-escape, while I was searching the classrooms upstairs. He couldn't have got in the building again, whoever he was. And Anderson came up out of the cellar. They weren't the same person—and that means that we have to account for the person who slid out of the fire-escape . . . or at least who opened the door of the fire-escape and set off the alarm."

Swarthout nodded. "I see that. Do you suppose they could have been hiding in the same place in the cellar?"

"Impossible. Because at the time our unknown friend made a getaway via the fire-escape, the cellar was full of officers. He must have hidden somewhere on the second floor after hitting the Inspector, and then waited his chance to go on from there. He had time to leave the cellar while I was out phoning the police."

"But wait," objected Swarthout. "The janitor could have hit the Inspector over the head, and then gone back to wherever he hid out. And this other person might have been hiding on the second floor all along—for some other purpose."

"The person who hit the Inspector wasn't dead drunk," Miss Withers reminded him. "And the doctor says that Anderson was full to the brim. That means another criminal— or an accomplice."

The basement lights, such as they were, were still on. The two intruders looked at the furnace, commonplace enough now. They poked among piles of old benches, stacked scenery from last year's pageants and class plays, and all the other lumber which accumulates in an old schoolhouse. But nowhere was there a cubbyhole big enough to hide a man.

They surveyed the half-dug grave, in the far corner of the dank expanse. "I should think digging into this hard earth would sober up anybody," Swarthout suggested. "Couldn't Anderson have been drinking, but still quick enough to swing a shovel or whatever it was?"

"The doctor says he showed signs of being very drunk indeed. Besides—there was something else that made me sure he was drunk. His eyebrows, that was it! His eyebrows had bits of straw in them when he was arrested, I remember noticing." Miss Withers stared speculatively at the young detective. "I should think a man would have to be pretty intoxicated indeed before he'd tumble face down in the straw. And straw in the eyebrows isn't a detail that a person would likely think of faking, either."

"Hey, wait a minute," said George Swarthout. "We forgot something. We've been all over this place, from the little

room under the stair to the grave up at the other end. Would
you mind telling me *where* there was any straw?''

Miss Withers looked blank. ''Straw? Why—that's right.
There wasn't any straw! How could Anderson roll in the
straw when there is nothing here but dust and coal?''

''I'll give you odds that the janitor was the guy who slid
down the fire-escape,'' offered Swarthout eagerly. ''And he
came right back in a cellar window, bringing the straw from
wherever he'd been!''

''Excellent,'' Miss Withers told him. ''Only those windows are no more than six inches wide, and they don't open.
Look for yourself.''

Swarthout doggedly investigated each of the four narrow
slits at the top of the west wall. Through the thickly grimed
glass he could glimpse the playground outside, but there was
no way on earth a man, or even a mosquito, could have
entered. The roar of the ''El'' came faintly to his ears, and
somewhere in the street a boy cried ''Extra!''

Miss Withers rubbed her nose vigorously. ''Do you happen
to have a flashlight?''

Swarthout pulled out of his overcoat pocket a long black
tube, with a powerful lens that threw a circle of blinding
white light.

''Somewhere,'' Miss Withers began, ''somewhere in this
place there's got to be some straw. Maybe it's only a particle,
so small that neither the police nor you and I today noticed it.
But it's got to be here. Let's find it.''

''Okay,'' said Georgie Swarthout. ''Say, I got an idea.
There's a lot of territory to cover here. Let's get Sunshine
Willis, the flatfoot at the door, to come down and help us.
The boys call him Sunshine because he's got a face like a sad
bloodhound, but he's a thorough old codger, and maybe he'll
strike a scent. He's not serving any purpose at the door, and
one flash of your badge ought to fetch him.''

It fetched him, though not without certain grumblings.
''Never worry about that,'' Swarthout told him. ''A little
smart detective work on your part, and a lucky break or two,
and you'll be jumped up to the second-class. Fifty bucks
more a month, Sunshine.''

''Yeah, and if the Sergeant finds this out, I'll be transferred to a bicycle beat somewhere in the suburbs,'' Willis retorted. But he came along, his own flashlight in his hand.

"Georgie, you start along the wall to the right from the foot of the stairs, and, Willis, you go left," Miss Withers directed. "I haven't got a flashlight, so I'll work· down the center of the room, where the overheads cast a little glow. Lend me a box of matches, one of you, and if I see anything that looks interesting I'll light a match and get a better view. Go slowly, now, and make sure you don't miss a thing. If this doesn't work we'll mark the floor off in squares and go over every inch of it systematically."

The hunt began. Officer Willis squatted down on his hams, made an inch-by-inch survey of the floor about him under the rays of his flash, and then hopped froglike for a few feet and made another. Georgie Swarthout's technique was to move forward on hands and knees, forgetting the damp cement and the damper dirt floor in the excitement of the chase. Miss Withers moved ahead more swiftly down the center of the room, her angular body bent almost at right angles.

Willis disappeared into the janitor's room under the stairs, but came out after a few minutes. "There's some four-leaf clovers over the door, but no straw in there," he called out. Then he squatted down again along the wall near the corner, alongside the shelves marked "Stores."

Georgie Swarthout moved swiftly enough along the west wall until he disappeared among the piles of heaped furniture and scenery, now and then calling out to announce a distinct lack of results.

There was a long silence as the three of them moved along their separate courses. Then Sunshine Willis announced that he had found a rat-hole.

"Do you know enough to pound sand in it?" called out Georgie cheerfully, across the room.

"I ain't got any sand," Willis retorted. "Will dirt do?" The sound of his thumping came clearly, and then died away. Miss Withers repressed a smile.

In spite of her pains she discovered nothing more interesting than some burned match stubs and the fragments of a label engraved in green and reading "United States Bonded Wareh—" The rest was missing. She tossed away her match and moved on.

Willis called out again. "I'm at the first coal bin," he announced. "Do I got to shovel the coal around?"

Miss Withers shouted to him that she didn't think it necessary. "You might try and see if you can reach the coal-hole from the inside," she suggested. "I think it's too high, but the murderer might have pulled himself through and into the street that way."

There was a roar of falling coal, and a subdued crash, followed by some very forceful language from Sunshine Willis.

"You're blank blank right it's too high," he shouted out. "Beg your pardon, ma'am, but I've got an egg on my forehead. I'll swear to it nobody tried this and made it."

And the chase went on. Willis made a great rattling around the furnace, and then the roar of falling coal signified that he had reached the second coal bin. Now and then Miss Withers caught glimpses of Swarthout against the farther wall, between the thick arches which supported the first floor. She had moved on in advance of the others, and was already at the end of the floored portion of the basement. Ahead of her stretched the black dirt floor of the unfinished portion, with a narrow board walk in the middle of it. She moved slowly along the walk, her eyes peeled for signs of a bit of straw. The light was bad, and she found herself at the bottom of her box of matches.

She paused beside one of the stone pillars, and felt for the last match. At that moment the lights in the basement of Jefferson School flickered once, and went out.

Hildegarde Withers gasped, and dropped the match.

"What's the matter?" she called out. "Who turned out the lights? Where are you?"

"Just a moment," Swarthout's familiar voice answered her, from a long distance. She saw the faint light of his flash against a wall.

Willis still rattled among the coal. Miss Withers stood still for what seemed an interminable period. She could hear her heart beating in her ears.

"The lights, somebody! Bring me a match!"

She heard the creak of a board on the walk behind her. She whirled around. "Is it you, Georgie? Who's there?"

There was no answer. Miss Withers drew back against the

stone pillar, wishing with all her heart for the cotton umbrella that she had left at the foot of the stairs.

There was another creak of the board walk, and Miss Withers knew with a sickening intensity that this was not Georgie Swarthout. If only she had not let that last match slip from her hand! She bent swiftly, fingers outstretched, hoping to touch it where it had fallen. At that moment there was a crashing impact above her head, and a shower of sparks and stone particles. She crouched quietly, too weak at the knees to move, as she heard the walk creak again. There was the sound of muffled, running footsteps toward the stairs, and then the flashlight in Swarthout's hand fell upon her.

"Miss Withers! What's the trouble? What happened?"

"Nothing happened," she replied testily as she rose to her feet. Something brushed her hair, and she looked up in astonishment to see a hatchet embedded in the mortar between two stones of the pillar. It was where her head had been before she leaned over searching for the match.

"Well, for the love of God!" Georgie reached for it, and then drew back. "There may be fingerprints! Somebody missed you by inches, lady!"

He turned away. "Willis! Quick, to the door! Somebody's in here!"

But Miss Withers caught his arm. "You stay here, you and your flashlight," she ordered. "Let Willis go to the door. He'll be too late anyway. Whoever did that is out of the building by now."

It was only too true. Willis returned empty handed. "I heard somebody running down the hall when I was at the foot of the stairs," he announced. "But when I got to the main door there wasn't a soul in sight."

Miss Withers took her eyes from the hatchet. "Not a soul in sight? You don't mean that, do you? This isn't a very busy street, but there must have been somebody?"

Sunshine Willis shook his head. "Nobody that matters. Only that little guy who keeps the candy store across the street. He was just going in his door. I called him and asked him if he seen anybody running, and he said no, why should he?"

Miss Withers looked at Swarthout. But she did not voice the question in her mind.

"This is what we get for my leaving my post at the door," Willis announced.

"Very well, you get back there quick as ever you can. Turn on these lights on your way," Miss Withers told him. "You stay at the door, and let nobody in. We'll finish the search alone."

Georgie cast his flash on the hatchet. "I'll get a fingerprint man on it in a little while," he promised. "One thing, this sure as shooting proves that the janitor is innocent. He couldn't sling this hatchet from his cell."

Miss Withers nodded. "But there's something wrong about this," she said slowly. "I recognize this hatchet. Notice the red paint on it? This isn't a real hatchet, it's a dummy, a model, that belongs in the show-case on the second floor. It's part of the George Washington exhibit, and it belongs with the cherry-tree!"

"A dummy my eye," said Georgie Swarthout. "It's been painted up bright, but that blade is steel if I ever saw it. Besides, carved wood wouldn't slice into the mortar like that." Miss Withers touched the blade and found it chill metal instead of the wood she had expected.

"Come on," she ordered. "I've got to know if that model hatchet is still in place. This is a dead ringer for it."

They climbed swiftly to the second floor, and stopped in front of the case marked "Lives of the Presidents."

The door hung open, and the cherry tree stump was alone. George Washington's hatchet was gone.

They returned in silence to the cellar, pausing at the main door long enough to make sure that Willis stood there, a stalwart Gibraltar.

Down in the semi-darkness again, they took up against the wall where Georgie had left off at Miss Withers' call.

"I'll hold the flash and you get down there and look," she told him. "Somebody didn't want us to finish this search, so that's just what we'll go on and do."

Slowly they worked their way along the west wall, crouched under the narrowing ceiling, until they reached the south corner. Here was nothing more than a maze of cobwebs.

"I'm sure there's straw here somewhere, and straw we've got to find," Miss Withers insisted. "We'll keep on keeping on."

They came along the south wall, covering a path no more than three feet wide along the cement. The dirt beneath their feet was soft and soggy and there was hardly room to stand erect. Miss Withers was sure that the place was inhabited by thick hairy bugs.

"This is a wild goose-chase," Swarthout told her. "There's no more sign of straw here than . . . wait a minute!"

He flung himself down. "Quick—the flashlight!"

Miss Withers sent the white beam where he pointed. They were in a little recess in the wall, beside a pile of boards and near the southwest corner of the basement. There was no sign that anyone had preceded them here since the workmen took away their tools, some eighty years or so ago, and left the half-finished job. But all the same, Georgie Swarthout pointed out two or three wisps of yellow straw.

"We've got it!" he announced triumphantly.

"Eureka, so we have." Miss Withers looked all around. "And just what does it mean, after all?"

"Mean?" Georgie looked at her, his face a grinning mask in the glow of the flash.

"Exactly. I was looking for the straw because I was sure it would point out to us an exit we hadn't suspected. And this wall looks firm enough."

Miss Withers patted the rough cement. Georgie came closer, crouching so that his hat would not brush the ceiling above them.

"Say, look here," he told her. "This wall looks newer than the others."

"Suppose it is? You don't mean to insinuate that the janitor, or anybody else, escaped through it and built it up after himself, do you?"

"No, but it's funny, all the same." Swarthout poked at the pile of boards. "You don't suppose there's a hiding place under these, do you?"

The flashlight disclosed a maze of cobwebs binding together the ancient pieces of lumber.

"We've struck another blind alley," Miss Withers announced, wistfully. "All the same, there was straw here." She bent over to get a better look at the tiny particles, and carefully picked them up and put them in her handkerchief. "Well, we've seen all there is to be seen here . . ." she began to say. As she spoke, she straightened up to her full height, and banged her head unpleasantly against the ceiling. Her hat was jammed down over her eyes, but Hildegarde Withers forgot even that in the excitement of her discovery.

For the ceiling had moved!

"It lifted slightly when I hit it," she exclaimed delightedly. "Here, Georgie, help me."

Together they fumbled at the boards above their heads, finally forcing them up and away. A narrow black square was disclosed, through which came down particles of dust and straw.

"I'm going up!" announced Miss Withers. "We've ridden our fox to earth!"

XII

Let's Play House

(11/17/32—11:30 A.M.)

"Wait a second," objected the young detective. "Got any idea what's up there?"

Miss Withers hesitated. "This is the south end of the building," she figured. "We ought to be coming up somewhere in the first floor hall, or maybe under the stairs. But it's dark through this opening—maybe there's a space between the floors."

Miss Withers made violent efforts to draw herself up so she could see into the dark square above them.

"I'd like to know how anybody made it without a ladder," she complained.

Georgie's eyes narrowed. "I got an idea. Let me try."

The pile of old lumber was very near. As Miss Withers watched, he fumbled and tugged at the boards until one of them slid out several feet, waist high. For all its age, it held his weight without cracking. Georgie, using this as a foothold, drew himself up into the darkness overhead.

Miss Withers heard his thumping about, and then saw the light of his flash. In a moment his face appeared in the opening.

"First floor hall my eye," he announced. "Say, you ought to get a load of this. You wouldn't believe me if I told you about it."

"I'm going to get a load of it, as you call it," Miss Withers retorted. "If you'll help me...."

With much grunting and bustling, together with a certain amount of damage to the lady's serge skirt, Miss Withers clambered to the board and from that eminence managed to squirm through the hole in the ceiling.

She stared, open-mouthed in amazement, at what she saw.

They were in a little cul-de-sac, a cubby-hole, formed by

the rearrangement of some of the wooden cases with which the place seemed to be filled. From a nail in the side of one of the cases, which stood in ranks almost to the invisible ceiling, hung a kerosene lantern, now being lighted by Swarthout. Straw littered the floor, together with one or two open cases and a well-worn lounge chair, of the folding canvas type.

"Why—this isn't the same building at all!" Miss Withers gasped.

"I'll say it isn't! Somehow the cellar has been extended under a warehouse—didn't you say there was a warehouse next door to the school? You didn't mention that it was a bonded liquor warehouse, did you?"

Swarthout pointed to the legend burned into the sides of every case. "Dewar's Dew of Kirkintilloch—Prime Scotch Whiskey."

Miss Withers, still panting, sat down suddenly on an upended case. "Now I know why Officer Tolliver mentioned that he'd rather have been assigned to guard the building next door than the school! But what in heaven's name was the janitor doing in here?"

"He was building a quiet corner for rest and relaxation," Swarthout explained. "It must have taken him months to work this out. First he heaped up the dirt floor in this end of the basement—though it must have been uneven when he started. Then he tore a hole in the school foundation wall, cut through until he found a space between the piles of the warehouse foundation, and arranged a little recess in the end of the cellar, with a brand-new wall which he put up himself. He had plenty of time, remember. Nobody would question anything he did in the cellar with tools.

"So far, so good. He arranged that pile of old boards to conceal the unevenness in the cellar wall, smoothed over the places where he'd torn out wall and ceiling, and cut his trap door through. Luckily he came up into a corner of the warehouse far from the corridor where I suppose a guard makes his rounds. He simply took down cases, smashing the wood in the school furnace, until he had a space here. Then he rigged up things for comfort."

"Comfort is right," Miss Withers agreed. She was speaking in a whisper, well aware that they had no more right here than the janitor. She noticed a jar of tobacco on a case near the chair, together with three venerable looking corncob pipes and a box of kitchen matches. A tin cup and a corkscrew stood beside them. There were even rude attempts at decoration, in the shape of several photographs of somewhat voluptuous ladies scantily attired, which had been tacked around on the liquor cases. Swarthout scrutinized them, and shook his head. "He goes in for the Billy Watson type of beef burlesque queens," the young man observed. "A little hefty for my taste."

Miss Withers watched as Swarthout drew a straw-wrapped bottle from a nearby open case. "What I don't understand," she said, "is what Anderson did with the liquor in all the cases that had to be removed? I suppose he did his best to drink it up, but there must be a hundred cases gone if this space was once filled up."

"Sold it, probably," Swarthout decided. "Or maybe he poured it in the furnace, too, which is a rotten shame." He shook his head. "Imagine that fuzzy Swede working away here for months, just to get a cozy little nook for getting drunk in! And never getting caught at it...."

"The man's a regular Sybarite," Miss Withers whispered. "I'm beginning to rearrange my idea about that janitor. And yet—he must be innocent of the crime, because being in jail he's certainly not the person who hurled a hatchet at me half an hour ago...."

"Listen!" Georgie Swarthout's hand caught her wrist, and his finger was on his lips.

Somewhere in the distant reaches of the liquor warehouse they heard a voice, dim and muffled. "The watchman, on his rounds," whispered Georgie.

The voice came closer, louder. It was raised in song. "Oh beat the drum slowlee and play the file lowleeeee, and play the Dead March as you carry me on, take me out on the praireee and pile the sod o'er meeeee..."—there was a decided hiccup at this point—"For I'm a young cowboy and I know I done wrong...."

Closer and closer came the voice, and then it began to fade away. "Oh, I first took to drinking and then to card playing, got shot in a fi-ight and now I must die...."

There was the sound of a metal door clanging shut, and the warehouse was silent again.

"No wonder Anderson had such an easy time," Swarthout

observed after a moment. "That watchman reminds me of old John Twist, a patrolman up in the Tenth Ward. He heard a shot in a railroad warehouse, and went over to investigate it, without any particular eagerness. He poked his head in the door and yelled, 'If you're in there get out of there because I'm going to count three hundred and then come after you.' "

"Very funny," Miss Withers told him. "And now I think I'd like to get out of here. It smells like my Uncle Henry used to smell on the nights when my mother wouldn't let me kiss him goodnight."

With even more difficulty than on the trip up, Miss Withers was lowered through the trap door again. Swarthout extinguished the lantern, not without a wistful eye at the straw-covered bottles. But Miss Withers waited below, and he had a very clear idea of what her attitude would be.

"Get behind me, Bacchus," he whispered, and dropped down through the hole. It was only the matter of a moment to pull the trap shut again, and to replace the board in the pile as it had been before.

They found Sunshine Willis faithfully guarding the main door, a yellow newspaper in his hands and his sad face sadder than ever.

"I'll use the phone in the Principal's office to notify Headquarters of what we found," Swarthout told Miss Withers. "They'll send a man down to take pictures of that hatchet before it's moved."

Miss Withers paused beside Willis. Silently he extended toward her the newspaper. "Want to read it while he's phoning?"

She shook her head. "No, thank you. I've been through too much excitement to do any reading now. I've got to think. . . ."

Willis still held out the yellow sheet. "It's an extra," he explained patiently. "They were yelling it when we were in the cellar. You better read it."

Miss Withers took the sheet, and fumbled for her glasses. But she needed no glasses to peruse the screaming black headlines that announced with amazing clarity and conciseness . . . . "MURDER SUSPECT SOCKS DOC AND SCRAMS"

"What in heaven's name. . . ." She sat down on the stoop and read on, breathlessly. "Suspected of Being Grade School Fiend, Janitor Knocks Distinguished Alienist Galleywest and

Does Human-Fly Act From Window.... Olaf Anderson, arrested as a suspect in the murder of Anise Halloran, beautiful schoolteacher, made a clean getaway from the hotel room of Professor Augustine Pfaffle, eminent Viennese criminologist, at eleven o'clock this morning, first striking the professor unconscious. Anderson had been taken by police to Professor Pfaffle's apartment for examination at the request of local police authorities and in the midst of a psycho-analytic test while alone with the professor, Anderson leaped to his feet, knocked the distinguished scientist unconscious, and made his escape through the window and down the oranmental façade of the Park View Hotel to the court. At an early hour this afternoon he had not been apprehended, although every exit to the city is blocked and the police state that an arrest is imminent... fiddlesticks!'' The final word was added by Miss Withers herself, as she thrust the paper back at Willis.

"Psycho-analyzing Anderson! Visiting criminologist or not, that man is pure daffy! Anderson is no deeper than a mud puddle—'' Miss Withers broke off short. She remembered something. At that moment Swarthout came out of the door.

"Look at that,'' she said. He nodded.

"What else do you think they're stewing about over at Headquarters?''

"Bother Headquarters,'' said Hildegarde Withers. "Do you realize what this means?''

He nodded. "We were so sure that the janitor was innocent of the murder because he couldn't have been in the cellar and taken that crack at you! And now—it's a thousand to one that he was the only person who could have done it!''

"I'm not betting, even at those odds,'' said Hildegarde Withers. "Come on, I'm going on an errand. If you don't mind, I'd like you to go along. That hatchet made me a little nervous.''

"Made *you* a little nervous!'' Swarthout grinned at her. "Say, it didn't come anywhere near me, and I'm plenty nervous myself. A good clean bullet isn't so bad, even in the dark, but a tomahawk has never appealed to me.''

"By the way,'' the young man continued as they sought an uptown subway, "I suppose we're going on a manhunt for the janitor? Got any idea where he might be hiding?''

"I have not,'' declared Miss Withers. "Let the police

chase Anderson. The less I see of him, the better. There's more point in searching for that missing Curran girl, to my mind.'' She stopped as she saw Georgie Swarthout's face.

''Lord, I forgot to tell you,'' he announced, above the roar of the train. ''They did find her!''

''What? Where? Is she dead?''

Georgie shook his head. ''Not exactly. The police up in Niagara Falls nabbed her in a rooming house, hiding out under the name of Mrs. Rogers.''

Miss Withers leaned back in her seat. ''This is surprise number two today,'' she admitted.

''It was a surprise for the girl, too,'' Georgie went on. ''The Lieutenant told me all about it over the phone when I called him from the school. You see, this Curran girl was hiding out under the name of Mrs. Rogers. Only it seems there's a Mr. Rogers in the picture, and a wedding ring and everything. The Niagara police have 'em both in the hoosegow, which is a hell of a place to spend a honeymoon. But the Commissioner is wiring them to let the kids go, because it's all on the level and they were married ten days in Hoboken. The names were phonied up a little, and the ages. But they're married, sure enough.''

''A secret wedding, I'll be bound, and they had to do it because of course Betty Curran would lose her job if the Board knew she was married!'' Miss Withers eagerly caressed the handle of her umbrella. ''Nowadays young couples find it hard enough going with two salaries coming in—but the Board decided that preference must be given the unmarried teachers, because they needed the work worse! That's it— that's why Betty Curran left her rooming house, and told everybody at school that she was going to have an operation. That's why the Strasmick girl started to object when I suggested sounding the alarm. I'm ashamed of myself—but somehow I was certain sure that the disappearance of Betty Curran had something to do with the Halloran case. And all the time the girl was only human—she was trying to eat her cake and have it, too. Marriage and her job—both.''

''Sure,'' agreed Swarthout. ''If it's no secret, where are we bound, and why?''

''We're bound for an apartment house on West Seventy-fourth Street, where I'm going to ask a question backwards.''

''Huh?''

"I'm going to ask a question by telling the answer first," promised Miss Withers. "Come on, here's Grand Central. Let's catch the Shuttle across town."

They finally reached the old brownstone house on 74th Street. Miss Withers started up the steps, but Georgie halted on the edge of the sidewalk.

"I'll just stick around here," he suggested. "You'll do better with your questions if I'm not around."

"You come along, young man," she ordered. "I'll do all right. Besides, I want to get your reaction to a young lady. A very beautiful young lady."

"If I must I must," said Georgie Swarthout. He followed her up the steps, waited while she rang, and then climbed on up the two flights of stairs.

The door was answered by Janey Davis herself, clad in shimmering cerise pajamas. Her hand went swiftly to her well-rounded throat. "I didn't know anyone was with you," she gasped. Then she turned and ran for a dressing-gown, stepping out of the closet in a pale green wrap that Miss Withers disapproved of, and envied a little. It showed practically all the pajamas, and a good deal of Janey.

"You were right," Georgie Swarthout told Miss Withers. "And I was going to stay outside on the cold sidewalk!"

There were introductions, and Janey let the young man hold her hand for the merest fraction of a second. It was not hard to see that she had been crying recently, and that she was only waiting their departure to start crying all over again.

"I know why you've come—I suppose," she burst out as soon as the two guests had seated themselves. Janey leaned against the mantel, her arms outstretched and her head thrown back.

"This thing is terrible! It's driving me crazy! At first you broke the news so calmly that it stunned me. I didn't believe it, I didn't think it was true. I didn't realize that poor Anise would never come home any more. But I wasn't able to sleep a wink since, nor eat anything today. It seems wicked to go on living with Anise, who loved life so much, lying on a marble slab somewhere while doctors desecrate her body. . . ."

"Well, well," broke in Miss Withers. "You mustn't let yourself go, my dear. Try to think of pleasant things. Don't stay alone too much. I know this is terrible, but it could be worse."

"I don't see how!"

Miss Withers saw, very clearly. "If a certain somebody had been a better axeman, or if I hadn't fumbled with a match this afternoon—but never mind that. You say you knew why we came?"

Janey Davis nodded. "The police were here, and they say they're coming back. About the lottery ticket. They don't believe me when I say that half of it is mine, and my money bought it. They hinted—terrible things. As if I'd do anything like that for money!"

"Of course not," agreed Miss Withers, tongue in her cheek. She'd seen practically everything done for money, including bloody murder.

Georgie Swarthout tore his eyes off Janey's face long enough to chime in. His voice had the ring of sincerity. "We know you didn't have anything to do with it, Miss Davis. We just want your help, that's all."

The girl gave him a grateful look. Then she turned back toward Miss Withers. "I must have seemed a cheap, common thing to you the other night. About the lottery ticket, I mean. But I'd been praying so for it, and I needed it so. . . . You see, my father and mother live in a little town upstate. They're quite elderly, and they're losing their home because they can't get it refinanced. It wasn't for myself."

Her face softened. "But I see I can't take the money, even my half of it, now," she went on. "Not since the ticket was in Anise's name, and since it won just before her death. It would be . . . grave robbing."

Miss Withers nodded approvingly. "A very worthy attitude. But, my dear child, this is an important decision to make. Have you thought it over?"

Janey nodded. "I've thought it over and talked it over. With Bob, I mean. He thinks I'm a little goose, I guess. But I think he's proud of me, too."

"Bob, I infer, is Mr. Stevenson?" Miss Withers inquired.

Janey Davis nodded. She smiled, as though she knew a deep, delicious secret.

"All the same," Miss Withers proceeded, "we didn't come up here to talk about the lottery ticket. Let that lie between your own conscience and the lottery commissioners themselves. I came up here to ask you, as Anise Halloran's roommate, why it was that you didn't tell me the other night that she bought whiskey from Anderson, the janitor?''

"You mean the brown bottle—what she called her medicine?"

Miss Withers nodded. ''Yes, that and the bottle in her desk down at school. Why didn't you tell me, especially since the janitor is involved in this business?''

Janey Davis' eyes were very wide and very innocent. ''I didn't tell you it because it wasn't true! Anise never bought any liquor from Anderson. I didn't know he sold it, and neither did she. The only thing she ever bought from him was the lottery ticket, and that was unpleasant enough. It turned out that she chose the number that he wanted for himself, or something like that. Anise was quite upset about it but she got her own way, as usual.''

Miss Withers shrugged her shoulders. ''Suppose I happen to tell you that I know positively that it was Anderson from whom she bought her liquor?''

Janey Davis shook her head, so that the curls danced about her ears. ''No, not Anderson. It was Tobey, the candy man across the street, that she bought her liquor from.'' Her hand went to her lips. ''I—I didn't mean to tell that.''

"And why not?'' Miss Withers wanted to know.

"Because I didn't see why it mattered in this case. Anise is dead, and she's suffered enough without having her name dragged through the mud any more. Her secrets are her own. Besides, she only drank because her nerves were bad. She bought the stuff herself because she said other people's liquor tasted like cleaning fluid. She was sick, really she was. It was just in the past two or three weeks that she took to drinking.''

Janey Davis was almost crying. ''Why can't you and the police search for her murderer, and forget about her little— failings? There isn't a person living who doesn't have something in his life that he isn't proud of. I have, and so have you!''

Miss Hildegarde Withers let that pass without committing herself one way or the other. ''These things are bound to come out sooner or later,'' she said slowly. ''It would be better if you gave us all the help you can, instead of hindering.'' But her remarks fell on stony ground.

Janey sobbed quietly into her handkerchief, while Georgie Swarthout made vague gestures of comfort. The situation was relieved by a shrill buzz of the doorbell.

Janey Davis came out of her sobbing spell, and went to the door. Her face lighted up at what she saw there—Bob Stevenson, his dark Chesterfield coat flecked with snow. He began to shake the wet drops from his hat, but the girl clutched his arm and drew him through the door.

He looked up, and saw Miss Withers' eyes boring into his own. "I see that the Spanish inquisition is still on," he observed. "Janey here didn't have anything to do with the case. Why can't you leave her alone? They've got the murderer, or at least they did have him until they let him get away. I don't see . . ."

"You don't need to see, young man," Miss Withers told him. "The investigation is bound to go on, whether we like it or not. I'm trying to be as human as possible about my part of it, but I'm going right straight ahead. Also, having learned what I came to find out, I'm going home. Oh, you must pardon my forgetfulness. Mr. Stevenson—Mr. Swarthout, of the police also, I might add."

The two young men nodded, and mumbled their delight at meeting. Miss Withers marched toward the doorway. Suddenly she hesitated.

"It's another nasty cold day," she observed. "Janey here is all unstrung, Mr. Stevenson is chilled and wet through, and we're both of us likely to be before we get a block away. I think under the circumstances, and to show that there is no hard feeling in all this, we ought to have a drink together."

Georgie Swarthout stopped as if shot. "What? Say, my ears must be going back on me. What you just said sounded like 'we ought to have a drink together'!"

"That's what I did say." Miss Withers made her best attempt at a convivial smile.

Bob Stevenson was smiling vacantly, his eyes wide. Janey Davis was the first to move.

"I—I'm sorry, but there's nothing to drink here. The police came and took Anise's medicine. . . ."

"Heavens, child, I didn't mean that." Miss Withers reached beneath her coat, and after much tugging she brought forth a single tall quart bottle.

Georgie's eyes widened. The label was *Dewar's Dew of Kirkintilloch*—and that bottle was from the liquor warehouse they had just left.

She set it on the table with a flourish. "Have you some glasses?" she asked Janey.

The girl looked questioningly at Bob Stevenson, and then moved woodenly toward the kitchen. Miss Withers had certainly dropped a bombshell into the conversation.

Stevenson began to be amused by the whole situation. "And to think that all this time I'd figured you for a Puritan," he told Miss Withers. He accepted one of the three glasses that Janey Davis brought. She herself didn't want any.

Georgie Swarthout tossed his off first, his eyes still on Miss Withers with wonder and amazement. Miss Withers took one gulp, but her eyes welled up with tears. Only Georgie, who stood beside her, saw that she poured most of the contents of her glass into a little Japanese garden that stood on the telephone table.

But A. Robert Stevenson sniffed his with considerable gusto. "It isn't often one gets liquor like this nowadays," he admitted.

"Very seldom indeed," agreed Miss Withers, who had never tasted this or any other kind in all her life. She put her empty glass on the table.

"I was just thinking," she said slowly, her eyes on the ceiling, "how Anise Halloran would have enjoyed being here, if she were alive. Congenial company—two of you with whom she's often drunk in the past—and really genuine liquor—"

Miss Withers let her voice soften. "Suppose she is here, trying to touch us, peering over our shoulders, trying to scream into our ears the name of the person who sent her into the shadows forever. . . ."

"Oh, for God's sake, stop!" Janey flung her lithe young body into a chair, and crouched there, her head buried in her hands. Georgie moved toward her, but Miss Withers waved him back.

There was the faintest trembling of Bob Stevenson's hand as he put down his partially emptied glass and knelt beside the girl.

"That's all right, Janey," he told her comfortingly. "Miss Withers didn't mean to frighten anybody. . . ."

"Miss Withers jolly well *did* mean to frighten somebody," said that lady under her breath.

Janey's hand clutched Stevenson's shoulder, pulling his well-tailored coat out of shape. He stroked her arm, comfortingly. "That's all right . . . all right. . . ." He looked up at Miss Withers. "You'd better leave her to me," he suggested. "Come back some other time; the child is hysterical now."

"I'm afraid you're right," Miss Withers admitted. "Come on, Georgie. We've put our foot in it again."

They went down the stairs in silence. Miss Withers looked at her young companion, her eyes twinkling.

"What do you make of our visit?" she asked.

Georgie shook his head. "I've got a hunch you suspect the smart young instructor of something or other, only I don't know what. Was that why you rang in the act about the dead girl listening in and so forth? If it was, he never batted an eye."

"Somebody else did bat one, though," said Hildegarde Withers. "I could see you were surprised at my sitting up the drinks . . ."

"Setting, you mean?"

"All right, setting up the drinks?"

"I was," admitted Swarthout. "I still am. Did you figure on getting them drunk enough so they'd talk, or what?"

Miss Withers shook her head. "I just wanted to see their reaction when I brought out the bottle with that special label on it. And neither one of them was at all surprised, in spite of the fact that that was the liquor Anise Halloran made a practice of drinking. I suppose I'm now as bad as the janitor, because to steal one bottle is as bad as to steal a whole warehouseful. But I had a hunch, and it didn't work. I'm not used to my hunches missing fire."

"What gets me," complained Georgie Swarthout as they walked on up 74th Street, "is why you left the bottle sitting on the table up in that cute little Janey Davis' apartment."

As it happened the quart bottle with the Dewar label was no longer resting on the table in Janey's apartment. It was lying scattered across the roof of a garage in the rear, its amber contents mixed with the falling snow.

The young lady who had just hurled it from an open window was leaning with her cheek against the frame.

"Oh, Bob, what'll we do?"

The young man came over beside her. "We'll keep on doing just as I suggested, dear."

"But Bob"—she moved her cheek from the windowframe to his shoulder—"they even suspect *me*! Miss Withers does, I know she does."

"She suspects everybody, and quite right, too," said Bob Stevenson. "Probably she goes home at night and asks herself questions until she gets herself in a corner and nearly confesses. Don't you worry about Withers, she's a smart old girl. Prides herself a bit on being a sleuth, but why not?"

"Oh, Bob, I wish I were as sure as you are!" She snuggled a little closer, and he ventured to enclose her shoulders with his arm. "Sure about it's all coming out all right, and everything. I'm frightened, Bob."

She looked up at him. Her eyes were moist, and her hands trembled.

"Say something, won't you?"

He swung away and faced her. "What can I say, you darling? It's the wrong time to say what I want to say. But—Janey, you know what it is. When all this is over and forgotten, and Anise's murderer has paid the penalty and we are all allowed to be ourselves again, will you . . . will you, Janey?"

Janey's soft fingers brushed his lips. "Don't say it, don't ask it now, Bob. When this is all over, after you know everything there is to know, then come and ask me—if you still feel the same way—come and ask me the most important question in all the world."

Bob Stevenson laughed. "As if there'd be anything to find out about you that could make me change! That's a joke!"

But joke or no joke, Janey Davis joined very little in his open laughter. She held out both her arms to him.

"Oh, Bob," she cried brokenly. "I'm so alone! I want something so terribly, and it seems to be you!"

XIII

Dunce Cap

(11/17/32—4:15 P.M.)

"It's all like a puzzle that won't work out," Miss Withers was complaining. The Inspector, still swathed in bandages so that he resembled a turbanned Mohammedan, watched her through swirls of blue cigar smoke.

"And I've got a feeling that when finally I'm given the solution, I'm going to find that I've been butting my head against a stone wall—as I did once in a newspaper crossword puzzle only to learn the next day that the word *iris* had been defined by the nitwit who made it up as 'the Greek god of love.'"

Miss Withers nibbled at a grape from the basket at the head of the Inspector's dismal looking white iron bed.

"It seems to me that you're getting along fine," Piper told her. "You've got pretty fair grounds for suspicion of five or six people, and a clear case against one, the janitor, even if that pompous ass of a criminologist from Vienna did let him get away. My boys will pick him up, though."

"Yes," Miss Withers agreed. "And what good will that do? I tell you, the janitor didn't commit the murder! He couldn't have, he was drunk as a lord. And that was no crime of impulse. The murderer knew the school, and my habits. The murderer knew that Anise Halloran would be the last person to enter that Cloakroom in the afternoon, since I never used it. He not only knew that I was mixed up with the police, he counted on it . . . or she did, whichever it was."

"Yeah? Well, there's lots to figure out. If my head didn't ache so, I'd take a whirl at the thing from here, but as it is I can only listen." The Inspector puffed at his cigar, almost happily. It was the first time in years he had had the energy

114

and leisure to smoke a cigar through to the butt without letting it go out a dozen times. He was making the most of it.

"You haven't told me yet how Anise Halloran managed to walk down the hall and out the building, as you say you heard her, and yet reappear instantly in the Cloakroom, a bloody corpse. Do you think she tiptoed back, so you wouldn't hear her?"

"I've got my theory of that," Miss Withers told him. "But I want to mull it over a little more. If my hunch is right, it's added proof that Anderson had nothing to do with the murder, directly at least."

"I'll make one suggestion," said Oscar Piper meekly. "You're making a hell of a mistake to take up this case with your mind made up that the janitor isn't guilty because he is so obvious a suspect. Everything points to him, so out of pure contrariness you want to prove him innocent, and somebody else guilty. You're fitting facts to the theory, not theory to the facts. And wouldn't it be a good joke on you and on the newspapers if in this case the obvious, dumb suspect happened to be the real murderer, after all?"

"Maybe," said Hildegarde Withers. "But Anderson didn't kill Anise Halloran. There was straw in his eyebrows, his feet are too big, and besides, he doesn't act like a murderer!"

"I told you some years ago that murderers never do," said Oscar Piper. "How about the hatchet that somebody swung at your head a little while after Anderson broke away from his guards and gained his freedom? Doesn't that pin it on him?"

Miss Withers nodded. "It certainly seems to pin it on him. But suppose somebody else thought of that!"

"You're making a whole lot of this lottery-sweepstakes business," the Inspector went on. "I don't see where that gets us anywhere. Janey Davis wouldn't commit a murder in order to get the other half of the money, and if she did she wouldn't give up her prize."

"She hasn't given it up," Miss Withers reminded him. "I think she would very much like to be persuaded not to give it up. She's got some weeks yet before the race is run, you know. I feel it deep down in my bones that Janey Davis is going to change her mind."

Miss Withers rose to her feet and walked rapidly the length of the room. "There's so many angles to the case," she complained. "So many parts that don't fit into the jig-saw picture. Why and how did the janitor get his collection of old shoes—Anise Halloran's old shoes? Where was Macfarland that afternoon when he says he was home and his wife says he was taking a walk and gathering material? How did the wooden hatchet in the exhibit case come to be a steel hatchet when it whizzed past my head? Why did Anderson have an endless supply of good liquor, and not sell any, and why did Tobey across the street sell quantities of the same liquor without any big booze ring hookups? Why did a sweet kid like Anise Halloran take to drinking straight whiskey, and start running down physically at the same time?"

"Wait a minute, wait a minute," pleaded the Inspector. "I'm afraid you'll have to flunk me in this test. Isn't there one question I can answer?"

Miss Withers was thoughtful for a moment. "Yes," she said. "Answer me this. Why did Anise Halloran stay after school to put her next morning's scales on the blackboard, and then go to the Cloakroom with the last one unfinished and a fragment? It went like his, you know. . . ."

She tried to whistle. "Whoooo-wheeeeee, whooo-wheee. . . ."

"Not much tune to that," the Inspector told her. "I'd about as soon listen to a crooner. And I don't see any clue in it, either. It doesn't mean a thing to me."

"It might to somebody else," said Miss Withers. "That is what Anise marked on the blackboard a few moments before she died. Thanks to my right idea of calling in the manicurist, we know that the body is hers, anyway. I was sure for a while that the major clue lay in the disappearance of Betty Curran, but now that is explained away. Don't those two notes suggest a song, a popular song perhaps, that might be a clue, a hint to guide us?"

"It sounds like a sparrow twittering to me," Piper admitted. "But you might try it on your suspects."

"I certainly intend to." Miss Withers rose to go. "I'll see you tomorrow, Oscar. That little nurse of yours keeps walking past the door, and I suppose I've overstayed my limit."

"So long," the Inspector called to her. "I'd give anything to be going out of here with you, if only to hear the eminent Professor Pfoof—"

"Pfaffle," corrected Miss Withers.

"That's what I said. The joke's on the Commissioner, who should have known better than to turn a murder suspect over to a visiting expert. I'd like to hear Pfaffle alibi-ing now. He'll be in a pretty spot, or I'm no judge."

"A clever little people, these Viennese," misquoted Miss Withers. "He may sneak out of it yet. Well, toodle-oo."

"What?"

"Toodle-oo. It's an expression I picked up from Georgie Swarthout."

The Inspector nodded. "Has that young scamp been any help to you?"

"He certainly has. He's out this afternoon doing a little investigating on a new lead." Miss Withers smiled proudly. "That young man shows promise, Oscar, if only he can be kept away from going the way of all flatfoots. Association with me has done him worlds of good—why, he got this idea for a new lead after only one day on the case. Said he'll tell me about it tomorrow."

With a wave of her hand, Miss Hildegarde Withers departed, whistling the trenchant, plaintive notes that Anise Halloran had marked upon a blackboard in the last few minutes of her life.

Though doormen looked after her inquiringly, and a stray dog or two came bounding toward her feet, she marched on down the Avenue, still whistling—"Whoooo-wheeee. . . ."

XIV

Finders Are Keepers

(11/18/32—9:30 A.M.)

"Hello? Hello, this is Miss Davis . . . who? . . . WHO? . . . Mr. Swarthout? Why, I don't remember . . . oh, yes. Yes, you're the detective who came up here with Miss Withers. What? Oh—I'm awfully sorry, but I have an engagement for lunch today . . . yes, and dinner, too. I'm sure what you have to tell me would be very interesting, but it's quite impossible. You'll have to excuse me now, I'm taking a bath."

Janey Davis, with a turkish towel wrapped insufficiently around her fair white body, hopped from rug to rug toward the bathroom, whence clouds of steam were issuing. "Of all the colossal nerve!" she remarked to herself.

A moment later, with her curly hair loosened from its tight bathing cap again, she stood with a comb and surveyed herself in the mirror.

"I wish I knew what he wanted!" Then she tossed her head. "Well, I haven't got anything to worry about!"

* * * * * * *

Across the town, in a luxurious hotel-apartment overlooking the Park from an eminence on the Avenue, Professor Augustine Pfaffle was doing worrying enough for two. His living-room was swarming with the gentlemen of the press—gentlemen by courtesy only, since they steadfastly refused to leave him alone, no matter how profusely the great criminologist's manager, representing the Thatcher Lecture Bureau, poured out drinks and offered sandwiches.

"Can I quote you as saying that American morons are quicker-witted than the morons over where you come from?"

"Did Anderson sock you once or twice?"

"What did you do for the eye, raw beef or a leech?"

"How come, with all your experience in investigating crime, you stayed in this room alone with a murderer?"

"Was it anything in your examination of Anderson, the janitor, that made him sock you in the eye and then beat it?"

"Is it true you said he was descended from the Jukes family?"

"May we quote you as saying that you consider Olaf Anderson a greater and more bloodthirsty killer than Landeau or the Marquis de Sade?"

"Pose for another picture, Professor . . . smile!"

Finally the Herr Professor raised both his skinny talons above his shining bald head and shrieked the pack of them down.

"Zentlemen! Blease!"

His eyeglasses dangled on their long black cord almost to his knees, and at every step he took a little cascade of cigarette ash fell from his vest.

"I do not wish to make a statement now. My manager tells me that it will conflict with my lecture tour. All this business is very unfortunate. In Vienna it would be impossible for a criminal to escape through the windows and down a wall."

The Professor twisted his slightly simian face into a grimace significant of the fact that he was wishing himself back in Vienna right now. "Zis unfortunate accident, zentlemen . . . it is nothing! It is only a matter of hours, perhaps minutes, before the prisoner will be back in his cell. I assure you!"

"Oh, yeah?" A fat and somewhat unshaven young man thrust his face almost into the Professor's. "If you're the big shot crime expert, why don't you psycho-analyze where the janitor has beat it to? Come on, Professor, let us see the great brain in action!"

"Yeah! You say it's only a matter of minutes before Anderson is caught and back in his cell. Give us a break, Prof. Where is he?" Other voices began to chime in.

"Where he iss?" Professor Pfaffle was stalling for time, and they knew it.

"Come on, Professor. You let him get away, now why don't you figure out where he's gone? It ought to be easy for the greatest crime expert in the world. . . ."

"Sure—where would Anderson go? Back to his school, or where? That ought to be pie for a criminologist. Why, haven't you ever heard about the little boy on the farm who could always find the pig when it got loose? They asked him how he managed it and he said, 'I always stop and think where would I go if I were a pig, and I look there, and there she is!' "

Professor Pfaffle drew himself to his full height. He looked at Mr. Thatcher of the lecture bureau, but Mr. Thatcher gave him no help in his crisis.

Professor Pfaffle waved one arm in the direction of the window. "Of course I know where it iss he went," he announced. "The movements of the criminal are an open book to the expert. He iss . . . there . . ." Pfaffle's gesture took in all of Greater New York.

The reporters moved toward the window. "You mean, in Central Park?" They seemed oddly impressed with the idea. The Professor made a quick decision.

Professor Pfaffle nodded energetically. "Ja, the park. The man is a claustraphobiac, of course. His crime has made him fear closed walls and the sight of his fellow men. He is, therefore, hiding in the wide reaches of Central Park since he knows he has no chance to leave the city while every exit is guarded."

"Say . . . you're good!"

"There's a story lead—Pfaffle the Hungarian Bloodhound spots lost trail by absent treatment. . . ."

"Pose for a picture pointing at the park—give us that old smile!"

"Who's got a nickel—wait, it isn't a pay telephone. Hello . . . hello. . . ."

Finally they were gone. The Professor wiped his brow. Thatcher, the exquisite man-about-town in spats and wing collar, came over to him.

"You got out of that neatly, Pfaffle my boy," he said. "Maybe we won't get cancellations of your bookings after all! The only thing is, I hope that janitor really is in the park!"

The Professor hoped the janitor was somewhere not in the park, and said so in two languages, combining the worst epithets of both.

"Why not he iss in der park? If the police do not find him there, that is their fault. Besides, by that time we are aboard a train, no?"

Thatcher patted him on the shoulder. "You're a regular master-mind," he admitted. "For a while I was sorry I'd arranged the whole thing with the Commissioner, when you let the prisoner make a laughing stock of you. But now you've stalled off the papers so that they'll play up the park, and lay off you. The newspapers will forget the case in another day or two anyhow—and by then, as you say, we'll be aboard a train and a fast one. The audiences in Chicago and Detroit will eat this up, watch 'em."

"Ja," agreed Pfaffle. "So I thought."

"Tell me," Thatcher inquired. "Was that on the level? I mean, did you just happen to see the park out of the window and think it a likely place, or did you really figure out the criminal psychology of the man?"

"Anderson has no psyche worthy of the name," insisted the Professor. "He is the most stubborn, surly *hund* I have met in some time. I hope they never find him. I have never had more trouble in analyzing a subject than I did with him. It is like beating on a stone wall."

He paused for a moment. "All the same, the man is a low-grade moron and if they wish me to, I shall testify in the court, provided I am not out on tour at the time."

"You could go on a dozen tours and come back before his case is ever tried in court," Thatcher told him. "The docket is filled months ahead."

The Herr Professor made no reply. Owing to the suddenness with which the newspapermen had departed, there was still a little something in the way of refreshments left behind. To these dregs and fragments Pfaffle applied himself as if he needed them.

•   •   •   •   •   •   •

As was her habit upon mornings when school did not keep, due to regular or accidental holidays, Miss Hildegarde Withers was sitting at that moment upon a bench near the 72nd Street gate of Central Park, her nose buried in a copy of the New York *Times*. In spite of the bright sunshine, a chill wind tugged at the sheets of her newspaper and whipped the collar of her modest coat about her ears.

A newsboy came, crying his wares, just as she was in the middle of an extremely interesting letter on the editorial page, signed "Irate Citizen." "Paper, lady?" The boy stared at her morning paper unpleasantly. '*Afternoon* paper', lady? *Worl' Telegram, Sun* an' *Post*?"

She frowned, disapprovingly, and then changed her mind. After all, she ought to read up on everything now. She handed the boy three pennies, and tucked a folded paper under her arm. Then she returned to Irate Citizen, who was openly in favor of legible house numbers and against dry-sweeping.

The boy passed on, down toward the peanut stand where even at this late season a few nursemaids with baby carriages had congregated, surrounded by swarms of begging, bulging pigeons. He was yelling something gleaned from the news columns, but Miss Withers made an effort to keep her attention on her *Times*.

It was not an easy matter, due to the swooping flight of the ever-hungry birds, and the merry cries of the be-sweat-ered and be-legginged children, who ran back and forth over Miss Withers' feet, pursuing each other with misplaced zeal.

At that moment a man, by his hangdog air and the state of his clothing a permanent member of the army of the unem-ployed, came furtively out of the bushes nearby, crossed the lawn, and stepped over the fence onto the sidewalk. Miss Withers did not notice him, no one noticed him. He was of the type whom no one notices, and it seems that even the Creator himself has forgotten.

He paused beside the peanut stand, and one hand went into his pocket. A nickel was produced, and exchanged for a brown paper bag.

This was routine procedure. The pigeons near by communi-cated, in their own mysterious fashion, the news of the approaching bounty to their more distant kind, and the air was immediately darkened.

And then it happened. The peanut vendor shook his head,

as if to clear his vision, and cocked it on one side. Several hundred birds did exactly the same thing, their amazement and surprise only too evident. This was unheard of! This was unthinkable!

The silence and the nervous tension of the moment communicated itself to Hildegarde Withers, and she put away her *Times*. She looked down toward the peanut stand, past the wheeling, cheeping birds—and saw that the disheveled, hatless little man had broken the unwritten law of the place.

He was walking swiftly on, toward the center of the park—and he was busily *eating* the peanuts he had bought!

Several hundred pairs of eyes followed him out of sight— but one pair was sharper than all the rest. Hildegarde Withers rose to her feet, with her newspapers tucked under one arm and her umbrella gripped in her hand. She moved after him, quickly and implacably.

She came around the curve of the sidewalk, to find the little man engaged in climbing the fence that set off the shrubbery.

"Anderson!" she commanded. "Olaf Anderson, you come straight here!"

He turned, his face paler than the shock of tumbled hair above it. There was little fight left in Anderson the janitor. His knees trembled, and he sniffed continually.

"I bane come quiet," he promised. "Don't shoot!"

She did not shoot. Miss Withers, however, did something even more drastic than shooting would have been. Her eyes piercing as gimlets, she leaned close to Anderson. "Listen to me!" she commanded.

Then, pursing her lips, she emitted the fragment of a tune which had already become the theme song of this demented drama—the two notes thrice repeated that Anise Halloran had written in her last few minutes of life.

"Whoooo-wheeeeeee—whoooo-wheeeee. . . ."

Anderson blinked, but no shadow of terror nor glint of intelligence showed in his face.

Miss Withers tried again. "Didn't you ever hear this before? Doesn't it mean anything to you? Listen—whoooo-wheeeeee. . . ."

Anderson's face lighted up. He took a stealthy step in the

direction of the shrubbery. "Cuckoo," he responded. "Cuckooooooo." Then he suddenly turned and ran for his life.

It was at that opportune moment that Motorcycle Officer Michael Vincent Cummings chose to come noisily down the Parkway, a freshly sharpened pencil and a new book of summonses in his breast pocket. He looked upon an angular lady waving a black umbrella frantically in the air, and then, at a glimpse of the janitor's flying heels, Officer Cummings flipped his machine up on the sidewalk, through the fence wires, and up the slope toward the shrubbery.

His motorcycle, like many another steed, balked suddenly at the barrier, leaving Officer Michael Vincent Cummings to transcribe a parabola in the air. His descent, however, brought him into contact with a pair of rapidly moving denim overalls, to which Officer Cummings clung with grim tenacity.

"I gotcha!" he cried out, with that passion for stating the obvious which characterizes so many of us.

From that point on Anderson the janitor spoke not at all, except to affirm his intense hunger, but he sneezed often and loud.

Miss Withers watched the departing "wagon," and shook her head sadly. Never in her life had she found her duty as a citizen so unpleasant to the taste. She tried to tell herself that this man had taken one life, and attempted two more, within the space of the last four days, but she could not make it stick.

It was not until that moment that she turned to the afternoon paper which she had purchased. A two column box at the upper left caught her eye, and the heading held it. "I'll Have the Last Laugh, Says Pfaffle. . . . Viennese criminologist from whom suspect in Halloran killing escaped yesterday says psycho-analysis will find him—look in Central Park, declared Augustine Pfaffle late this morning. The Professor went on to explain that his interrupted examination of the school-janitor showed him to be a pronounced victim of claustraphobia, or fear of closed spaces. . . ."

"Closed fiddlesticks," declared Hildegarde Withers. She dropped the newspaper carefully into a Keep the City Clean container, whimsically modelled of concrete in imitation of a tree trunk, and marched off across the park toward the east. It was after eleven and she had promised to meet Georgie Swarthout at the Inspector's room in Bellevue surgical ward at noon.

She came silently through the door and seated herself by the head of Piper's bed. The Inspector put aside his cigar and stared at her.

"You look like all three of the Furies," he told her. "What's up?"

She told him briefly of the events in the parl. The Inspector raised his eyebrows so that they disappeared in a maze of bandages, and whistled softly.

"Bravo! Three cheers, and other congratulations. Although it's ten to one that the traffic cop you called in will get all the credit. Possibly he'll mention that a feminine bystander aided him in spotting the wanted man."

"He can have the credit," said Hildegarde Withers. "I don't want any acclaim for dragging a man back to a cell out of the great outdoors. It makes me feel like something very low. As my children say, I could put on a top-hat and walk under a snake. The look in that man's eyes when I called his name . . . it haunts me."

"This is going to be a feather in the cap of our visiting friend from Vienna," the Inspector told her. He motioned to a litter of newspapers around his bed. "My X-rays came out so well this morning that they said I could read up on things a bit, which is how I happened to run across it. You know, I was just wondering if maybe there's something in this psycho-analytical method of solving crimes?"

Hildegarde Withers sniffed, audibly. "There's everything in it except common-sense," she announced. "Why, if I—"

She was interrupted by a cheery hail from the doorway, and Georgie Swarthout arrived, a box of cigars under his arm for the Inspector, and a meaning look for Miss Withers.

Piper opened the box, and sniffed at the aroma of Havana which rose to his nostrils. "You know," he observed with a twinkle in his eye, "Vice-president Marshall was wrong, after all, when he said what this country needs is a good five-cent cigar. What this five-cent cigar needs is a good country."

Miss Withers ignored this, and turned to Georgie. "I can see that you're full to bursting with something," she told him. "Come on, get it out of your system. Did your new lead come to anything? What was it, the murderer's monogrammed cuff-links at the scene of the crime, or another missing ruby eye from the idol of the secret cult in Tibet?"

"Neither one," said Georgie Swarthout. "This isn't out of an Edgar Wallace thriller, but it thrills me, all the same. I played my hunch, see?"

"Begin at the beginning," Miss Withers told him. "Go on until you get to the end, and then stop."

"It began when I saw that Stevenson guy," said Georgie Swarthout. "I didn't like his looks, see? Too fussy about his clothes. . . ."

"They don't hang men for wearing tab collars and spats," Miss Withers reminded him. "But go on."

"Well, it didn't take me long to get wise to him," Georgie announced. "That guy was concealing something."

"If there's anybody in this case who isn't," Miss Withers observed wearily, "I don't know who it is."

"Yeah. Well, anyway, I didn't like his looks. The idea of a swell girl like Janey Davis mooning around after him!" Georgie shook his head. "I got suspicious of him right away. So I went down to where he lives, in the Village, and I had a talk with the little wop who sells ice and wood in the basement. . . ."

"And *gin, a dollar a fifth,* if I remember his quotation," Miss Withers put in.

"Huh? Yeah. I gave the wop a dollar to tell me if he'd seen any dame answering the description of the dead Halloran girl come down there with Stevenson. But that doesn't get me anywhere. The wop swears that he never saw Stevenson bring a dame into his apartment, big or little, blonde or dark."

Georgie rose from his chair, and leaned across the foot of the bed. "But get this! I wasn't satisfied with that, so I go upstairs. Stevenson isn't home, and I pick his lock the way we did Dana Waverly's last year in the bus murder case, and I go in."

"You are one up on me," Miss Withers conceded. The Inspector leaned back on his pillows, but his hands clenched and unclenched at his sides.

"Well, I went through the dump. Nothing much in the line

of furniture. Mostly second-hand junk from the uncalled-for warehouses. Fireplaces full of burned newspapers. Bookcases full of books.''

"What books?" Miss Withers judged people, first by their hands and feet, and next by their libraries.

"Oh, just books. Nothing much. Mostly books on family trees and so forth. All about the Stevenson family, and the Addison family, and so forth. The living room didn't get us anywhere, and the bathroom was also a blank, except for a few bugs in the tub. But there was a kitchenette in the wall, and in that kitchenette I found this!''

With a flourish, the young detective pulled from his pocket a nearly-full bottle, and handed it to Miss Withers.

"Ever see that label before?''

She nodded slowly. "Dewar's Dew of Kirkintilloch" had entered the case again.

"And that proves Mister Stevenson isn't the white-haired boy you thought he was," declared Georgie Swarthout. "This liquor isn't kicking around everywhere. I guess this is pretty good evidence that somebody besides the janitor knew about that secret entrance through the school cellar into the warehouse next door!''

Miss Withers picked up the bottle, smelled it, and made a wry face. "This case is getting to have a pretty high alcoholic content," she said slowly. "So far it's been nothing but bottles of whiskey. If I weren't a strict teetotaller already, I would be now, for certain.''

The Inspector sat up against his pillows. "Swarthout, can't you dig up some clues that are White Rock or seltzer or something? Discover a jar of buttermilk that points straight to the murderer, and Miss Withers will be ever so much happier.''

"I'd be happier at anything that pointed straight to the murderer," that lady told him acidly.

At that moment the white-capped nurse knocked on the door. "A message for you, Inspector. It just arrived.''

She brought a blue and white envelope, with the familiar Postal Telegraph monogram, and put it in Piper's hand. He opened it savagely, and as he read its contents he ground his strong teeth deeply into Swarthout's innocent cigar. Then he shoved his missive toward Miss Withers.

It was signed by one Jasper Abbott, who had risen from

street-car motorman to the elevated position of Assistant Commissioner of Police, by virtue of an inability to earn a living in any other fashion and a cousin high in the rolls of Tammany Hall. Mr. Abbott was not the Inspector's closest buddy, and his wire did nothing to cement their friendship.

It read: "THE COMMISSIONER DESIRES ME TO CONVEY TO YOU HIS PLEASURE AT HEARING THAT YOU WILL BE BACK ON DUTY WITHIN THE NEXT THREE OR FOUR WEEKS IN WHICH WE ALL JOIN STOP YOU WILL BE GLAD TO KNOW THAT IN YOUR ABSENCE PROFESSOR AUGUSTINE PFAFFLE OF VIENNA HAS BEEN APPOINTED ACTING INSPECTOR OF THE HOMICIDE SQUAD AT THE SUGGESTION OF DISTRICT ATTORNEY ROCHE AND GIVEN A FREE HAND IN THE HALLORAN CASE."

"Glad?" said the Inspector bitterly. "I'm practically tickled pink."

XV

I Know Something I Won't Tell

(11/19/32—11:00 A.M.)

Janey Davis was asleep, a vaguely troubled sleep, when the telephone rang. Her curly red-brown hair was tumbled across the pillow, and her body curled like a kitten's. She reached out a smooth white arm and fumbled with the alarm clock. But the ringing went on.

Then she sat up straight in bed, stark terror in her eyes. She was staring at the door. For a moment she remained there, soft, warm, terrified and lovely. Then the instrument across the room on the desk attracted her by its frantic vibrations, which almost lifted the receiver from the hook. She slipped her feet into a pair of mules, and crossed the room to the window. Once the wintry blasts were shut away, and the curtains raised to admit the dim glow which passes for daylight in Manhattan, she lifted the telephone.

It was the voice of her chief, Mr. Waldo Emerson Macfarland, and by his tone he seemed very upset indeed.

"Miss Davis? Janey? Listen to me carefully. I want you to get down to the school just as quick as ever you can. . . ."

"But—" the sleepiness left the girl's voice. "But I thought there was to be no school until Monday! You said so yourself!"

"Never mind what I said, pay no attention to that," Macfarland told her. "I've just got my instructions, and I am giving you yours. When you get down there, telephone every teacher and every employee of the school—excepting poor Anderson, of course—and tell them to be there at one o'clock. No, I don't know what it's for. Something to do with the police. If any of them object, tell them there will be an officer after them if they are not down there at two o'clock. The officer on guard at the door will have his instructions to let you in. Am I making myself perfectly clear, and do you understand me?''

"Yes, I understand you," said Janey. "But I don't see—I thought the case was closed? They arrested the janitor, didn't they? Even if he got away, they caught him again . . . who else do they want?"

"*Whom* else," Macfarland told her absently. "And Janey—"

"Yes, Mr. Macfarland?"

"Be very careful what you say and how you act!"

"As if he needed to tell me that," said Janey Davis to herself. She went into the bathroom and brushed her teeth, vigorously. Then she turned on the shower, and let her pajamas slip from her body. Gingerly she stopped under the stream of water, tucking the last shreds of her hair under a green bathing cap.

It was at that inauspicious moment that the telephone chose to ring again.

Wearily, the girl stepped out of the tub again, wrapped a scanty bath towel around herself, and slopped over to the phone.

"Hello? . . . Who? . . . Yes, this is me . . . Mr. Swarthout? . . . Say, with all night and all day to choose from, is there any law that you always have to phone me right in the middle of a bath? Besides, I'm in a hurry. . . ."

She wrapped the towel more closely around her shoulders. "What? No, I can't have lunch with you today, either. I have to work. W-O-R-K, work. Yes. No, I don't know when I'll get through. Yes, at the school. No, I don't think so . . . really, I can't. . . ."

    •   •   •   •   •   •   •

The faculty of Jefferson School had gathered faithfully in response to Janey's telephone calls. By thirty-five minutes after two the narrow seats of Miss Vera Cohen's classroom, always used for faculty meetings because of it nearness to the Principal's office, were almost full.

Even Betty Curran Rogers was there, a frightened smile on her lips and a shining new wedding ring on her left hand. Her knees were up at her chin, due to the lowness of the seat which was meant for second-graders, and her heart was in her mouth, due to the fact that at any moment she expected to receive official notice from Mr. Champney and Mr. Velie of the Board of Education that on the expiration of her contract at the end of the semester her services would no longer be required at Jefferson School. Since the new Mr. Rogers was a salesman of power cruisers, with a drawing account of twenty-two-fifty a week, the situation was not one to be taken lightly.

Today Mr. Macfarland did not sit at the desk, with Janey Davis at his side to take dictation or make notes on his remarks. He was, like the rest of them, dutifully waiting on a bench. He fiddled with his eyeglasses.

Janey Davis sat across the aisle from him, her pencil busily drawing little circles and whirligigs. Young Mr. Stevenson, in the seat behind, watched her anxiously, but she did not turn around.

He leaned forward once to whisper, but she shook her head. "For Heaven's sake remember where we are," she whispered back.

Miss Rennel was busily talking. "I'd like to know why we're down here in the first place, and why we're waiting in the second place? Land's sake, nobody is any more anxious to cooperate than I am, but in my opinion this is highhanded, very highhanded. . . ."

Mr. Macfarland, thus appealed to, shrugged his narrow shoulders. "I told you that it was none of my doing," he reminded her.

"Well, but what are we waiting for?"

Mr. Macfarland said that he didn't know.

"I suppose it's Hildegarde Withers! I don't see what authority she has to gallivant around all over town questioning us as if she were a prosecuting attorney! Just because she knows a policeman. Tell me"—Miss Rennel was voicing the thoughts of them all—"tell me, Mr. Macfarland, has Miss Withers any official authority?"

"None as far as I'm concerned," that gentleman said wearily. "Before I knew of the arrest of the janitor I had some idea of asking her to undertake an investigation, but later events . . ."

He was interrupted by the arrival of no less a personage

than Sergeant Taylor of the Homicide Squad, at present acting as a vanguard for a small army composed of Professor Augustine Pfaffle, his stenographer, male, a photographer, likewise male, and bringing up the rear, the bulky figure of Mike McTeague, a Gibraltar in brass buttons.

"Folks!" announced Taylor dramatically, "I have the great honor—I mean, I'm glad to have the opportunity—I mean, this here gentleman is one of the world's greatest criminologists, and a gentleman with whom I am honored to have the opportunity of working with him. You all read in the newspapers about how without going out of his hotel room he was able to locate the missing suspect in this here murder case.

"Now it seems that there's one or two angles of this murder about which the Commissioner and the District Attorney aren't entirely satisfied, and so the case has been turned over to Professor Pfaffle here. He is going to iron out the wrinkles, with your help, ladies and gentlemen, so that a waterproof iron-bound case can be turned over to the District Attorney and the Grand Jury, so that justice will be satisfied and—"

"The Army and Navy forever, three cheers for Jack Dalton of the U.S. Marines," whispered Bob Stevenson into Janey's curls.

"What I vant is very simple," the great criminologist announced. "It is not enough for us to know that a murder was committed in this building at a certain time by a certain person. We must know vy! And we must know how! Also, we must present legal proof of der fact. For that reason I ask your help. I vant every one of you to try to remember what he or she did on that fatal afternoon when Anise Halloran was killed. It is very important, and besides, you may be interested to know that everything we do and say is to be taken down for inclusion in my new book on crime and criminals, as well as given to the newspapers." He nodded toward the secretary, who was busy with notebook and pencil, catching every pearl that fell.

"I vant you to just be natural, and go ahead as if your

classes were in the classrooms as they were that afternoon. You are all here, I trust?''

"All but our third grade teacher, Miss Hildegarde Withers," said the Principal. "However, she has been sent for, and should arrive at any minute."

"At any minute is not soon enough," fumed Professor Pfaffle. "I must have everybody here, at once! Everybody!"

He walked up and down in front of the blackboard, hands behind his back, and his high brow furrowed. His shoulders almost brushed against the musical scales which the murdered girl had marked upon this blackboard only a few days before, but Professor Pfaffle paid no attention.

"You promised me full cooperation," he stormed at Macfarland. "And now one of your teachers isn't here!"

"Two teachers aren't here," said Bob Stevenson softly. He was looking at the blackboard. Only Janey Davis heard him, and her head bent a little lower.

"Vell, vy don't you do something?"

Mr. Macfarland rose to the occasion. "You might send somebody after the missing teacher," he suggested. "After all, you've been given complete authority, Professor."

"Ja!" Pfaffle whirled upon the Sergeant. "You! Send that officer—" he pointed toward McTeague—"send him to get this Fraulein Withers. If she does not come willingly, arrest her!"

McTeague blinked. "A—arrest Miss Withers?"

A wicked smile flickered across the face of Bob Stevenson. "I'd give a month's pay to see him do it," he whispered. Sergeant Taylor opened his mouth, protestingly.

"You have your orders!" The Professor was imperious. "Send this man after her, at once!"

Sergeant Taylor nodded slowly. "Okay, Perfessor. Only, don't you think we'll need McTeague here? He's the only cop we've got to help us now."

"Need him? What for? The less police around the better for my plan. I want everybody to be perfectly natural, understand? They cannot be natural and act as they did on the day of the murder with a policeman before every door. Send him on."

"You're the boss," said Sergeant Taylor. McTeague left

the school, shaking his head. He had instructions to bring in Miss Withers, dead or alive.

Professor Pfaffle conferred with his satellites. Then he very ostentatiously referred to his massive silver watch.

"We haf already lost twenty minutes," he announced. "All because of this Fraulein Withers!" He stopped short.

There was the sound of quick footsteps in the hall, and then a cheery voice greeted the assemblage.

"Who's taking my name in vain? I'm so sorry, so very sorry that I'm late. I hope things didn't get cold!"

Hildegarde Withers swept into the room, her bonnet cocked over one eye, and her umbrella sticking out straight under her arm.

"Miss Withers?" Principal Macfarland half rose in his seat. "Where have you been? Didn't you meet McTeague? because we just sent him after you."

Miss Withers found a seat at one of the front desks, not without considerable hustling and rattling of her umbrella. "I saw somebody in uniform rushing out of the door as I came down the stairs," she admitted. "But I didn't dream it was McTeague looking for me. . . ."

"Down the stairs? What were you doing upstairs?" Macfarland was annoyed.

"Just looking around," Miss Withers told him. "I suppose this is Professor Pfaffle of whom I have heard so much?"

"Ja, I am him," admitted the Professor, slightly mollified. "We haf waited for you. Haf you been upstairs looking around all this time?"

"Yes, I was looking for a friend of mine—a red ant. But I'm here now. Let the fish-fry proceed."

Professor Pfaffle shook his head dubiously, and then rapped sharply on the desk with his knuckles. "You understand, all of you? Except for the fact that none of the pupils are at their desks, you will act as you did that afternoon. If you stepped out into the hall then, do it now. If you crossed your room to the window, do it now. But everything at its due place, you understand. Forget *nothing*—the slightest thing may be important. In the case of a pathological murderer such as this Anderson seems to be, every detail of the actions of those around him may be of the highest importance. Omit nothing!"

He looked at his watch. "It is almost three o'clock," he

told them. "Reenact the last half hour of that day, down to the most minute detail! *Everything*, remember!"

Miss Strasmick raised her hand.

"Professor, I cut my finger in a pencil sharpener that afternoon. Do I have to cut it over again? It was just getting well!"

But the teachers were already filing out toward their own classrooms, leaving Miss Vera Cohen alone in room 1A. That lady drew a copy of the *Saturday Evening Post* from a drawer of her desk, and opened it noisily.

"I read this story until I left Anise here alone putting her work on the board that afternoon, so I suppose I'll have to reread it now, though I know she marries him at the end."

The Professor and his satellites stood outside in the hallway. "Which is the lady I spoke to you about?"

Sergeant Taylor motioned toward the door of 1B, through which Miss Withers had just passed. The Professor raised his eyebrows.

Then he moved down the hall, followed by the photographer and the secretary—also the Sergeant, who was intent upon not missing a single thing.

Professor Pfaffle burst in upon Miss Withers without knocking. She put down her copy of the *Atlantic Monthly*, and stared at him through her glasses as if he were a noxious weed.

"I understand that it was you who stumbled upon the janitor's hiding place," he told her. "We shall require your cooperation for the next few minutes."

"But you gave me instructions to reenact the events of the murder afternoon," she reminded him. "I sat at this desk all afternoon."

He waved his hand. "Never mind that. We are already aware of your movements upon the afternoon in question—or at least what you say they were. I wish to take some photographs of the basement and of the janitor's hole in the wall where he slipped through into the warehouse. The Sergeant's men have been unable to locate this hideaway, and I wish you to show it to us."

"Find it yourself," she suggested. "It ought to be easy for a man who can tell where an escaped suspect is hiding. And another thing, nobody showed me where it was."

The Professor drew himself up to his full height. "You do

not understand my position," he told her. "I haf been appointed Acting Inspector of the Homicide Squad! The Commissioner of Police has himself given me this little symbol of my authority!" With a certain natural pride, Professor Augustine Pfaffle displayed a large silver badge affixed to his vest.

Miss Withers gave it a glassy eye. "How pretty!" She rose slowly from her desk, after putting the *Atlantic* carefully away. She felt of her own badge, but decided to keep that for an emergency.

"I suppose I'll have to show you what you want to know," she told him. "But I'm not wild about going down in that basement again. The last time I was there I very nearly had an accident. By the way—" She turned to the Sergeant. "Did the print men find anything on that hatchet?"

"Not a thing," admitted Sergeant Taylor. "They worked over it mighty carefully, too, because we need some concrete evidence to support the Professor's hypot—his theory. There weren't any prints on the shovel, either, though we did find some hairs and blood which belonged to the Inspector, and showed that the shovel was what the janitor used to whack him down."

"So it was the janitor?" Miss Withers followed the Professor obediently out of the room. "I've been a little skeptical about that, all along. There are a few things that don't fit in, somehow."

"Nonsense," retorted the Professor. He was genial again now that he had won his point. "I understand that you fancy yourself as an amateur detective, Fraulein Withers? Ah, the amateur! Always looking for abstruse meanings in the obvious. Who else but this janitor Anderson had the opportunity? The cellar was his territory, and he could dig graves and dispose of bodies there as he saw fit. Who else but Anderson was the pathological type to commit a sex crime of this nature? Ah, my *gnädige* Fraulein, it is as plain as the nose on your face."

Miss Withers flashed him a barbed look, but he sailed on blithely. "I shall never forget another case very like this one in some aspects—the shoes in particular. You are aware that several pairs of shoes of the dead girl's were found hidden in the janitor's room under the stairs? A very clear case of *fetishism*. In this case of which I was speaking, a poor fellow broke into a store in Berlin and stole nearly a hundred pairs of women's shoes. Not to wear them, *ach nein!* They were discovered in his room some time later, each and every shoe with its toe bitten off!''

''Mercy sakes!'' They were now descending the cellar stair. Miss Withers looked extremely perturbed. ''Then you think that Anderson is one of those—?''

''A shoe-fetishist? Ja, I know it. I understand that even when you found the body, the shoes had been removed and were lying in the center of the room. They were no doubt added to the poor demented creature's collection after he disposed of the body.''

Miss Withers was thoughtful. She remembered the blue sandals that she had stumbled upon so terribly in the darkness. They had not been among the shoes discovered in Anderson's room. But she held her tongue.

''Here's the furnace where the body was found, in flames,'' she said, in the tone of a rubberneck bus-driver. ''Ahead of us, in the corner, is the half-dug grave. And here . . .'' she left the board sidewalk and moved swiftly across the dirt floor where it rose toward the ceiling . . . ''here is the hole in the wall!''

She stood back in silence while the Herr Professor was with difficulty pushed up through the hole by the faithful Taylor. She watched while the photographer took picture after picture, and listened while the Professor dictated page after page of notes, instructions, and conclusions as part of his case-history.

Overhead she could hear the footsteps of the other teachers in the hall. For a time Miss Withers amused herself by trying to determine each teacher by her step, and by the part of the building from which it came. It would not be hard, she realized, for a man hiding here to know a good deal about events on the floor above him.

At last Professor Pfaffle expressed himself as satisfied. Sergeant Taylor, who had, as Miss Withers told it later, ''clung to the Professor's coat-tails like a puppy to a root,'' expressed himself as being thrilled and delighted with the privilege. ''It sure is great to work with you,'' he declared.

"It ain't often we get a chance to see how a great expert like you takes aholt of a job."

They paused at the foot of the stairs while the photographer replaced his camera in its shoulder case.

"It might interest you to know, Professor," Miss Withers announced, consulting her old-fashioned watch, "that the time is now exactly three-fifty-five, which is the hour when I discovered the body of that murdered girl. Now if you had only resorted to the usual theatric device of having somebody else impersonate the victim, this is the time at which the crime should be reenacted. . . ."

She broke off short as the tread of heavy footsteps came from the hall overhead. There was something menacing, implacable, and remorseless about them to the little group which stood in the dank cellar, and waited. . . .

The heavy tread halted, almost where the door of the Teachers' Cloakroom was, and then after a moment came on.

"Hello . . . hello, there. . . ."

The voice was muffled and strange, filtering as it did through closed doors and solid walls. But at least it was human.

Sergeant Taylor gave a somewhat quavering answer, and then the door at the head of the stair swung open to disclose the figure of a tallish, broadish man in formal afternoon wear, with a gardenia in his buttonhole and a whangee in his hand.

Taylor came to attention. "The Commissioner!" he gasped.

"I just thought I'd drop in and see how you're getting along," came the cheerful booming voice. "What is this, a wake? I expected lots of excitement and fireworks."

"The fireworks come later," Professor Pfaffle assured the Commissioner. "You shall see for yourself. I now go upstairs to question the teachers. They have reenact the events of that afternoon—if any one of them do anything different today, another will notice it. I shall from this afternoon get a case history which will make the excursions of Freud and Jung into criminology look like the picnic of a child. From this afternoon we are learning much, *nein*?" Taylor agreed heartily and quickly.

"Unless I very much miss my guess, you are going to learn even more than you expect," said Miss Withers, sotto voce, "before this afternoon is over."

The Herr Professor smiled patronizingly at Miss Withers as they climbed the stair. "Is it possible that you, Fraulein, have made a study of abnormal psychology?"

"I've read William James," she retorted acidly.

"James? James? I haf not heard of him. Pre-Freud, I imagine."

"In more ways than one," Miss Withers told him cryptically.

The Herr Professor had hardly reached the Commissioner's side when he took his stance and began another speech.

"I am glad and happy that you haf come here to witness my triumph," he announced. "The same scientific principles which enabled me to trace the hiding place of the escaped janitor . . ."

"What man wouldn't make a break for the park if he'd been in a cell for a day or so, and saw it spang in front of him as he came out of the window?" Miss Withers was losing her temper. But the Professor plunged on.

"Those same scientific principles, I repeat, which told me that Anderson had been for a long time a victim of claustraphobia as well as fetishism. . . ."

"I suppose that his little nook between the liquor cases which you thought so significant was also chosen by him because of his fear of closed spaces?"

"These principles . . ." the Professor glared at Miss Withers . . . "have made perfectly clear to me the motives, the mental causes and causations, and the whole secret of this crime. It was a love crime, the love of Caliban for a star. . . ."

Miss Withers looked puzzled at this, but let it go by. The Professor, on his mettle, really opened up and got down to business. He had already nodded to the secretary to take this down, as he could use most of it in the press statements he intended to give out in time for the morning papers.

"I know every thought that went through the mind of the janitor, Anderson," he announced. "I know how he committed this crime. I know his every movement on that fatal afternoon, or I shall know it as soon as I question the teachers who have just reënacted their own motions on that afternoon.

"I know that Anderson had a warped love for Anise Halloran, so far above him that she was out of his reach. He was, in his mind at least, a stone beneath her feet. He was only worthy to lick her shoe . . . note the fetishism? . . . and the next step was for him to start his collection of these beloved objects. Perhaps she bought new shoes during her lunch hour, and threw the old ones into her waste basket. At any rate, his duties as janitor gave him many opportunities. He was a voluptuary anyway, notice the comfortable little hideaway he made for himself where he could drink and smoke and gloat over his photographs while he should have been on duty. You follow me?''

"Yeah, I guess so," agreed the Commissioner. "Sounds reasonable."

"Ja. Well, then a change comes over the janitor. Perhaps slowly, perhaps all at once. If all that he may possess are the shoes of his beloved, no one else shall have more. He will destroy her! He lurks in the hall until all the teachers haf gone home, he thinks, but her alone. In his hand is the hatchet— for the warped and twisted mind of this poor man makes this killing an act of worship, a supreme sacrifice!

"He enters the Cloakroom, and strikes her down before she can cry out. A moment in which he attempts to remove her shoes, the object of his love now that the perversion has overwhelmed him—and then he realizes that Miss Withers is still in the building, perhaps through hearing her voice. He flees . . . without the body. Miss Withers enters, finds it, and goes for help. While she is gone he attempts to go through with his plan of burying the body in his basement. But the Inspector returns too soon, and the madman strikes him down with the shovel, and realizes that he has only a matter of moments. The grave is forgotten, as there is no time to dig it deeper. Only the furnace remains as a place to hide the dreadful remains. In goes the body, and the flames catch it in their teeth. Anderson runs to his hideaway, filled with panic. He drinks—and the liquor fuddles what is left of his mind so that he walks out upon the detectives, like a child, forgetting all his deep-laid plottings. That is typical of this type of delusion."

"It might also be typical of innocence," Miss Withers suggested. But nobody paid any attention.

"There is your case," Pfaffle finally concluded. "It only remains to substantiate it, and the evidence which these teachers will give me is to do that. They must have noted many details this afternoon which will fill in the blanks in that other afternoon. Now for the final chapter of our little story—Sergeant, call everybody into room 1A again.''

The Commissioner looked puzzled. "I say, I didn't see anybody around when I came in. . . .''

"Sergeant, get them here—everybody. I want the Commissioner to hear this. Go through the building and bring them all down, every single teacher." Pfaffle was booming with enthusiasm. He led the way down the hall, but the Commissioner lingered beside Miss Withers.

"And what do you think of all this statement of the case?''

"I think it's splendid," Miss Withers told him. "Only it isn't true. Anderson couldn't be the murderer. His feet are too large, and there was straw in his eyebrows. Besides . . .''

She broke off suddenly. They were standing in the door of Miss Cohen's classroom, with Pfaffle bustling about the desk, when the loud and excited voice of the Sergeant sounded on the stairs.

"Professor! I've looked in every classroom in the building, and nobody's here! They've scrammed, every last one of 'em!''

The Herr Professor dropped his eyeglasses to the floor with a sickening crack, and the blood rushed to his face.

"*Du lieber Gott! Der Schweinhunds!* I'll haf by the scruff of the neck every one of them dragged to the jail!''

The Commissioner, his professionally impartial face struggling to keep from a smile, voiced his surprise. "But I don't see why . . .''

"*Dumkopfs!* They shall answer for this!" The Professor was giving a good example of one of his own case histories in dementia.

Miss Withers sniffed, and gathered up her umbrella preparatory to departure. She had stood a good deal from the Professor this afternoon, but she felt amply rewarded.

"Your own instructions, if you remember, Professor," she told him gently. "I heard you order us, in the faculty meeting, to act exactly as we did that afternoon of the murder. Teachers go home at three-thirty, you know. And the officer whom the Sergeant meant to place on guard duty at the door was sent after me. So when three-thirty came, they all calmly walked out. Which, if you ask me, is the most sensible idea that has been brought forward this afternoon.''

XVI

Ach, Du Lieber Augustine!

(11/19/32—4:00 P.M.)

"You really have no cause to complain of the behavior of the faculty of Jefferson School," the Commissioner was reminding Professor Pfaffle. "You told them to reenact *everything*, and they took that to mean departure, too."

"Somebody varied the procedure by departing earlier today than he did on that other afternoon," Miss Withers observed. "Somebody remained here that day until long after the police arrived, and then left noisily but quickly by means of the fire escape. I'm afraid that person was not as punctilious about obeying you as the rest of them seem to have been. Unfortunate, Professor."

That gentleman was in a fine fury. He removed his shiny badge, and threw it on the desk. Then he beckoned to his photographer and his secretary, who had remained by the door, at attention.

"We go," he announced. "I resign from the position of Acting Inspector of the Homicide Squad. Augustine Pfaffle is not accustomed to being a laughing-stock."

He marched down the hall, and the front door of Jefferson School closed with a tremendous bang.

Miss Withers looked at the Commissioner, and that gentleman looked back at her. "I wish Oscar Piper was on the job," said the Commissioner wistfully.

"I wish so too," said Miss Withers. Only Sergeant Taylor seemed unhappy about the whole thing. "Aw, he's gone, and I was figuring on learning from him how to be a psycho-criminologist!"

At that moment the door of Macfarland's outer office opened, and the Principal appeared. "What was that noise

142

—a shot?'' Miss Withers noted that his hands trembled more than the slamming of a door would seem to necessitate.

"Gee,'' said Sergeant Taylor. "I looked in all the classrooms, but I clean forgot to look in there. And he was there all the time!''

"Of course I was there all the time,'' said Macfarland testily. "How much longer is this nonsense to keep up? Where's the Professor?''

"The Professor and the nonsense are both gone, along with everybody else,'' Miss Withers remarked. "But you're still here. Were you here this late the afternoon of the murder, by any chance?''

"Of course not! I told you that I left early—Janey will substantiate that—and that I walked the streets gathering material for my daily essay.''

"But it didn't occur to you that your orders were to reproduce exactly our activities of that afternoon?'' Miss Withers' voice was very casual, but Macfarland hesitated in answering.

"My wife will be worrying about me,'' he suggested hopefully.

The Commissioner suddenly consulted his watch. "I must be off,'' he told them. "I only stopped in to see how my new appointee was getting on, and now I know. My car is outside, Miss Withers.''

"You may drop me at the Tombs,'' Miss Withers suggested. "I understand the janitor has been booked for murder and taken there. I'd like to have a chat with him, if you can pass me through the red tape.''

The Commissioner had a sudden idea. "You've shown the only intelligence in this case so far,'' he told her. "Here . . . this ought to cut all the red tape you meet.'' And he handed her the bright badge that the Herr Professor had thown aside. "I'll make it official if you wish,'' he suggested.

She pinned it beside the gold one which was Oscar Piper's. "I guess two honorary decorations ought to equal one official appointment,'' she remarked.

Waldo Emerson Macfarland let his eyes widen, saucer fashion, and the Commissioner bowed.

•   •   •   •   •   •   •   •   •

"You can talk to him for just fifteen minutes," said the guard. He clanged the iron grill behind him.

"Ten will be plenty," said Hildegarde Withers. She turned to the man who stood with his hands in the pockets of his coat, and his head lowered.

"Good afternoon, Anderson," she remarked.

The janitor stared at her. "Why d'you come here? Why don't you leave me alone? I got nothing to say to you."

"But I have something to say to you," Miss Withers told him.

Anderson slumped into a chair. "It's fonny you aren't afraid to be here alone with me," he growled. "Don't you read the newspapers? Don't you know I'm the Hatchet Fiend?" Something in her calm presence loosened his tongue.

"Nonsense," Miss Withers told him. "The worst thing you've done, as far as I can see, is to steal liquor from the warehouse and sell it to your friend Tobey across the street."

The janitor remained unruffled. "So Tobey talked, did he? Well, I don't care. Everybody talk talk talk all the time. That German doctor, he says I'm queer—that I'm a nut. He ask me questions I won't answer for any man! He wanted to know what I dream!"

"Was that why you hit him and went out of the window the other day? I thought so. Now listen to me, Anderson. I haven't got much time. But you're going before the Grand Jury in a little while, and if something isn't done about it you're going to be tried and executed for the murder of Miss Halloran."

"I don't care if I am," said Anderson.

Miss Withers' voice was stern. "Don't you talk that way to me! I won't have it. Why in Heaven's name do you want to die?"

He shrugged his wide shoulders. "Why should I live? For forty years my luck is bad. Then once, good luck comes . . . but I miss it. I always miss it."

"Yes? What good luck?"

"The best luck in the world . . . money! I don't want to

spend my life a poor man, a janitor, tending furnaces and cleaning schoolrooms. Bad luck cannot last always, so I keep on trying for the great lucky break.'' Anderson was letting the words tumble forth, like a pent-up torrent. ''I play the stock market, I lose. I play the Mexican lottery, I lose. I play the Chinese lottery, I lose, again and again. I bet on Dempsey in Philadelphia, and on Al Smith in the election. Always I lose. I play the Irish sweepstakes for three years. This year I have no money. The man who sells me my tickets last year tells me, if I take a book of tickets and sell them, I get one free for myself. But I must sell every ticket in the book, understand, except that last one. So I sell them. I work, I talk, I argue, but I sell them. All but two tickets—the final one I must sell, and the one I mean to keep.

''Miss Halloran, she buys liquor from Tobey. I know she is sporting, see? I go to her, I tell her about the ticket and what she might win. So she borrow the money from another girl—but she insist on taking the ticket I want, instead of the other one. She take ticket 131313 . . . and I am left 131319, the only other one. Three thirteens are solid fourteen carat luck . . . and she wins. But me, I lose. I know that ticket will win, but I have to let her choose, it is the rules. The last ticket left is mine . . . and then, just as I knew it would happen, I read in the newspaper that my number wins. My number—but her ticket! She snatches my fortune from my hands. That afternoon I go crazy! I can't think, I can't think, I can't do anything. So near I have come to a fortune!''

''So you killed Anise Halloran for that?'' Miss Withers was incredulous.

''I kill nobody. I crawl into the warehouse and get drunk. I drink to forget. I drink more than I ever drank all my life . . . and when I come out, they tell me I kill somebody.''

Miss Withers nodded. ''One more thing, Anderson. Who knew about the little hole in the wall by which you got into the liquor warehouse?''

''Nobody!''

''How about Tobey, the candy store man? You sold the stuff to him. . . .''

''I told him a friend bring it off the Scandinavian-American liner for me.''

"Which he may not have believed. It's not impossible, of course, that some one of the teachers, or even Mr. Macfarland himself came into the cellar looking for you while you were climbing in or out of your little secret hideaway. Well, I'm going now, Anderson."

He clutched at her sleeve. "You believe me?" Then he turned away from her impassive face. "No, you don't believe me. You're just like the others. You want to make me talk, but you think I kill that girl because I want her shoes or something. You think I'm a Hatchet Fiend!"

"I do not," Miss Withers told him, as a parting shot. "Whatever you are, you're not a fiend, and you're no more pathological than the rest of us, the Professor included. As for your being a murderer—the courts will decide that. Good luck, Anderson."

Miss Withers passed out of the Tombs, and on to the Criminal Courts Building. Hesitating a moment at the head of the stairs, she finally decided to pass by the familiar office where Lieutenant Keller, she knew, must be waiting eagerly to discuss the Viennese criminologist and his meteoric rise and fall. On she went to the very last door of the long hall, which bore the simple legend—"Van Donnen."

She found the famous little laboratory expert measuring the rifling marks on a leaden bullet, preparatory to comparing them with those on another bullet shot out of a suspected gangster's gun. He rose to greet her, bewildered and a little embarrassed at being caught without coat or collar.

"Never mind that," she told him. "I want some information. I've been asking doctors and reading medical books all week, but I don't get anywhere. Tell me, Doctor. What is the best thing to kill ants with?"

Dr. Van Donnen raised his eyebrows. "But my dear lady! Do you come to me because of ants in your cupboard? Any commerical poison—Flit or the like. . . ."

"I don't quite mean that," said Hildegarde Withers. "Is there any poison which would be instantly fatal to an insect, say an ant, but of which he would enjoy the taste?"

Van Donnen was thoughtful. "The best commercial ant poisons are sweet syrups loaded with sodium arsenite. But those would not come under the specification you mention, because they are slow to work. The ant carries them to his nest, and poisons the whole food supply of the swarm. Let me see—something which an ant will eat or drink from preference, but which will kill him instantly. . . ."

He snapped his fingers. "I would say that it must be some petroleum derivative, such as kerosene, which would act upon the respiratory functions of the insect. The odor is so strong that ants and all insects like it, but before he would even taste it he would be dead."

Miss Withers nodded, thoughtfully. "And what would be the effect of kerosene, say, upon the human system?"

"Perfectly harmless. It is often used as a remedy for sore throat. The more highly refined petroleum products, however, can be dangerous. Ethyl gasoline, for instance, if concentrated, is one of the deadliest of lead poisons. But what has this to do with the investigation you are undertaking? I understood that the unfortunate girl met her death through a hatchet blow on the skull?"

"I'm just nosing around," said Miss Withers. "These refined gasoline products such as you spoke of before—what would their effect be on the human system? Suppose I drank a glass of gasoline or naphtha?"

"Your system would reject it, instantly. Only a very minute dose could be retained by the stomach. If that were not true, common cleaning fluid or benzine would be a dangerous poison. But no more than a drop or two could be kept down by the stomach, and such a minute dose would have to be repeated every day for two weeks or more before death would ensue . . . and that death would be a long and lingering one."

Dr. Van Donnen clasped his hands, and his round little face took on a cherubic beam. "It is very interesting that you have brought up this subject, Miss Withers. I have for many years in the subject of the petroleum poisons been interested. Nothing is known by the general medical profession of their action, owing to the fact that the characteristic taste is so strong and the stomach so easily upset by them. But a pamphlet was published last year by Dr. Emile Ladrue of Paris announcing that he had succeeded in producing the symptoms of pernicious anaemia of the bones in a monkey by daily minute doses of benzine for only one week. The monkey survived as an invalid for several months, but Ladrue was of the opinion that if the doses had been continued for another week, death would have come very shortly."

"That's what I wanted to know," said Miss Withers grimly. "Dr. Van Donnen, I'm going to insist on the Coroner's ordering an exhumation and a stomach analysis of the corpse of Anise Halloran!"

He blinked. "But Miss Withers! If you suspect a petroleum poison, stomach analysis will prove nothing. Everything is absorbed by the blood. There is no trace left, as in the inorganic poisons, which can be analyzed!"

Miss Withers paused by the doorway. "Doctor, suppose you wanted to conceal the taste of a strong petroleum poison, how would you do it? In coffee, as my mother concealed castor oil?"

He shook his head. "Liquor would the the best thing," he told her. "So much in these times it tastes like benzine anyhow!"

Georgie Swarthout waved his hand in a gesture which implied that the entire Alps restaurant, from the orchestra in the distance to the balcony on which they sat, was a special creation of his own for this particular event.

"This isn't so bad, now you're here, is it?"

The three sad young ladies who comprised the orchestra struck up something very Strauss, and the waiter produced the soup tureens as a magician might have caused a rabbit to appear out of a hat.

Janey Davis drew an intricate little design on the tablecloth with her fork. "It isn't so bad," she agreed. "But I still don't know why I came."

"I'll tell you," said Georgie Swarthout. "You came because you knew I'd go right on phoning you until you agreed to have dinner or breakfast or lunch or something with me. And some of the moments I chose to phone you were a little inopportune. . . ."

"Very inopportune," said Janey Davis.

"Have it your own way. I heard about a girl who said she had to take four baths one Sunday afternoon before the phone would ring. What do you think of that?"

"I think you're impossible," said Janey Davis.

"At least highly improbable," agreed Swarthout. "Dance?"

"Oh, no, I couldn't."

"Come on, forget that I earn my salary by working for the city, will you? You look worried, young lady. This case has been gruelling for you. Relax."

Janey pushed back her chair. "Oh—all right." She smiled a little. "This is a waltz; do you waltz?"

"No, but I'll hold you while you waltz," promised Georgie. They waltzed.

In his arms the girl was stiff as cardboard, and trembling a little. Georgie leaned toward her ear, hidden in a mass of red-brown curls. "Is it as bad as all that? You act as if I was medicine."

"Why did you bring me here?" she insisted. "What do you want to know?"

"Believe me, this is purely a social venture on my part," he said. "I told myself the first moment that I saw you—here is a girl who can waltz. And now you stiff-arm me."

Janey Davis relaxed, flinging her head back and closing her eyes. "Is that better?"

"You know it is." They finished the dance in silence, and then returned to their table.

"But listen to me," Janey insisted. "I've told the authorities everything I know about this case. Really—what do you want to know?"

"I want to know where you want to go for the rest of the evening," Swarthout told her between bites. "My badge takes us past the box office at most of the theaters."

Janey shook her head. "I can't go anywhere, I'm sorry. . . ."

"Another date?"

She nodded.

"With that Stevenson chap?"

She nodded again. "But I don't see what business of yours it is."

"It isn't," Georgie admitted. "He's an awfully good friend of yours, isn't he?"

"Of course he's an awfully good friend—of both Anise and me."

"Known him long?"

"Only since the beginning of school. This is my first year as Mr. Macfarland's secretary, and his first year as assistant principal at Jefferson. But Anise met him last summer at Mr. Macfarland's place up in Connecticut!"

Georgie did not conceal his interest in that fact. "Then Anise Halloran knew Stevenson—and Macfarland, too, for that matter—before school started?"

Janey put her hand to her lips. "I—I didn't mean to say that!"

She half rose in her hair. "Why did you have to make me say that? Mr. Macfarland has been so kind to me, and Bob Stevenson is one of my best friends. . . ." Ready tears sprang to her wide eyes, but there was something calculating behind them.

"I'm sorry," Georgie Swarthout told her. "This asking questions gets to be a habit. Come on, break your date tonight. Let's forget the whole mess, shall we, and just be gay?"

"I can't be gay," the girl told him. She reached for her handbag. "I don't think I'll ever be gay again. And you'll have to excuse me—I'm not at all hungry. And I can't forget that you're a detective, either."

"But not a very good detective," Swarthout reminded her.

Janey Davis let him help her with her wrap. "I'm not so sure about that," she said bitterly.

XVII

Blind Man's Bluff

(11/20/32—12 noon)

Miss Withers walked nervously up and down past the hospital bed, watching the Inspector polish off the last of his lunch. For the time being, the familiar hospital odors of ether and antiseptic were submerged in the rich aroma of chicken and mashed potatoes.

Piper pushed aside the plate and reached for a cigar. Miss Withers took a box of matches from the bedside table and struck one for him. Then she cast a mountain of Sunday papers from the side of the cot, and placed an ash-tray there.

"Pretty soft for you, Oscar," she told him. "The rest is doing you good. I guess this was the only way in the world to make you take a vacation."

"It's soft enough," Piper admitted. "Too soft, in fact. I've had all the vacation I want. I don't see why I had to get socked on the head just at the time when there was a big murder investigation beginning."

"You're like the old lady who said it was too bad we had to have a depression during these hard times," Miss Withers remarked.

The Inspector puffed fretfully at his cigar. "And I lie here on my back, with my hands tied, while the Commissioner turns that phoney professor from Vienna loose in my office!"

"Well, Professor Augustine Pfaffle turned himself out in a hurry," Miss Withers reminded him. "He's sent in a bill for three thousand dollars as a consultant's fee, I hear. It would have been considerably less expensive for the people of the city of New York to have bought a copy of a book on abnormal psychology. . . ."

"Or for that matter, to have electrocuted the janitor fellow,

Anderson, without trying to find out what mental quirk made
him bump off the girl.''

"As a matter of fact, he didn't," Miss Withers announced.
"I've said so all along. I've told you and I told the Sergeant
and I told Professor Pfaffle himself, though it didn't do any
good. But I know that Anderson didn't kill Anise Halloran."

"Yeah?" The Inspector's nerves were not what they might
have been. "I suppose you know who did?"

For a long moment Miss Withers did not answer. She was
staring at the pitcher of ice water on the Inspector's table, in
which a little oblong reflection of the window danced merrily
up and down.

She smoothed out her gloves. Then at last she spoke, her
voice quiet.

"Oscar Piper, I do know!"

In spite of his bandaged head, the Inspector very nearly sat
upright. "You know who killed that Halloran girl? And
you're sitting here, doing nothing about it? For the love of
God, *who* did it, and *why*?"

Miss Withers pursed her lips very tightly. "I only know
who."

"Well, spill it!"

She shook her head. "What good would it be for me to tell
you, or anybody down at Headquarters either? It's too fantas-
tic, too impossible. Nobody would believe me, and I haven't
got any proof. It's just a hunch, but I know it's right."

The Inspector forgot himself so far as to hurl his dead cigar
across the room. "Tell me . . . who is it? The flower of the old
South, Mr. A. Robert Stevenson? Waldo Emerson Macfarland,
who writes an essay every day and two on Sunday? One of
the other teachers—say that big husky Pearson girl who wears
low-heeled shoes and mannish clothes?"

"I'm making no announcements now," insisted Hildegarde
Withers. "If I told you what I'm thinking, you would have
the Sergeant and probably those two blundering detectives
Allen and Burns making an arrest within five minutes. And
then you'd discover, after a few weeks, that there wasn't
sufficient evidence against that person to convict, and the case
would be dropped."

"Maybe it would and maybe it wouldn't," the Inspector
argued. "Say, I bet I know who you're putting the finger on!

A woman could have done this job, hatchet and shovel and all!"

Miss Withers kept her face impassive. "Remember one thing while you're guessing, Oscar Piper. The murderer of Anise Halloran was smart and clever. This is one of the most diabolic and ingenious plots I've ever heard of, but also the most confusing. Because things are not what they seem. . . ."

"Skim milk masquerades as cream . . ." chimed in the Inspector, finishing the old ditty.

"Exactly. And the whole thing was planned to represent a crime of passion, but there was about as much passion in it really as a butcher shows when he does whatever is done to a steer. The murderer figured on everything, and provided for every possibility except bad luck."

"And that bad luck?"

"Was being too careful of details like shoes," Miss Withers finished. "Now if you can figure out anything from that point, you're welcome to it. . . ."

She broke off suddenly as the door opened and the round, inquiring face of Sergeant Taylor showed itself.

He touched his hat to Miss Withers, and then went to the foot of the bed. "How'r yuh, Chief?"

"Don't 'chief' me," said Piper bitterly. "You're graduated out of my class now into the psycho-criminology class, or so I hear. Go back and take your orders from Professor Pfoof, or whatever his name is."

"That's what I came up here about," said Taylor unhappily. "All that psycho-what-you-call-it business is washed up, Chief. The Commissioner is sore as a boil about Professor Pfaffle's resigning before he could fire him, and then running straight to the District Attorney with his pet theory about Anderson. They say the D.A. is going to have Anderson indicted before the Grand Jury according to Pfaffle's statement of the case, and the Commissioner said I was to come up here and get any suggestions you or Miss Withers might give me. He says we need a new angle on the case. . . ."

The Inspector smiled grimly. "So that's the theme song, eh? The honor of the dear old department is at stake again. And so the Commissioner wants me, lying here in bed, to dope out a new Hatchet Fiend for him and show up Pfaffle! Well, he can . . ."

"Oscar!" Miss Withers rubbed her nose, vigorously. "I have the germ of an idea. Now if the Sergeant will follow it. . . ."

"Yeah," said Taylor bitterly. "I followed one of your ideas, and now I'm going to be sued for false arrest by that Curran girl you were sure had something to do with the case!"

Miss Withers stopped short. "That's true. I did think she had something to do with the case. And all the time she was getting married, secretly. Sergeant, that was a joke on me . . . a joke on me. . . ." Her voice faded away.

Suddenly her eyes lighted up. "I've got it! Eureka, I've got it. I mean I have it! I've been blind as a bat! But now I've got it!"

The Inspector looked at her as if she had gone daft. Miss Withers was dancing a quiet little buck and wing all by herself.

"You've got what, Hildegarde? Ants? Or the shakes or something?"

She nodded, happily. "Ants do come into it. At least one does. Oh, it fits, it all fits! I not only know *who* now, I know *why*!"

She stopped short. "Proving it is a different matter, I'm afraid. The hunt has only just begun, but at least I'm not hunting blind any more. I know what I'm after, which is a help. All we need is a decoy. . . ."

"A what?" The Sergeant was obviously skeptical and bewildered.

"We need a goat," Miss Withers told him sharply. "When they hunt tigers in India, I've read that they first tie a goat to a tree. The goat blats and wails at night, and the tiger hears it, comes prowling around, and thinks he's found some easy meat. But while he's eating the meat, the man up in the tree shoots him dead. It's very simple and easy."

"Except for the goat," the Inspector put in. "I suppose you've picked the Sergeant here for that part?"

"I have not." The Sergeant looked considerably relieved. But Miss Withers continued.

"You, Oscar, are going to be the goat!"

"What's that?" the Inspector very nearly put the hot end of his cigar in his mouth.

"You've been complaining that things were dull, and that you were left out of the picture, weren't you? Well, I'm going to put you back into the picture." Hildegarde Withers smiled on him, benignly.

"Me? But what can I do? With this damn bandage across my head, and the doctor saying that I've got to stay in bed two more weeks. . . ."

"You can play goat in bed," Miss Withers told him.

XVIII

Homework

(11/20/32—8:30 P.M.)

"I feel cold," said Janey Davis. "Bob, I don't want to walk in the park, even if there is a moon. Can't we just stay here in the apartment?"

Bob Stevenson laughed. "Of course, honey. I forgot that you're a little hothouse flower, and this is November going on December." He elbowed his way out of the tiny kitchenette, in which he had been helping Janey prepare a light supper for the two of them, and felt of the radiator.

"Cold as ice," he announced. "Would it do any good to pound on it?"

Janey shook her head. "It's not that kind of cold, Bob. I feel cold inside. And sort of frightened."

He came quickly toward her, and held out his arms. She let him hold her for a moment, her face against his shoulder, and then pushed him away.

"Don't mind me," she said. "I know there's nothing to be frightened of. I'm afraid I'm bad company tonight." She went over to the empty fireplace.

He leaned back in his easy chair, facing her. "I know what's the trouble, honey. It's the idea of going back to the old routine tomorrow, back to Jefferson School . . . back where Anise was—"

"Don't! Please don't! I can't stand it, Bob." Her face was white and desperate. "Bob, let's go away somewhere, now, tonight! Let's go where nobody will ever mention Anise's name again—where nobody will ever ask questions and wonder and pry! Can't we, Bob?"

"There are some things you can't run away from," said Bob Stevenson. "I feel the same way, and I suppose the others do, too. Hold on a little longer, Janey, and we will go

156

away—far away. Ships sail down past the Goddess of Liberty bound for Majorca and Bali and Timbuctoo. . . ."

"Timbuctoo is in the desert," Janey reminded him. But she was smiling.

He waved his arm. "How does Persia sound then, or Rangoon? They say the Irish lakes are the most beautiful lakes in the world . . . and Cambodia has temples that were just as they are today long before our ancestors came down out of the trees. One of these days, Janey—"

"Oh, Bob!" Then a practical note entered her voice. "I don't know what we'd use for money, though. Unless I cashed that lottery ticket. . . ."

"Well? I don't think Anise would mind, Janey. She had no people, you know. Nobody that she'd want her money to go to more than you. And half of that ticket was yours. . . ."

Janey sat on the arm of his chair. "Maybe I am being a little foolish about it, Bob. And I do want to get away from it all, so very badly. . . ."

The telephone interrupted her.

Janey Davis whirled around, her finger pointing at the innocent instrument. "There! That's what I mean. We can't get away, even in dreams. I feel like a hunted thing, day and night. The police, or the reporters, or Dr. Macfarland . . ."

"I imagine poor Mac feels a bit hunted himself these days," Bob told her. "Hadn't you better answer it? It's probably the wrong number."

Savagely, her lithe body moving like an angry panther's, she crossed the room and raised the receiver.

"Yes?"

It was Georgie Swarthout's voice at the other end of the line. "Is that you, Janey?"

"Yes, it's me." She pressed her hand over the mouthpiece, and looked helplessly at Stevenson. "That fresh detective again, Bob. He hounds me half to death, trying to make me go out with him. What will I do?"

"My advice would be to go," Bob Stevenson told her. "You can't afford to antagonize any fly cop, darling. He seems a harmless kid, and you could use a friend at court, as the saying goes."

Janey shook her head, rebelliously. Swarthout's voice was

booming cheerfully in her ear. Suddenly she realized that he wasn't trying to make a date this time.

"Will you say that again?" She listened now, with all her might and main.

"Sure I will. Get this, Beautiful. I just wanted to find out whether you were in or not. I've got to see you for a moment. On business, official business. Something has broken in the Halloran murder."

"Where are you?... come right up," Janey gasped.

"I'm on my way." And the line went dead. Janey told the young instructor what had transpired.

"I'll be running along, then," suggested Stevenson.

"You'll do nothing of the kind," said Janey Davis. "I want your moral support. Georgie Swarthout has a hot brown eye, and there is no discouraging him. If this visit is official, there's nothing he could have to say to me that you can't hear. And if it isn't, I think it's just as well that you're lurking in the background."

"Okay," agreed the young man. He put on his coat and straightened his tie. He was hardly back in the easy chair again when the downstairs bell broke into a clamor, and Georgie Swarthout raced up the stairs.

If he was disappointed to see Bob Stevenson sitting there, he concealed it like a true philosopher.

"Listen," he said breathlessly. "I've only got a few minutes. Lucky for me I found you both here. Saves me a trip to the Village."

"I don't understand..." Janey faced him defiantly.

"You're taking a trip to Bellevue, both of you," Georgie explained.

"But why both of us?" Janey wanted to know.

"And why Bellevue? That's a hospital, isn't it?" Bob Stevenson was alert.

"Listen carefully," said Swarthout. "We've got a big break in the Halloran case. It's going to be washed up tonight. You'll both be glad to know that. And here is how."

Bob Stevenson stood up and crossed over to the fireplace, where Janey was. Georgie dropped into the easy chair, and fumbled for a cigarette.

"Are *we* in luck!" he exclaimed. "Piper is over there with a mending skull, you know. At Bellevue, I mean. It was a pretty close one for him, but he's beginning to come out of it. Which is why both of you, and every other person implicated in this Halloran case, is going to gather at Bellevue tonight— as quick as you all can get there. Because''—Georgie lit his cigarette, carefully and thoroughly—''because it's ten to one that the murderer of Anise Halloran is somewhere in that crowd. And Piper is going to identify the guilty party!''

Janey Davis was clinging to the mantel, her fingers white at the knuckles. For a moment she swayed, and then her body was tense again.

''Identify? What do you mean? How can the Inspector identify anybody?'' Bob Stevenson was frankly puzzled.

''Well,'' explained Georgie, ''you heard that the Inspector walked into the cellar of Jefferson School while the murderer was still at work, didn't you? And got hit over the head with a shovel for his pains?''

''Yes, I heard all that,'' agreed Stevenson. ''But he didn't get a glimpse of whoever struck him!''

''So the papers said. And that's what he thought when he first came to. A crack on the head like that affects the memory of events that happened shortly before, so the medics say. Anyway, it's beginning to come back to him. He did get a glimpse of the face . . . and he remembers it! So all we have to do is to round up everybody and walk them through the hospital room. He'll pick out the murderer, and the rest of you will go free of suspicion.''

''So we're arrested, huh?''

Swarthout shook his head. ''I've no authority to arrest you, and no warrant. You don't have to come over to Bellevue. The only one in the whole party who has to come is Anderson the janitor, because he is already under arrest on suspicion of homicide. But of course, anybody who refused to come would be in a pretty tough spot. It would be sort of confessing that he or she was afraid to. . . .''

Bob Stevenson looked at Janey, whose wide eyes were filled with panic. ''Steady, girl. There's nothing for us to be afraid of.'' He turned to Georgie. ''I suppose there isn't any chance that the Inspector, on account of the blow on the head and the resulting illness, would make a faulty identification?''

''I doubt it,'' Georgie told him. ''Piper has been identifying crooks and criminals and murderers for years. He's got a photographic eye. Don't worry, he won't pick you by accident. Besides, he says that the face of the person who hit him was engraved in his memory as if burned in with acid. It's been hazy until now, but he says it is clearing. The doctor doesn't know when he may have a relapse, as his condition is still very serious, and that's why the order has gone out for the party being tonight."

"In that case, Janey and I will go with you," Bob Stevenson accepted. "I suppose you have the police wagon downstairs?"

Georgie shook his head. "Nothing like that. I'm not even going to take you over there, because I've still got a few calls to make. This whole thing is very sub rosa, and Sergeant Taylor and I are working the round-up alone. Hop in a taxi, and get over to Bellevue before ten o'clock. And remember, this is just a little formality—except for one person!"

Janey opened the door for the departing detective. "I'll be glad," she said, her voice trembling, "I'll be glad—glad—to get it all over with! I don't much care how!"

"Will you ditch the boy-friend and have a bowl of chop-suey with me afterward?" Georgie whispered.

But she closed the door, gently and firmly. Georgie Swarthout hitched up his pants, and plunged down the stairs. He had work to do tonight.

Waldo Emerson Macfarland was next on his list. A taxi rolled him swiftly north along Amsterdam Avenue, cutting toward the park along 96th Street. The residence of the Principal of Jefferson School was certainly dark and seemingly deserted, but Georgie leaned on the bell with a hearty good will.

Just as he was about to give it up as a bad job, a light went on over his head, and he saw a face peering through the glass of the door. "Let me in," Georgie shouted.

Then the face disappeared, and the light went out. Georgie leaned on the bell again. Finally he took the badge from his pocket, and with it rapped resoundingly upon the pane.

At last the door swung inward into darkness, and Georgie stepped gingerly through in response to a throaty "Come in."

The door swung shut behind him. At that moment something hard was pressed against the small of his back.

"I have you covered," came the Principal's voice. "One false move and I'll shoot."

Georgie made no moves of any description. After a long interval, the pressure was momentarily removed from his back, and the lights in the foyer snapped on. Georgie looked over his shoulder and stared with disfavor into the pale eyes of Waldo Emerson Macfarland, watery and red without their accustomed glasses. The Principal was attired simply but modestly in a brown woolen bathrobe and narrow ladylike patent-leather slippers.

Macfarland returned his stare, also without enthusiasm or welcome. They stood thus for a few minutes, and then Georgie spoke.

"It won't do, you know," he observed.

"What won't do?"

"Trying to palm off a pipe as a revolver. The mouthpiece doesn't feel the same, even through an overcoat, as the muzzle of a gat. What is that, a Peterson's? I thought so."

Georgie moved away, and Macfarland stared blankly after him. "What's the idea of treating the law this way?" Georgie flashed his badge.

"So? I have made a mistake, I am afraid. But the events of the past week have been very unsettling. I was of the opinion that perhaps someone might come seeking my own life. Besides, this evening I was locked in my study, engaged in writing one of my daily essays, this time upon the subject of Assassination. . . ."

Swarthout explained why he had come. "I've still got one more call to make," he told Macfarland. "So the less fireworks you pull the better I'll like it. You understand, this is just a formality in your case. But you're to show up over at Bellevue, on the third floor, just as quick as you can. Unless, of course, you want to stand on your constitutional rights. I won't make you go—but of course we'll draw our own conclusions of why you aren't willing."

Macfarland smiled. "But why should I refuse? No one could be more anxious to have this case cleared up than I am. Besides, I might very possibly secure material for the last few paragraphs of my essay on Assassination!"

Swarthout thought it was very likely. "Then I can count on your being there within the hour?"

"Absolutely! You couldn't keep me away with a squad of strong-arm men," promised Macfarland. "I'll go and dress at once...."

The taxi was still waiting outside. Georgie leaped in, and gave the Martha Washington Hotel as an address to the driver. That gentleman looked surprised.

"Say, you don't want to go to that dump," he objected. "Leave me steer you to a place I know over on One Hundred and Tent'—the dames is better."

Georgie leaned forward and scrutinized the chauffeur's identification card which hung in a little frame on the rear of the front seat. "Roscoe Doolittle" was the name beneath the unflattering photograph. He spoke to the driver, his voice heavy with reproof.

"Roscoe! I'm ashamed of you! What do you take me for?"

"I take you for a guy who wants to go to the Martha Washington," said Mr. Doolittle resignedly. "But don't say I didn't tell you."

Down through the city they plunged, and up a side street to the canopy bearing the familiar cameo representation of her who had been Martha Custis before she became the step-mother of her country.

"Stick around," said Swarthout to Mr. Doolittle. He went swiftly up the steps and came face to face with the stern-visaged lady at the desk. Georgie Swarthout had known and worked with many police-matrons in his short but busy career as a detective, but never had he met a lady who looked more like one than this.

"I want to see Miss Pearson," he announced.

The police-matron looked pointedly at the clock. "It's nine-thirty," she reminded him. "No callers after ten, and no gentlemen allowed upstairs at any hour." She made it clear that while the classification might not include him, the rule did.

Georgie was in a hurry. "You can get her down here so I can talk to her, can't you?" He toyed with the badge for a moment, which seemed to have a salutary effect.

"I think she went out to a movie," admitted the Cerebus. "But maybe she's come in." She lifted a telephone from the desk beside her, and pushed a plug into the switchboard.

"Four-eleven? Miss Pearson? There's a gentleman down

here to see you." The telephone was replaced. "Says she'll be down in a few minutes," Swarthout was told. "You can wait in the parlor." She indicated a room to the left. "No smoking."

"Thanks," Georgie said. He leaned against the counter, and wondered if once more he had been unlucky enough to disturb a lady in her bath. But it was only a few minutes before the bulky form of Miss Pearson, art teacher at Jefferson School, appeared on the stairs. She had been hurrying, and she was out of breath.

Miss Pearson came directly to the desk. "A gentleman to see me?"

"This." Cerebus indicated Georgie with a nod. "He's got a badge."

Miss Pearson's face may not have fallen, but it slipped considerably. "Oh," she said vacantly. "I remember you. You're the detective. I thought it was a gentleman to see me, and I ran all the way down stairs because the elevator was in use."

"I want to take you for a ride," Georgie explained.

"What?" She stared at him curiously. "Gangster, social— or what?"

"Just a ride," said Georgie. "I'll tell you about it in the taxi."

XIX

Final Examination

(11/20/32—10:30 P.M.)

"Is everybody here?" Sergeant Taylor stood by the doorway of the Bellevue Hospital reception room, checking names against a list which he held in his hand.

"All okay," Swarthout answered him. "We were lucky to find everybody in town and at home."

"They had instructions to stay in town, and as a rule on Sunday evening nobody who has a job stays out very late. That's the advantage of having the party at this hour. Another thing, since regular visiting hours are over here, there'll be nobody butting in. Well, we seem to be set."

"What are we waiting for?" Swarthout wanted to know. His question was taken up and echoed by a dozen voices inside the waiting room.

"Where's that Hildegarde Withers?"

"Has she got anything to do with this—I might have known!" The voice was Miss Rennel's.

"Why don't they let us parade in front of the Inspector and get it over?"

"We can't stay all night. Officer—OFFICER! What are we waiting for?"

The Sergeant poked his head in the doorway. "Be easy," he advised them. "It won't be long now. We're only waiting for another guest or two." Swarthout showed his surprise, but the Sergeant kicked him forcefully.

"I'll go upstairs and see how things are coming on," promised the Sergeant. "Everybody sit tight till I come back. Swarthout, you stay here and keep an eye on things in general."

The Sergeant disappeared down the hall, and Georgie Swarthout entered the waiting room, much after the fashion of Mr. Clyde Beatty going into his cage of mixed lions and tigers. The only difference, Georgie thought, was the fact that the famous lion-tamer had a chair and a blank-cartridge pistol to protect himself with.

They were a mixed lot, these men and women who awaited their turn at being identified as the Inspector's attacker and, naturally following, as Anise Halloran's murderer. But they shared one emotion at the present moment, and that was impatience. If one among them was guilty, he or she concealed it most effectively, Swarthought thought.

He leaned against the door, and waited.

Across the room Janey Davis and Bob Stevenson were whispering. Georgie saw the young manual training instructor reach for Janey's hand, and was wickedly happy when he saw her withdraw it.

Miss Cohen, ever bent upon self-improvement, was trying to read a copy of *The Modern Instructor,* but she turned very few pages. Beside her Miss Mycroft, she of the first grade, was staring with a worried expression at the design of the carpet. Miss Jones and Miss Casey were looking out of the window, which opened onto a rolling sea of fog that might have concealed the East River somewhere far beneath its blanket.

Betty Curran Rogers was busily engaged in rolling the new wedding ring around and around the third finger of her left hand. Her face showed, perhaps, the least excitement of anyone present, for she and she alone could prove a perfect alibi for the afternoon of the murder. But all the same, she was here.

Waldo Emerson Macfarland sat alone in a corner, as befitted the Principal of the school. He was smiling, a very nervous and insincere smile, and his mild and vacant stare implied that he was not particularly intent upon gathering material for his essay on Assassination, after all.

Miss Rennel, as usual, was talking, with only a tearful Miss Murchison as a listener. Alice Rennel considered the whole matter an imposition, and said so.

Beyond her, Miss Hopkins and Miss Pearson sat together upon a divan, both looking remarkably uncomfortable in spite of the fact that they had the most comfortable spot in the room. Miss Pearson now and then made a remark indicative of her admiration and respect for the dead girl, no doubt under the natural impression that this was a wake.

Across the room Miss Strasmick walked up and down, eyeing her fellow teachers and Georgie alike with an alien eye.

At that moment the door opened and a newcomer entered, somewhat urged from behind by the strong arm of the Sergeant, who immediately withdrew. It was Tobey, a very unhappy and seemingly bewildered Tobey. Away from his musty candy-shop, he was like a strange species of spider plucked from its web. He immediately scuttled toward the most distant corner and remained there, as if hoping to be ignored and unnoticed.

His arrival, instead of causing a general outbreak, had the strange result of bringing the conversation in the room, sketchy as it had been, to a complete stop. Only the low whispers of Janey and Bob Stevenson continued.

"I suppose *that* was who we were waiting for," Alice Rennel finally observed. "Why don't they do something?"

"Any minute now," said Georgie Swarthout.

"That's what you said half an hour ago!"

"Well, I'm not the sort of a man to say one thing one minute, and another the next." Georgie leaned back against the door. He remained there, undisturbed, for another twenty minutes or so. Finally it opened again, this time to produce the denim-clad figure of no less a personage than Anderson, the janitor!

There was an immediate uproar, as a result of which Georgie went outside where the Sergeant was talking to detectives Allen and Burns, who had brought the prisoner down.

"You boys can wait outside in the car," the Sergeant was saying.

"Hey, wait a minute," objected Swarthout. "I don't want to speak out of turn, Sergeant. But that janitor will make a break for it as sure as God made little apples, if you leave him around unguarded."

"You don't say so?" Taylor nodded sagely. "Well, I wouldn't be surprised if you're right, kid. Okay, boys, go on and wait in the car." The two precinct detectives departed, and Georgie shook his head sadly.

"This is too fast for me," he remarked. "I don't savvy."

"You don't have to," he was told by his immediate

superior. "Go back and tell your palsy-walsies that it'll be only a minute now."

"I don't dare to," said Georgie. But he reentered the room, all the same. The janitor, pariah-like, had been left the far corner of the room for himself, and Tobey and the others were grouped near the windows.

"If something doesn't happen immediately, I'm going home," announced Alice Rennel savagely. "I don't fancy being locked up here with"—she glanced at the dejected figure of Anderson—"with a murderer! Even if he is at the other end of the room."

"He may not be at the other end of the room, Miss Rennel," Swarthout reminded her happily.

The teachers all moved a little away from one another, as if the sudden change of electric current had caused them to repel. Suspicion, hitherto aimed at Anderson, flashed right and left. No one spoke, and for the first time that evening, even Janey Davis and Bob Stevenson were not carrying on a whispered conversation.

The minutes dragged by. Georgie went out into the hall again, but the Sergeant had disappeared. The young detective returned, and to keep his guests busy, began to assign them numbers according to their initials.

"Anderson, you're first on the list," he announced. "Then Miss Casey, Miss Cohen, and Miss Curran. Then you, Janey—I mean Miss Davis. Then . . ."

He was interrupted by the opening of the door. For the first time that evening, Miss Hildegarde Withers came in view. She was followed very closely by Sergeant Taylor and a portly gentleman in a white coat who looked like a doctor, and was.

Miss Withers showed weariness in both her posture and voice. "It's no use," she announced after a moment. "The party is off, ladies and gentlemen. I've been arguing with Dr. Horman here for almost an hour, but he says no."

There was a gasp from her audience, but Miss Withers held up her hand. "The Doctor refuses to permit us to go ahead with the little plan that Sergeant Taylor and I worked out. You see, Inspector Piper is in a very serious condition, and the excitement was too much for him. Merely remembering the face of his assailant was a great shock, and now he is asleep and the Doctor refuses to permit us to waken him. We shall have to postpone the party until tomorrow.''

There was a long minute of silence. One person in that group was relieved by her announcement, but there was no sign of it.

''Miss Withers asked me to speak to you myself,'' said the Doctor after a moment. ''She was afraid that you might blame her for the postponement. Rest assured that she had nothing to do with it. The Inspector is in a very weak condition, and the slightest shock might be too much for him tonight. I have given him a hypo, which has put him into such a sound sleep that I think it best he remain so until morning. Perhaps then it will be possible to attempt the identification, but now—impossible. I shall not waken him even to give him his necessary medicine at midnight—it remains by his bedside to be taken only when he wakens. So you see how important I consider this sleep?''

They saw. Instead of relief at the avoidance of an unpleasant event, the group seemed to be disappointed. Macfarland particularly stressed this point.

''I did want to finish my essay tonight,'' he complained. ''Tomorrow I must take a new subject, as I have not failed to do every day for years. And now—everything goes flat like yesterday's ginger ale.''

''Sorry, but it can't be helped,'' cut in the Sergeant. He crossed the room and took Anderson's arm. ''Come on, Olaf. It's back to the cell for you.''

The others watched while the Sergeant led his prisoner out through the door. Then they began a confused bustling, and making ready to don coats and hats, which was rudely interrupted by the sound of a distant crash, followed by shouts of ''There he goes! Stop him, somebody . . . !''

They all rushed to the door, Miss Withers in the lead. But they saw only the perspiring face of the Sergeant, his hat over his eyes and his right hand dangling an empty handcuff.

He was running down the hall toward them, his legs moving like pistons, but making very poor time. A floor nurse followed him, temporarily shocked out of her usual poise.

''He's got away and escaped!'' the Sergeant announced, unnecessarily. ''Hit me over the head, and then ran back up these stairs and down the front ones!" The Sergeant was near to collapse.

"After him!" shouted Bob Stevenson. He set out down the hall at a fast sprint, with Georgie Swarthout trotting leisurely behind, and Macfarland and Tobey in the rear. Miss Withers could hear Stevenson's feet pounding down the stair, and then suddenly stop on the lower landing.

The young man was at the window when Georgie and the others caught up. "Which way did he go?" they demanded. "Did you see him below in the street?"

Bob Stevenson shook his head. "I thought so, for a minute. But I guess it wasn't he. I'm afraid it's no use—he's got clean away."

The men climbed the stairs again, to where Miss Withers and the others were waiting. The floor nurse had already returned to her desk and her doze. Miss Rennel had something to say about it all. "The idea of letting a dangerous maniac run loose among us, with only one or two half-witted officers in the whole building! I shall write a letter to the *Times* about this!"

"I'm really awfully sorry about the whole thing," Miss Withers apologized. "Our intentions were the best in the world. Well, good night, everybody. If it is possible to have the Inspector go through with this tomorrow, we'll be notified at the school."

Bob Stevenson lingered a little behind the others. "Miss Withers," he suggested, "I'm taking Janey Davis home, and there's plenty of room in the cab. Won't you ride with us? She lives quite near you."

"Not tonight, thanks," she refused him. "You two children run along together. Two is a company, you know. . . ."

She put on her hat and coat, and followed the procession down the stair, oblivious of the fact that there was a good deal of hostility rampant about her. In the lower hall she paused.

"Good night, everybody," she said. "I think I'll just run back up and see how the Inspector is." The Sergeant paused, dejected and disheveled.

"Bang the door when you leave," he advised. "The lock is set."

She had a last glimpse of Macfarland's face, strangely haunted, as she turned away. She stood on the lower step of the stair for a moment, making note of the lower hall, now half-darkened and completely deserted. Up toward the front of the building, she knew, the night phone girl was on duty, but this rear hall, used in the daytime for deliveries and ambulance cases, was left to its own devices.

After a few minutes had passed, Hildegarde Withers crossed the hall again intent upon releasing the spring lock of the door. Much to her surprised gratification, she discovered that someone had been forehanded, and that she had been beaten to it.

Leaving the door as it was, she climbed the stairs again. But this time she did not go down the hall to the waiting room, but went on up to the fifth and top floor. At the far end of the long hall, a sleepy night nurse was bent over a magazine. Through the windows, violent howls resounded from the violent ward of the Mental Wing, but all was quiet here. Not a red light showed above a single door.

The Inspector's room was at the end of the hall, the first door from the rear stair. Miss Withers opened it, and stepped inside.

Inspector Piper, far from being in the state of coma so touchingly described by Dr. Horman, was calmly reading a copy of Real Detective Tales, with the blue smoke of a cigar eddying above his head.

Hildegarde Withers brusquely removed the cigar from his mouth and tossed it from the window, which she opened to its fullest capacity. Then she put away the magazine.

"How do you expect anyone to believe you're sick when the place simply reeks of tobacco?" She tucked him carefully in, smoothed his pillow, and emptied his ashtray.

"Everything go all right?" he wanted to know.

"Like clockwork," she answered.

"Anderson make his getaway?"

She smiled. "It was a narrow squeak. Allen and Burns were pretty slow to grab him, and I was afraid for a minute that Bob Stevenson, who is quicker on his feet than I thought, was going to queer the works, as you say, by recapturing the fugitive. But it all went off perfectly. The Sergeant is coming up the front way, and he ought to be here any minute. There's someone now—yes, it's he."

The door opened, and Taylor appeared. He was grinning

from ear to ear. "Boy, I should of been an actor," he announced. "Did I put over the phoney escape! Say, they ought to give me six curtain calls."

"The last act isn't over yet," Miss Withers reminded him. "Everything quiet outside?"

"Like a tomb," said the Sergeant. "The floor nurse up at the other end of the hall goes out for coffee every half hour or so, as you told her, and in between she sleeps. And that isn't acting—she didn't even hear me go by, and I came up the front stairs, right by her desk!"

Miss Withers moved toward the light switch near the door. "Everything all set? Oscar, do you feel like a goat?"

"I'm practically Billy Whiskers himself," said Oscar Piper. "This excitement will probably set my convalescence back a week or two, but it's worth it. Fire away."

But Miss Withers stopped short. "I almost forgot your medicine," she announced. She poured some water from the pitcher at the bedside into a glass, and then shook her head. "It doesn't look like medicine," she decided. "Even in the dark it wouldn't look like medicine. . . ."

She stepped out of the room for a moment, and returned with a tiny vial of iodine. Three drops in the half glass of water produced a remarkably medicinal looking concoction.

"Don't make a mistake and drink this," she warned the Inspector. He grinned up at her.

"Don't you make any mistakes yourself," he retorted. "If this scheme of yours backfires, don't blame me. . . ."

"If it backfires, you're the goat," she reminded him. He patted his pillow, under which was a comforting lump made by an automatic .44.

A last minute survey of the room showed everything shipshape. Miss Withers pulled down the shade, in case the fog should clear and the moon come out again. Then she motioned toward the little clothes closet across the room, in which the Inspector's tweeds awaited his recovery.

"To your station, Sergeant," she ordered. "Is the cord long enough? Good." She tested the bedside lamp, screwed the bulb in as tightly as it would go, and then made sure that the cord which ran across the floor and under the closet door was not tangled around anything.

"Remember, Sergeant," she said. "No matter what happens, no matter what you hear or think you hear, don't turn on that light or come out of the closet until you hear me call your name. Get it?''

"Got it," answered the Sergeant. She made sure that the door was tightly closed upon him. "Remember to breathe heavily and deeply, Oscar. You're in a coma. Well—here goes!"

She crossed the room to the door, and turned out the overheads. Instantly the place was as black as a sea of pitch.

Awkwardly she felt her way along the wall to the door which opened into the next room, now vacant by arrangement. There were some advantages in being in a city hospital. She stepped through the door into a room as black as the one she had left, leaving it open. She fumbled for a few moments in the darkness, finally finding the chair she sought. It was a cushionless, wooden chair with a straight back. She had chosen it so—for Hildegarde Withers did not mean to sleep this night.

Something heavy and chill lay against her heart—it was the little gun that she had found in Janey Davis' desk so few days and so many centuries ago. She pressed it to her, finding a solid comfort in the knowledge that it no longer held blanks, as Janey had left it, but that it was now capable of sending forth ten soft-nosed missives of death within as many seconds. She thought she knew how to use it, but she was not sure.

She wished heartily that she had remembered to acquire a wristwatch with a radium dial. But at any rate her old-fashioned timepiece ticked cheerily away on her wrist, and she felt a certain companionship from its familiar sound. The ticking seemed to resound through the empty room—finally merging, against her will, into a dull, muffled roar as of many waters. . . .

She awakened sharply, a moment or an hour afterward. For one terrible second she forgot where she was, and why. Then it came back to her, and instantly she knew that a sound had roused her.

It came again, a soft but definite knocking at the door of the room in which the Inspector lay.

XX

Tag!

(11/21/32—1:15 A.M.)

"Confound those meddling nurses," Miss Withers whispered. It was up to her to do something about it, since Sergeant Taylor had his orders to stay in the closet until she called his name, and the Inspector could not move.

She rose from her chair and tiptoed softly through the open doorway and across the other room. She paused for a moment by the door, and then threw it open.

The face of Bob Stevenson met her own. For a moment they stood there, speechless. "Don't be startled," he whispered. "But I thought you would probably decide to keep a vigil here tonight, and I had to talk to you."

"But—" she protested. This was not what she had expected.

"I know what you're thinking. You were afraid there might be an attempt on the Inspector's life, weren't you?" Stevenson was strained and excited.

"Perhaps I was," admitted Miss Withers.

"So was I." His voice was tense. "Listen, you ought to know this. I didn't tell anybody what I saw from that landing when I was chasing the escaped man—not even Janey. I took her home first, and then came back here. You've got to know. There's a plot of some kind on foot—how do I know? I know because from that window I saw Anderson being led into a waiting auto by two men—a prisoner! His escape was faked, or else somebody planted the whole thing!"

"Good heavens!" said Miss Withers.

"And I know why it was faked," Bob Stevenson continued. "Don't you see! With Anderson at liberty—or a captive somewhere away from the police—he would be blamed for anything that might happen to the Inspector tonight? Suppose the real murderer arranged for Anderson to get a chance to escape, and then had him kidnapped so that he could never prove any sort of an alibi! His next move would be to kill the Inspector, who is the only living person who could ever identify the murderer . . . and then the janitor would shoulder the blame, and the murderer of poor Anise would go scot-free!"

"I suspected as much," Miss Withers confessed. "That's why I'm here."

Stevenson looked at her, and real admiration shone in his eyes. "You're one woman in a million," he said. "I only hope Janey turns out half as big as you are if such an emergency ever arises . . . with us. It takes real nerve to wait here alone in the darkness, knowing that a murderer may come at any minute . . ."

"But I'm not alone," Miss Withers told him.

"Oh, yes—the Inspector." Stevenson looked over her shoulder. "Is he—all right?"

Oscar Piper's heavy breathing filled the room, as it had for an hour. Miss Withers nodded slowly. "He's all right, so far," she said. "But young man, we can't stand here."

"Of course not." Stevenson was apologetic. "On my way here I stopped off at home and picked up my own gun," he explained. He brought it out of his pocket. "Want to take it, just in case?"

Miss Withers shook her head. "I won't need it," she told him. "But I think you could help me, if you will. Want to stand guard duty with me till morning—or until something happens?"

"Now you're talking," said Bob Stevenson. She pulled him through the doorway, her hands trembling with excitement, and guided him across the room to the connecting door. "There's another chair," she told him. "It's comfortable, so don't go to sleep."

He found it, by striking a match. But he insisted, in polite pantomime, that she take it. "Neither of us will sleep tonight," he told her. He was right.

They took up the vigil where Miss Withers had left off, and again the ticking of her watch and the slow breathing of the Inspector were the only sounds that broke the stillness of the night.

Once or twice footsteps sounded in the hall outside, but it was only the nurse on her infrequent errands. The watch ticked on—and on—

"If anybody comes now, we'll be ready for 'em," Bob Stevenson whispered in the darkness.

Miss Withers hushed him with a sibilant "shsh." More seconds, minutes, hours went by. Hildegarde Withers began to wonder if it had all been a failure after all, a trap baited and set, but all too evident to the eye of the Hunted—who was also the Hunter.

"It must be nearly morning," whispered Bob Stevenson in her ear. She did not answer, though her body was as tense as a steel spring. The first faint flickerings of dawn were already showing beneath the shades of the windows. It was now, or never. . . .

There was no sound of a turning knob, and the hinges of the door did not creak. But all the same, there came a faint sound from the other room, a sound like the falling of a leaf upon the water. . . .

Miss Withers rose to her feet, her voice for a moment strangling in her tight throat. Then she gasped, weakly— "Taylor! TAYLOR!"

The room was suddenly plunged into brilliant light by the shadeless lamp at the head of the bed, and Sergeant Taylor's solid bulk appeared in the closet door. Her own hand was clasped around the chill butt of the little .32, but she did not draw it.

For Bob Stevenson stood by the head of the Inspector's bed, a glass in his hand. He had removed his shoes, and his brow was beaded with perspiration.

"What's this?" came the voice of Oscar Piper, heavy with sleep.

"I—only wanted—a glass of water," said Stevenson, his eyes upon Miss Withers. "I didn't want to disturb anyone, and I was certain that there would be water here on the bed-table." He looked down at the brownish liquid, in which a white pellet was almost completely dissolved. "But it seems—it seems that I have a glass of medicine by mistake."

There was a moment of silence. Then Miss Withers spoke. "Why don't you drink it, anyway?" she said softly. "It's good medicine—for you."

The pleasant brown eyes lighted up. Bob Stevenson smiled a weary smile, and then inclined his head toward the white-faced woman who watched him. "Your health," he said. Then he raised the glass.

"Stop him, Taylor, you fool!" roared the Inspector, wide awake now. But it was too late.

Stevenson put down the glass, empty. It tinkled against the porcelain of the table as his weakening fingers let it go. For a moment longer he held himself erect, the color fading perceptibly from his eyes. But the smile remained—even after his body lay graceless and twisted across the floor, its convulsive movements dying away.

The sickening-sweet odor of bitter almonds filled the room. "Quick," ordered Piper from his bed. "Taylor, get the nurse! Get the house doctor—get a stomach pump. He'll not cheat the Chair this way!"

But Hildegarde Withers stood with her back against the door. "This is my doing," she said, through dry lips. "Let it end my way, Oscar. I'm wearing the badge tonight. There is nothing to be gained by a legal execution to titillate the morbid and the depraved. He has cheated nobody—there is no price greater than that he has paid. And the hemlock cup was invented centuries before the electric chair."

XXI

Loose Ends

(For those who care to know Why *and* How *as well as* Who)

"When did you know it was Stevenson?" the Inspector asked weakly. He had been given two hypos, and still found sleep beyond him. Miss Withers sat at the head of his bed in the full glow of the morning sun.

"I suspected him for a long time," she countered. "But I could not conceive of a motive until the Sergeant rallied me in this room about my hunch on the Curran girl's disappearance. It did have something to do with the case—indirectly. For if one girl pretended an appendicitis operation to conceal her marriage and her honeymoon, it suddenly occured to me that Anise Halloran might have had the same sort of a secret.

"I suspected, of course, that Bob Stevenson knew her better than he pretended. But so did Macfarland, at whose summer place in Connecticut they first met. He makes a practice of inviting the young teachers who are to be under him the next year, I suppose. Or perhaps he uses his influence to secure jobs for the young people he likes. At any rate, I'll wager anything that Stevenson and Anise Halloran were married at Greenwich last summer, probably under false names. On his salary alone they would have been very poor, but with both of them teaching, they were well off. But the fact that they taught at the same school made it necessary for them to live apart. You remember what I told you about Anise's complaint about her landlady in her former place objecting to the frequent calls of young men—or a young man? Well, the only young man who called frequently after she moved in with Janey Davis was Bob Stevenson—ostensibly calling on Janey, so that Janey's boss, Macfarland, would not come to know of it.

"I'll run briefly through what happened, or what I'm pretty sure happened. The married life of the Stevensons wasn't very happy. The separation and the constant concealment was not an aid to harmony, and Bob Stevenson was an unbalanced, erotic and neurotic type. But let's start at the beginning. What were the motives?

"The lottery ticket puzzled me for a while. It offered very little motive for the murder, even though on the day she died Anise Halloran won a prize certain to be large and possibly a young fortune. Why should Bob Stevenson kill her, supposing that he was her sweetheart? Why should Janey Davis kill her, for Janey owned half the ticket anyway?

"But supposing Anise was married to Bob Stevenson! Still it did not make sense that he'd kill her to get the ticket when naturally he would share in the wealth as her husband.

"I mulled and mulled over the problem. There were a dozen little details that didn't fit in. Anise had been looking very badly for the last few days, even I noticed that at school. She had also, we discovered, taken to secret drinking, which was entirely out of character. The liquor was not enough to have caused her ill health. I figured that there must be something deeper, more sinister.

"What puzzled me most was the murder being committed almost under my nose. The murderer must have known that I pride myself on snooping in such cases. Therefore, either he had no choice, or else he desired my intervention. Or both!"

"It makes my head ache," complained the Inspector. "But go on."

"Well, it was the latter possibility that made me sure Anderson could not have committed the murder. Whoever did it carefully planned everything to point in a certain direction—but not too obviously. I was supposed to start sleuthing around, and to happen upon the chain of clues leading to Anderson. A crime of violence—the body buried in the cellar, where only the janitor was at home—the shoes hidden where they were sure to be found—everything spelled janitor. Except that the janitor was really drunk, judging by the doctor's report and the evidence of the straw in his eyebrows. Besides—his feet were too big. Remember the shoes that I found on the floor near the body of Anise Halloran? Professor Pfaffle was sure it was a sex murder because of that. And actually, the murderer, knowing that I was in my room and guessing that I might become suspicious, removed the shoes from the corpse and put them on his own feet! Carrying his own shoes, he walked down the hall past my door, inadvertently arousing my suspicion by the shuffling sound he made. I thought Anise was ill—and rushed out to make sure. The murderer stopped in the doorway to put on his own shoes again, and then tossed Anise's back through the window into the room with the corpse from outside!''

The Inspector nodded. "So far so good. Go on."

"I figured that out quite easily. Well, then the murderer slipped back into the building, figuring on burying the body where it would be found later and sending the janitor to the death house."

"Wait," objected Piper. "How did he know that Anderson would not surprise him?"

"He knew of the janitor's little hideaway," Miss Withers insisted. "He must have learned that by accident, when coming down to the cellar for manual training supplies or lumber for his classes. That was the premise upon which he built everything else. And he knew that Anderson got dead drunk there, every afternoon.

"But he didn't count upon my finding the body in the Cloakroom. He knew that I never use the room, but keep my hat in my desk. He was in the cellar, digging his grave, preparatory to putting the body under ground, when we upset the whole apple cart. You walked in on him—and he hit you with the flat of the shovel, from behind. He had the hatchet with him, but he didn't want to kill you.

"He knew that if one detective came, others would follow. So he had to give up the idea of burying the corpse. The furnace was handy, and he thrust it in, built up the fire, and hid himself somewhere on the upper floors—probably on the second, where he placed the murder hatchet in the exhibit case, in place of the wooden one which he must have taken away with him and destroyed."

"Where did he get the real hatchet?"

Miss Withers shrugged her shoulders. "You forget that he had complete control of the manual training room, as well as the science laboratory. He alone knew how many hatchets there ought to be—and that's why none were found missing.

"Anyway, he hid on the second floor, afraid to try to make a break for it through the front door. Probably he did not think of the fire escape at the time. At any rate, he remained in the building until I had searched the third floor, and was almost ready to try the second! Wait—I've got it. He was waiting, trying to get into his own classroom. He wanted to destroy some evidence which he knew was there."

"And that was what?"

"A cigarette lighter and a can of benzine and some un-washed glasses," Hildegarde Withers explained. "All of which proves that his hand had been forced, somehow. He had not meant Anise to die that afternoon, but somehow it became necessary."

"The lottery ticket announcement in the paper?"

"Probably. Undoubtedly. You ask why he wanted to kill Anise when she was coming into a fortune?"

Miss Withers shook her head. "He didn't want to kill her, then. But he had to finish the job that he'd already started with minute doses of benzine. That was why he'd got Anise into the unhealthy habit of drinking every day—he got her into his room between classes and they drank together—with a drop of benzine in her glass, its flavor deadened by whiskey.

"If he stopped the doses then—she would remain a help-less invalid, a burden to him all his life. Remember the guinea pig that died, and the other one that became an invalid? He tested the doses on them first—God knows how he learned of the poison. He was a science teacher, remem-ber. He might have read of the Frenchman's report on the effect of refined petroleum products on monkeys that Dr. Van Donnen told me about. Anyway, he was quietly going about the job of killing his secret wife when he struck a snag. And this was it!"

Miss Withers jumped to her feet. "It wasn't entirely the lottery ticket. He had to kill Anise by violence, because while he succeeded in making her a dipsomaniac, she didn't like the taste of his liquor mixed with bezine. She knew where he bought it, from the stock Tobey had got from Anderson, and she went there and supplied herself with her own stock!

"His dosing of her was cut off in the middle—right where she was doomed to invalidism, but not to die. The lottery business was only incidental, he was killing her because he was tired of her, or because he had fallen in love with her roommate, or because he was burning to try the new method of murder he had learned about. There are men like that, Oscar."

"You're telling me!"

"Well, he was fairly well covered, he thought. The benzine can was explained by the cigarette lighter. Only I couldn't understand why the lighter had never been used, and yet the benzine can was nearly empty. As for the glass he forgot to wash, it was only luck that a red ant happened to wander into his laboratory, perhaps brought in by some specimens or dirt samples or something, and inadvertently tipped the whole thing off by drinking the poisoned residue in the glass, and dying.

"The rest is simple. All he had to do was to sit back and let the bright Miss Withers solve the murder of Anise Halloran by the wicked janitor, and let Anderson go to the electric chair for it. Only something slipped. Something always slips. It was dramatic justice in this case that it happened as it did. Anise Halloran, or Anise Stevenson as her name was, clung to the shreds of her marital happiness. Even though she had begun to fear her husband—witness the gun loaded with blanks that she had Janey Davis procure for her over in New Jersey somewhere—still she wore her wedding ring. And when he threw her body into the blazing furnace, she was still wearing it."

"You mean, he didn't know enough to take it from her finger?"

"It wasn't on her finger, silly. She couldn't let anyone see it. She wore it somewhere next to her body, probably on a cord around her neck. Bob Stevenson never thought of searching her for it in his haste—and that blackened and partly fused bit of metal was a terrible link in the chain against him!

"Another thing went wrong. The shoes—there was something wrong about the shoes. He planted them in the janitor's quarters that day—but they were Anise's shoes. And where would Anderson get five or six pairs of Anise Halloran's shoes? Who, besides Stevenson, could possibly acquire more than one pair at the most? He had access to her apartment. He had known her for a long time. And his passion for completeness and full detail tripped him neatly. The shoes fooled the detectives. They fooled Pfaffle, but they didn't fool me."

"I was neatly fooled," confessed the Inspector. "When you finally convinced me that Anderson was being framed, I was sure the guilty party was Macfarland. I think it was because of the sneeze you heard in the hall outside your door just about the time the murder was committed—when Macfarland was supposed to be at home writing his essay, and wasn't."

Miss Withers nodded. "It was like Stevenson to think of doing that. He knew I'd take it for Macfarland. Anybody would. It established that the principal was lying—or nearly did so. He was full of tricks like that. I seem to remember a rattling sound in the basement about that time too—which was probably done by him to impress me with the fact that Anderson was around and about.

"Stevenson must have relaxed when all that was settled. He settled down to playing the great friend and lover to Janey Davis—who stood a very good chance of cashing in on his dead wife's lottery ticket. But even if she threw up the ticket, she was young and lovely—lovelier than Anise, for that matter—and she was a woman that he hadn't had, and probably couldn't have, without marrying her."

"It's all clear except the alibi," Piper objected.

"You mean Stevenson's being at the library reading up on the Addison family? He planted that perfectly. He was a familiar visitor to the Genealogy Room. He simply signed for a book that he knew was very rare, took it to his little reading nook, put it into the drawer where the boy would not pick it up and return it to the main desk, and slipped out. He went back to Jefferson School—murdered Anise Halloran—slipped out of the fire escape when he knew it was too late to do whatever he wanted to do in his own laboratory, and returned to the library, where he unearthed his book from its hiding place and returned it to the desk. Thus he had an alibi—not a perfect one, he was too smart for that. But it was just the sort of alibi that an honest, innocent person usually has."

The Inspector nodded. "It all fits like a glove. Now that I look at it this way, I see that nobody else could have killed that girl. I suppose that Stevenson got panicky and came for you with the hatchet in the cellar that day because he was afraid you'd stumble on the truth?''

"Afraid? He was pretty sure I had. If the magnificent structure he had built to incriminate Anderson were to topple over, he was pretty close to hot water. That sounds tangled . . . but it states the case. And I had come around asking too many of the wrong kind of questions to suit Bob Stevenson. He read in the extra that the janitor had escaped, and the chance was too good. If I were killed in the basement that day, no jury on earth would fail to convict Anderson of both crimes. But the hatchet missed me. And Mr. Stevenson had to give up that little dream. . . ."

The Inspector shook his head. "The fellow certainly was thorough. Stevenson ought to go down in the annals of crime as the murderer without nerves."

"But he wasn't without nerves! He knew that you didn't get a glimpse of him when he attacked you from behind with the shovel. But he got to worrying. He weakened, and thus he gave himself away. He swallowed the bait, hook, line and sinker, and he returned to the hospital after he was sure we had all left, set upon putting you where you could never identify anybody again. Murder had got to be a habit with him by then. But the escape of Anderson was almost too convenient. He was on his guard. That's why he rapped on the door of this room—and nearly spoiled everything.

"If he had entered without knocking, and come over to the bed with gun or poison in his hand, the case would have been clear. But as it was I had only circumstantial evidence against him, and flimsy evidence at that.

"So when he knocked at that door, very softly, he was hoping and praying that there was no one here but you, and that you were in a coma. If you answered the knock, he'd have gone—knowing that you were wide enough awake to cry for help. But when I did, he must have been torn between stark staring terror, and relief that he had knocked and that he had a story all ready."

Miss Withers found her throat dry as a corn husk, and drank copiously from the water pitcher itself, avoiding the brown-stained glass which awaited the Medical Examiner.

"But he was an optimist, Oscar. He believed that luck was

with him when I accepted his help. I had no choice, for I knew this was my one chance to trap him. He hoped to slip the poison in your medicine, which he thought you would drink on awakening, and then to make me believe that we had both drowsed while the real murderer entered. He removed his shoes, and crossed the room without a breath of sound. But I knew what he was doing, because he spoke to me first to see if I slept. And I heard the tiny splash his pellet of poison made as it touched the water . . . you know the rest."

"I know the rest," agreed the Inspector. "But would you mind telling me one thing? Why in heaven's name did you go around whistling that insane little bird-call for days and days? What part did that play in this twisted business?"

"You mean this?" Miss Withers pursed her lips, and whistled her two notes, thrice repeated. . . . "Whoooooo-wheeeee. . . ."

The Inspector nodded. She smiled, shamefacedly. "That, Oscar, was the one essential clue that you always talk about. It was the little tune that Anise Halloran wrote on the blackboard underneath her regular scales and tunes for the morrow's class. When she wrote that phrase, Oscar, she tried to leave a message behind her. Somehow, she knew. Perhaps her suspicion of her husband went farther than ordering the little gun that Janey never gave her. Perhaps she guessed the dreadful secret behind the liquor which tasted so badly. Perhaps she knew what was waiting for her that night—but did not know where, or when. It will always be a mystery why she did not cry out for help, instead of putting that pathetic little clue on the blackboard. I think it was her pride. She married him, you see. She still wore his ring, next her bare body. She had faith, an insane faith, that everything would somehow come out all right. She intended to come back next morning and erase the pitiful evidence of her momentary terror and suspicion of the man she once loved—perhaps still loved."

"Yeah, but why the tune? What does whoooo-wheee convey?"

Miss Withers took a pencil from her bag, and the Inspector's chart from the foot of his bed. "I whistled it to every suspect in this case, until they all thought I was cuckoo. I made the natural mistake of reading the tune instead of the notes, Oscar. See here? She wrote the simplest, easiest message she could think of—just the notes A-D . . . A-D . . . *hold*

A-D. Notice the *hold*, Oscar? Stevenson's name was A. Robert Stevenson, in full. The A. undoubtedly stood for Addison, the maternal side of his family of which he was so proud. She must have called him 'Ad' as a pet name, and in her terror she forgot that no one else knew it! All the same, her message remained in plain view of all of us, on the blackboard, crying aloud Bob Stevenson's guilt for those who could read. See? 'If anything happens to me (it's understood she implied) *hold Ad!*' "

Miss Withers rose to her feet. "I'm going to leave you now," she said. "It's been a hard night for an invalid, even if you did sleep through it like a log while I was giving you credit for being a consummate actor!"

Piper grinned. "I knew I was in good keeping," he told her. Their hands met, across the coverlet.

"There's only one person I'm really sorry for in all this," Miss Withers remarked. "Janey Davis is such a sweet child, and this is going to be the hardest blow of her life. She was pretty close to being in love with that charming fiend. I wonder if I ought to go to her before the newspapers come out with all the gory details?"

"I think you ought to go home and go to bed," Piper told her, his voice strangely gentle. "Janey Davis is a young lady who can take care of herself."

•   •   •   •   •   •   •

At that moment a very sleepy Janey Davis was answering the telephone in her little apartment on 74th Street.

The voice at the other end of the line was very familiar to her by now. It was Georgie Swarthout's.

"I know it's early, Janey," he said softly. "But I've got something really important to talk to you about. Won't you get dressed and come out to breakfast with me?"

There comes a time in every girl's life when, having said "No" very definitely and very many times repeated to a certain young man, she says "Yes" from pure contrariness. Much to her surprise, Janey Davis said it now.

And
the
curtain
falls. . . .

Kinsey Millhone is . . .

"The best new private eye." —The Detroit News

"A tough-cookie with a soft center." —Newsweek

"A stand-out specimen of the new female operatives."
—Philadelphia Inquirer

Sue Grafton is . . .

The Shamus and Anthony Award-winning creator of Kinsey Millhone and quite simply one of the hottest new mystery writers around.

Bantam is . . .

The proud publisher of Sue Grafton's Kinsey Millhone mysteries:

☐ 26563 "A" IS FOR ALIBI $3.50
☐ 26061 "B" IS FOR BURGLAR $3.50
☐ 26468 "C" IS FOR CORPSE $3.50

and coming soon:

"D" IS FOR DEADBEAT